The Griffins of Castle Cary

The Griffins of Castle Cary

HEATHER SHUMAKER

Simon & Schuster Books for Young Readers
New York   London   Toronto   Sydney   New Delhi

SIMON & SCHUSTER BOOKS FOR YOUNG READERS

An imprint of Simon & Schuster Children's Publishing Division

1230 Avenue of the Americas, New York, New York 10020

This book is a work of fiction. Any references to historical events, real people, or real places are used fictitiously. Other names, characters, places, and events are products of the author's imagination, and any resemblance to actual events or places or persons, living or dead, is entirely coincidental.

Text copyright © 2019 by Heather Shumaker

Jacket illustrations copyright © 2019 by Yaoyao Ma Van As

All rights reserved, including the right of reproduction in whole or in part in any form.

SIMON & SCHUSTER BOOKS FOR YOUNG READERS is a trademark of Simon & Schuster, Inc.

For information about special discounts for bulk purchases, please contact Simon & Schuster Special Sales at 1-866-506-1949 or business@simonandschuster.com.

The Simon & Schuster Speakers Bureau can bring authors to your live event.

For more information or to book an event, contact the Simon & Schuster Speakers Bureau at 1-866-248-3049 or visit our website at www.simonspeakers.com.

Book design by Tom Daly

The text for this book was set in Adobe Caslon Pro.

Manufactured in the United States of America

0219 FFG

First Edition

10 9 8 7 6 5 4 3 2 1

Library of Congress Cataloging-in-Publication Data

Names: Shumaker, Heather, author.

Title: The griffins of Castle Cary / Heather Shumaker.

Description: First edition. | New York : Simon & Schuster Books for Young Readers, [2019] | Summary: "Siblings Meg and Will must uncover the haunted history of their aunt's quaint town in order to save their younger sister, Ariel, from a ghost intent on keeping her as a friend"—Provided by publisher.

Identifiers: LCCN 2018015659 | ISBN 9781534430884 (hardcover : alk. paper) | ISBN 9781534430907 (eBook) |

Subjects: | CYAC: Haunted places—Fiction. | Ghosts—Fiction. | Brothers and sisters—Fiction. | Aunts—Fiction. | Racially-mixed people—Fiction. | Americans—England—Fiction. | England—Fiction.

Classification: LCC PZ7.1.S518 Gri 2019 | DDC [Fic]—dc23

LC record available at https://lccn.loc.gov/2018015659

For my son, Xander.
My first and most loyal reader.

Contents

Ding dong bell
Kitty's in the well
Who'll get her out again?
Ding dong bell

CHAPTER ONE

Beginnings

If you know much about ghosts, you'll know that wait-ing is one of the things a ghost does best. Ghosts have the patience of eternity.

Each April the ghost stirred. It coughed, cried, and blew its nose, then rose to the surface. April is an in-between season, a time when cracks split open along the ancient path from winter to summer, from death to life. A time when accidents might happen.

This year the ghost dislodged a beetle from its ear and wafted up to the walnut tree. There it settled in a crook of branches. Leafless twigs scraped, the buds on the brink of bursting: poised, silent, and swollen.

This ghost was waiting for someone.

Someone to whisper to.

Someone to treasure.

It was waiting for a child.

❧

"Nothing but sheep," said Will, his nose squashed against the train window. "Look at them! What are we going to do for a whole week? What if the Griffinage doesn't have a piano?"

"Whistle," said his sister Meg. "That's what you always do."

"Very funny," said Will.

Meg and Will Griffin were constant companions and a little less than a year apart. Meg's hair was golden brown and curly. Very curly. Her hair was a mass of tightly coiled curls that bounced around her head when she ran. She had light tan skin, so light most people assumed Meg and her siblings were white, though the Griffins were a mixed race family.

Will was nearly as tall as Meg, with longish blond-brown hair that combed straight, and a wide grin that seemed too big for his cheekbones. Meg was eleven and Will was ten, but every November after Will's Halloween birthday, they were the same age for seven weeks. Then Will would joke: "We're twins, Megs! I'm as old as you."

Meg glanced over at Ariel. She'd formed a nest from their pile of coats, and was sitting cross-legged among them, poking in her crayon box. Ariel was five. She was what strangers called "adorable," which meant she had enormous brown eyes, and dark wavy hair that cascaded to her waist and was clipped with bows. Right now her left bow was sliding partway down to her ear, and she was trying to draw a picture as the train jostled along. "My red's gone," said Ariel.

"Use purple," said Will.

"But I *need* red," Ariel continued. "Red's for his tongue. He can't have a purple tongue." As usual, Ariel was drawing animals with round heads, stick legs, and impossibly large tails.

Meg sighed. She didn't mind helping Ariel, but she'd already rescued the green crayon from the floor twice, and dug out sienna from the seat crack. They'd only been on the train from London for ten minutes. If Ariel kept losing crayons at this rate . . . Let's see, it was nearly a two-hour ride to Castle Cary and Aunt Effie's house, so four crayons every ten minutes, that meant four times twelve, or forty-eight spilled crayons.

"Look on the floor," said Meg.

Ariel looked, but tipped the crayon box as she did, threatening to spill what remained of the sixty-four colors.

"There," said Meg, righting the box and retrieving the red from under the sleeve of Will's coat. "Now keep track of it, and color by yourself."

Meg stood up to change seats, but Ariel's hand flew out to stop her.

"Don't go, Meg," said Ariel.

Meg gently pried off her sister's hand. She wanted to talk to Will. It was a relief to know Aunt Effie would be taking care of Ariel once they reached the Griffinage. Mama always asked them both to look after Ariel, but it usually fell on her. "You'll be fine," she said. "I'm only moving a few inches."

Ariel slumped into the coat pile, but Will looked up as she sat down next to him.

"Nothing but sheep," Will repeated, tapping the window.

"What do you think he's like?" Meg asked.

"Who?" said Will.

"You know who," said Meg.

She knew what was bothering Will. It was the same thing she was worried about. Staying at the Griffinage with Aunt Effie would be a treat. She was the sort of grown-up who believed in ice-cream cones every day and staying up late. Their favorite aunt. She'd come to see them countless times in Minnesota, and now, finally, they would get to see where she lived in England. Will could probably even play a neighbor's piano, so that wasn't the problem. The problem was Uncle Ben.

"Why didn't anyone *tell* us about Uncle Ben before?" Will demanded, flopping back on his seat. "If he's married to Aunt Effie, you'd think we'd have heard of him at least."

"Maybe they're not married," said Meg. "Yo[u] maybe he's her boyfriend or something and [she] wants us to call him 'uncle.'"

"We still should have heard of him," said Will. "I'll bet he's a recluse."

"You mean like a hermit?"

"Yeah," said Will. "Maybe he doesn't like to be around other people."

"Or maybe he can't get out of bed or something," said Meg. "Why else would Aunt Effie have to take care of him?"

"He's probably a grump," said Will. "I bet he sits around the house and bangs his cane and we'll never have any fun. I thought it was just going to be Aunt Effie. This changes everything."

"No, it doesn't," said Meg.

"You know it does," said Will. "You're scared of him, too."

❧❧

Until that very day, the Griffin children had never heard of Uncle Ben. When their parents talked about the Griffinage, it was always Aunt Effie. Aunt Effie who called. Aunt Effie, who sent her love. Aunt Effie, who mailed them books and chocolates wrapped in red tissue paper on their birthdays. Aunt Effie's last name was Griffin too. That's why the house was called the Griffinage. "If a vicar lives in a vicarage, and an orphan lives in an orphanage, then a Griffin should live in a Griffinage," she proclaimed. "Much better than a house number, don't you think?"

Being Griffins, the children had always longed to see the Griffinage. But a Griffinage with Aunt Effie in it, not an unknown uncle. When Mama announced the news about their extra-long spring break—*you'll have to miss a week of school, Dad and I will be away at the geology conference, and you three will stay at the Griffinage*—nobody mentioned Uncle Ben.

"The Griffinage!" said Will. "Cool!"

"It'll be like living in our own family castle," said Meg.

"Hardly," said their father, who'd been there before. "You're not staying in the manor itself, you know. The Griffinage is a house, and the only true castle in Castle Cary is in ruins."

"But, still," said Meg, and she walked away to dream of castles with emblems of gryphons on the front door.

Mama sent away for passports. Ariel asked a million questions. Dad found his favorite rock-hound pants. Meg looked up Castle Cary and its county, Somerset, on the map, and Will packed and repacked his duffel bag.

"Save room for clothes," said his mother, examining the contents of his duffel. "Yes, Will, more than two pairs of underwear." Then she retreated to the basement again, where she and their father, both geology professors, spent hours preparing for the conference by writing speeches with words like "geomorphology," "petrology," and "paleoarchaeology."

Maybe it was the "ologies" that distracted the Griffin parents. Somehow it wasn't until the family arrived at Paddington Station, and the train to Somerset was inching up to its platform, that their father stopped midsentence (the full sentence was "When I was a boy, I rode trains at age eight without my parents," but he stopped at "rode," which didn't matter because the children had heard the story so many times before). Then he said something new and surprising: "See if you can help out with Uncle Ben. Aunt Effie will have enough on her hands taking care of you lot."

"Uncle Ben?" said Will, his mouth agape.

"Who's Uncle Ben?" asked Meg, just as the train whistle blasted. Why did grown-ups keep repeating old stories instead of explaining new things kids really wanted to know? Mama was bustling about, gathering luggage, kissing Ariel, and herding them toward the train platform. There wasn't much time. Hurriedly, Meg asked: "What's he like?"

"Oh, you'll meet him soon enough," said their father. "Uncle Ben is one of a kind."

"But . . . ," said Will.

"Listen up now," said their father. "You get off at Castle Cary. I've talked to the conductor, and he'll tell you when the station comes up."

"But what about Uncle *Ben*?" Will asked.

"What about him?"

"Will Uncle Ben be there too?"

"No idea," said their father. "I don't think she always brings him to a place like the train station. So many people and the noise, you know."

Will gulped. If this uncle didn't like people, and he didn't like noise, he surely wouldn't like children. This would be a terrible vacation.

"Does he drool?" Will asked.

His father gave him a strange look. "Well, sometimes. I suppose he can't help it."

The children spotted Aunt Effie right away at the Castle Cary train platform. She still sported a head of springy curls exactly like Meg's, the afternoon sun shining through her outer curls like a halo, and if that left any doubt about who she was, she was waving wildly in their direction.

Will scanned the platform to see if he could spy a drooling man propped up in a wheelchair with a cane between his legs. He saw Meg searching too, though trying to pretend she wasn't. No, it was just Aunt Effie who had come to the train station. The Castle

Cary stop was small and nearly deserted. "Guess he's not here," Will whispered, amid Aunt Effie's shouts of "hallo" and hugs of welcome. Ariel was smiling now, basking in Aunt Effie's attention.

"Shh," said Meg. "Don't be rude."

"I'm not being rude, I'm just stating a fact," said Will.

"Well, whispering's rude," whispered Meg.

By now, Aunt Effie had Ariel's hand in hers and was headed to the car park. She approached a tiny golden-yellow-colored car. Will couldn't help staring. At home, this little car would fit inside their family minivan. He eyed the pile of luggage dubiously. "Will we all fit?"

"Never underestimate a Mini," answered Aunt Effie. "You should see what I can jam in this creature. Why, in Japan they once fit twenty-one people inside. The world record for people in a Mini is held by the Pilobolus Dance Company in the States: twenty-six people! In the newer model, of course. More legroom. Did you know Pilobolus is the Latin name for a fungus? Grows on cow manure and shoots off ballistic spores like a cannon. Funny name for a dance company, isn't it?" She paused and stooped down to help Ariel, who'd tripped on the curb and spilled half her crayons. Meg grabbed two that had rolled under the Mini's back tire. When the crayons were back in the box, Aunt Effie grinned at Will, who was still holding his duffel. "Chuck it in the boot, love. Right. Off we go!"

The Griffinage cottage looked lovely and quaint at first sight, just like the painting on their mother's shortbread cookie tin. The Mini bounced to the end of the dirt drive, and they all tumbled out.

"Oooh!" said Meg and Ariel at the same time.

The front door was bright red and child-sized—so low, adults would need to duck. The roof was thatched. No shingles in sight, simply bundles of straw stacked like a mat. This thick thatch spread over the cottage like a warm blanket, swooping over the upstairs windows so the window panes could peer out. Like eyes, Will thought. Perched on top of it all was a fox-shaped weather vane.

"Call me Mrs. Thatcher!" Aunt Effie laughed and glanced at the children, who looked back puzzled. "Never mind. Before your time. Welcome to the Griffinage! Held together by Sellotape, I'm afraid," she added. "The thatch looks pretty, but squirrels muck about and it leaks a bit."

"It's a Goldilocks house," exclaimed Ariel.

"You mean the bears' house," said Will. "The bears lived there, not Goldilocks."

"Right you are, Will," said Aunt Effie. "Come and meet the bear!"

Will, who'd begun to feel better in Aunt Effie's company, felt his throat tighten, and he jammed his hands in his pockets. If Aunt Effie called him "the bear," Uncle Ben must be really bad. Aunt Effie sailed up the walk, picking up a suitcase and tucking Ariel's hand in hers.

"All this is Griffin land," she continued, setting the suitcase down again, and sweeping one arm out toward rows and rows of fruit trees beside them. "The orchard—damsons, plums, apples—and all the way out to the pastures. See that stone wall? That's the back border, so you'll have plenty of room to roam. Of course, those stones haven't always been a wall. Once they were part of the glory of the Roman Empire! Imagine that. The Fosse Way runs through here, a road the Romans built when they invaded England two thousand years ago, but after the Romans marched out, people gradually plundered the stones to build cow barns and wells, and these particular stones got stuck in a wall. How's that for the fall of an empire?"

Will gaped at the Griffinage garden, with its flower beds, hedges, wall that used to be an ancient road, and rows of fruit trees. He couldn't even see the full extent of the stone wall, the property was so big. Aunt Effie, by now, had reached the red door, and bent low by habit. Will hurried to catch up. The front door was the right size for him, and he entered the Griffinage with six inches to spare.

"Bring your bags upstairs," Aunt Effie called over her shoulder. "We've got bangers and mash for supper, and

I expect you're ravenous." *Bangers and mash?* thought Will. It sounded a bit like dog food.

"Don't people in England eat pretty much the same food as people in the US?" he asked. Aunt Effie and Ariel were already past the slate entryway and halfway up the stairs, Ariel chattering all the way. Will and Meg climbed after them.

"Pretty much, dear," Aunt Effie said. "Will, you're in the front room. You girls are back here in the east room." She showed them a room with a tremendously tilted ceiling. "Can't wear a hat in here," she said, ducking her own head. "You lot should be fine, though, if you promise to grow at the normal pace."

Before them they saw a crooked room with two beds, one just a folding cot. The ceiling seemed to have a desire to become a floor, for it slanted downward at a reckless angle. Meanwhile, the floor tilted upward, as if to meet it. Tucked around the corner was an alcove, a stray piece of the room with its own miniature window. Ariel ran to it. She ducked in and skipped back out, saying: "Oh, can I sleep in the cubby?"

"In here? Well, I suppose," said Aunt Effie. "I thought you'd want to be closer to Meg." She bent double as Ariel dragged her into the tiny space.

"Please, please. This could be my own little house," begged Ariel.

Aunt Effie answered by pushing the cot into the

corner spot. It fit perfectly, as if designed for a small child's bed. Ariel spun around in delight.

Will joined Meg, who'd drifted over to the window, her eyes fixed on an enormous tree in the back garden. Leaves sprouted from the other trees, but this one was still leafless, and its bare branches reached toward the house like human arms.

"That's the walnut tree," said Aunt Effie, coming up behind them. "Old as the hills. Well, not really," she amended hastily. "How can I say that with two geologists in the family? Glad your parents aren't here to hear me. The Mendip Hills themselves are three hundred million years old. That tree's old all the same."

"Must be a hundred," ventured Meg.

"Oh, much older than that, my dear," said Aunt Effie. "That walnut has stood there for ages. Might live to three hundred, I should think. It's withstood many a storm."

Downstairs, the Griffinage kitchen greeted them with wafts of sausage, its savory smell mixed with other mouthwatering scents, like fresh bread and hot chocolate. Aunt Effie dodged about, bringing steaming plates to the table. The table itself was built into the wall at one end, and instead of chairs, high-backed wooden benches ran along its sides, reminding the children of church pews or benches at grand railway stations. At the head of the table stood a single chair. *Must be for Uncle Ben*, Will thought. Since Aunt Effie had asked him to set the table, he set out five plates.

"Expecting somebody?" asked Aunt Effie, coming up with a pot of mashed potatoes. "Who on earth is the extra place for, Will?"

"Um, I thought Uncle Ben might be hungry," said Will.

"Oh, goodness me!" exclaimed Aunt Effie. "*He* won't be coming to the table." Will blushed and busied himself with straightening his silverware. Who was this strange uncle? Was he so odd that he couldn't eat with them?

"Now, let me see, where can he have got to?" Aunt Effie plopped the pot down. She poked her head down the hall. "Ben!" she hollered, then yelled again at the back door: "Ben! Come and meet the family!" Will braced himself against the bench. Beside him, he heard Meg gasp. Their mother never yelled at their father like that. Well, there was nothing to do now but meet him.

The back door pushed open and revealed a large brown foot. Not a shoe, not at all. The next moment, a creature lumbered in. He was a mountain of a dog, a huge, shaggy beast, with folds of skin wrapped around his sturdy neck like a lion's mane. He moved the way a mountain might move, and each leg ended with a massive bearlike paw. He was entirely brown.

"A giant chocolate dog!" cried Ariel, and was out of her seat in an instant.

"Ah yes, Uncle Ben," said Aunt Effie. Her voice softened, and her gaze lingered on the big, brown dog. "Uncle Ben, come meet your nieces and nephew."

Will stared as relief poured through him. "Oh," he said, and then "oh" again. He might have kept on saying "oh" the rest of the evening if Meg hadn't elbowed him.

"So that's the 'bear,'" Meg said.

"Or the 'man of the house,'" said Aunt Effie, as Uncle Ben politely sniffed them one by one. "He's so big he feels like a person, so I call him 'Uncle.' Where were you, Ben? Usually, you're underfoot and greet us at the door, you great clown. What were you doing out by the walnut? Didn't you know the children were here?"

Ariel was kneeling by Uncle Ben, nuzzling her head in the thick fur folds by his shoulders. "I love him, Aun' Effie," Ariel said. "He's the most biggest dog I've ever seen. Can he be mine for always?"

"Well, dearie, he's yours for the week, while you're here at the Griffinage. All of yours," she said, sweeping her hand around the table to include the others. "Uncle Ben will adopt you like puppies, I predict. Just like the Nana dog in the book *Peter Pan* with Wendy, John and Michael. Nana was a Newfie too, you know—a Newfoundland dog."

Uncle Ben lifted his enormous head at her words

and thumped his tail. Aunt Effie pushed the pot of mash in Will's direction. Despite its name, bangers and mash turned out to be delicious—sausage and potatoes, slathered in gravy.

Will scooped out a second serving. He ate slowly, soaking in the comfort of being in a thatched cottage with a full belly, newly acquainted with an uncle who was a dog.

"If you kids ever get into trouble," said Aunt Effie, "just look for Uncle Ben. These Newfies are known for saving children. Great protectors. Though, come to think of it, Nana was no match for flying children. Still, I don't expect any flying in and out of windows here. As I told your father back in January, 'What possible trouble can the kids get into? You just leave them with me, Davy, and go off with Marie following those rocks of yours. No worries. It's quiet as a graveyard here in Somerset.'"

"Oh, doggie," said Ariel. She was now on the floor with Uncle Ben, nuzzling deep into his mammoth neck. "You're the nicest uncle ever!"

"Well," said Meg. "That's the end of our mystery."

But, of course, she was wrong. It was only the beginning.

CHAPTER TWO

The Haunted Tower

The very next morning, Meg woke with a start. She gave a small cry and sprang up in bed. A prickly feeling had enveloped her. She swatted her hand over her head as if to push it away. "No!" she said sharply. "Go away."

And to her surprise, it did.

The next moment she saw the deep chocolate face of Uncle Ben peering at her with his soulful eyes. Morning light poured through the crooked window.

"Am I glad to see you," Meg said, allowing Uncle Ben to lick her face, even on the lips. The prickly feeling was gone, but a small wad of loneliness lodged in its place. With every lick of Uncle Ben's rough tongue, the lonely bundle diminished until it lifted away. His fur was soft, but soggy around his muzzle. Uncle Ben raised a massive paw to shake.

"Good morning, Uncle," said Meg, shaking his paw.

✑

Down the hall, Will was just stirring when he heard music. There it was again. A distinct musical phrase. Will lay perfectly still, trying to catch the notes. Melodies often came to him when he was alone; tunes simply entered his mind and demanded to be plunked out as soon as possible on the piano. It was thrilling when a new song arrived unannounced, so he burrowed under the covers with a warm feeling inside, preparing to trace the musical notes in his mind. This music reminded him of bells, a plaintive tune like a song belonging to a windswept night.

Will let the music flow through him. La de de la da. As he did, the notes grew clearer and more urgent. This was new. The melody seemed to be taking charge. Will gasped a bit as the tune gained strength. La De De La DA . . . La De De LA DA . . . The pattern repeated, insistent, drilling into his head. Then a buzzing noise disrupted the melody.

"Oh, get lost," he grumbled. He strained to hear the music but the buzzing increased. He began to hiccup, and the tune slipped. Down the hall, Uncle Ben barked.

"That's done it," Will groaned. "Too much noise. Now I'll never know how it goes." He realized the buzzing had also stopped, but it was too late. The song had fled. He hiccupped his way back under the covers. Will buried his head and lay still, trying to retrieve the notes, but it was like chasing the fragment of a dream that kept eluding him.

∘❧∘

After two such discouraging attempts, the little ghost drifted back to the branches of the walnut tree in a huff. It was rude to be batted away like a mosquito. Go away. Get lost. What was wrong with these children? Didn't they know she wanted to play? It had been so long. She didn't want to spend another year down in that hole alone. She'd braved the rooms despite that dreadful dog. Always sniffing around disturbing her airspace. Besides, she was sure there'd been another child. She sucked a ragged curl of hair that had strayed into her mouth and swung her legs from the tree branches. Down below, she could see the dog out in the garden. So. If the dog was outside, that meant the house was clear.

Well, there was one more.

She glided from the walnut tree through the window into the old east room where her own bed used to stand in the nook. There was the last child. The little one, asleep on a cot. The ghost lifted the covers to peer at her face. A girl, a bit younger than she was, but she'd do. Warmth from the sleeping child's body wafted up and swirled around her. The ghost gave a small sigh of pleasure. Company at last. She tucked her cold hands into the child's and watched as her eyes flicked open.

"Oh, hello," said Ariel.

Downstairs at breakfast the front door banged open and closed. Meg dropped her spoon. She was feeling jumpy this morning. She listened to the clump of boots on the slate entry hall. The tramping stopped, followed by a belated knock on the wall.

"We're in the kitchen!" Aunt Effie hollered. "It's Shep," she told the children, hastily brushing wayward crumbs from her clothes. "My neighbor. Also main Griffinage handyman."

In walked a big-bodied man with curly reddish hair. His curls were loose and wavy, the way Meg sometimes wished her hair could be. He wore a black vest and scuffed leather boots, and he dipped his head to fit under the door's low lintel.

"So these are the young Griffins!" he said, straightening to his full height and surveying the breakfast crew. He looked at Will and grinned. Next he smiled at Meg, sizing her up from her faint freckles to her head of curls. She'd only combed it with her fingers this morning, and could feel a tangle beginning at the nape of her neck. Meg looked down at her cereal bowl, waiting for him to compare her hair to Aunt Effie's, but he didn't say a word. She instantly liked him for that. Instead, Shep looked around the room, ducking his head here and there, pretending to search under the table and behind the stove.

"Hmm. One, two. I thought there were three of you," he said.

"Haven't seen Ariel this morning," Aunt Effie replied. "Zonked out from travel yesterday. Still sleeping like an angel up in the east room alcove."

"You put her up there?" asked Shep sharply.

"Yes, why ever not?" said Aunt Effie. "She's sharing with Meg."

Shep muttered something about old rooms having old memories. Aunt Effie didn't seem to hear him and began clanking the kettle at the sink. This handyman was not like the contractors who came to their house, Meg decided. Shep was already sitting down and joining them at the table with a steaming mug of coffee.

"Is Shep your real name?" asked Will, scooping a second helping of jam on his toast.

"Real as yours," said Shep. "Last name, actually. Short for Shepherd. My family has been shepherding ever since God made the first sheep. But me, I'm mostly a tech repair and computer programmer."

"Oh," said Will. "What's your first name?"

"Ah, now. That's a secret," said Shep.

"Best secret in Castle Cary," said Aunt Effie. "Everyone calls him Shep, or Shep Shepherd for formal occasions."

Shep winked at Will and Meg, who were facing him across the broad oak table. "Best town secret besides the ghosts," he added.

"Ghosts?" said Will. A large blob of jam oozed off his toast and onto his chair.

"The most famous is the manor ghost," Shep continued. "Not really a secret. The town holds ghost tours, makes money from it. Said to haunt the West Tower up at Mendip Manor. She's the active one. Shines lights and so on, especially in April. You're visiting at a good time to see her."

"Shines lights?" asked Will. "You think we'll see that?" Shep shrugged.

"Maybe that, maybe more," he said with a grin.

Will promptly dropped more jam from his toast. This time it landed on his pant leg. Meg stared at Shep. Back home, nobody talked about ghosts, especially not grown-ups. Well, maybe at Halloween, but not in regular breakfast conversations. There must be ghost stories galore in a country with so many old buildings. Maybe even here at the Griffinage. Maybe right here in this room. She shivered a little, and turned her head. Normally, she'd never look for ghosts flying around the kitchen, but back home their kitchen was an ordinary one with a linoleum floor. Meg was quite sure that ghosts and linoleum did not mix.

Aunt Effie, however, clanged the kettle lid shut and

glared at Shep like a bad-tempered schoolmarm. "Now, Shep. Don't go filling their heads with nonsense."

"It's history, Effie," said Shep. "Good, solid local history. As a history teacher yourself, you ought to encourage children taking an interest in days gone by. A bit of a ghost story won't harm them."

The kettle lid clanked again in disagreement. Aunt Effie turned her back to the group and rattled around at the stove. Shep sighed as he watched her, then pushed back his coffee mug and stood up. "Right, then," he said. "Sorry, Effie. Just introducing them to Castle Cary. Show me what trouble you're having."

Aunt Effie stopped to fill Uncle Ben's water dish, then set off down the hall to her back office, where she kept her computer. Shep paused before following. "Keep your eye out," he said, and winked at Meg and Will.

Meg saw Will was grinning and trying to wink back, but his winks came out like squints, with both eyes blinking at once.

"I like that guy," said Will, continuing to practice his winks.

"Who?"

It was Ariel, standing in the kitchen doorway. She still wore her nightgown. Her cheeks were flushed and her hair tousled. She swayed and leaned against the doorjamb.

"His name's Shep," said Will.

"I've got a new friend too," said Ariel.

"You can join me on my daily constitutional," Aunt Effie told them as she fussed over Ariel and fixed her a late breakfast. "Uncle Ben and I walk along the pastures and chase squirrels in Bibsie's Woods. At least he does the chasing." She paused to wipe up a fresh patch of dog slobber by Uncle Ben's breakfast bowl. "I'll show you the manor."

"The manor?" asked Will. "Where the ghost is?"

Aunt Effie pinched her brow and looked hard at Will. "The manor is easy to see," she said. "But no ghost. If it's ghost stories you want, I'm sure the manor tour guide will spin you tall tales filled with local folklore. They all believe it around here, swallow the fable hook, line, and sinker. Even Shep, as you see. Pity. Such a sensible fellow otherwise." She sniffed, and glanced down the hall, where Shep was working.

Will said nothing. He didn't know if he believed in ghosts or not, but a manor with a ghost seemed much better than a manor without one.

Half an hour later, the Griffin children were standing on the slate stones in the Griffinage entry hall. The air held the moist scents of spring: mud, damp coats, and daffodils. Ariel was wearing Will's hand-me-down rain boots, still two sizes too big for her, and the others stuffed their feet into their own boots, which had fit perfectly well last October, but were now a size too small. "Curl your toes and never mind," said Meg to Will.

Now they tromped through the Griffinage garden, past the orchard, and out across the first pasture. Aunt Effie stopped to snap on Uncle Ben's leash so he wouldn't worry the sheep. The pastures didn't belong to Aunt Effie. They belonged to local farmers, but anyone could walk along the footpaths that crossed them, as long as walkers left the gates the way they found them.

The pasture had looked green and idyllic from a distance, but up close Will discovered it was mostly mud with ragged clumps of grass. Like a Minnesota soccer field after a rain game. Hoofprints pocked the ground everywhere, as if a team of woolly soccer players had just tramped by. Even the sheep—so white from a distance—were yellowed, and dark patches of mud clotted their wool underbellies. Ariel gave a sudden cry.

"Oh, he's bleeding!" she said. In a trice, she'd dropped Aunt Effie's hand and run toward a sheep with a red splotch on its woolly back.

"There she goes again," muttered Will. Trust Ariel to run after a mucky sheep. She was always delaying things.

"It's not blood!" Aunt Effie called after her. But Ariel was out of earshot. They watched as she coaxed the sheep toward her, then sat squarely in the mud and fingered the ewe's dung- and dirt-stained body. When

they reached Ariel, both her boots were already missing, her face was smudged, and her clothes were two
shades browner.

"Not again," said Will.

"He's not hurt," Ariel reported, her eyes shining.

"No, dear, it's just paint," said Aunt Effie. "Well, dye,
actually. The colors help match the mothers with the
lambs. See? That's her lamb, there. When I was a girl,
they marked the sheep with colors to tell whose sheep
was whose, but they've changed to ear tags for that.
Now, where've your boots got to?"

Ariel shrugged. "They slip when I run. I had to run."

"Of course, you did," Aunt Effie said, chanting the
rhyme: "'Walking is slow and not much fun. Sensible
children always run.'" She spied a boot that had landed
in a heap of sheep dung, and watched as Meg fished
the other out of a rain-soaked ditch. Ariel was now
hopping in her socks, one heel landing in a new pile of
glistening sheep droppings.

"Hmm, you look a bit squelchy," said Aunt Effie
appraising her. "It's a long walk to the manor, and
though they might not mind a bit of good Somerset
sheep grime, I can't take you to the manor barefoot."
She reached for Ariel's grubby hand. "Time for an
Emergency Bath and Costume Change, miss."

Will groaned audibly. A bath! Just when they were
heading to a haunted manor, too. Ariel always messed

things up. Right now she was rubbing noses with Uncle Ben, unaware of the inconvenience she was causing. He and Meg used to have more fun together before Ariel was born. Grown-ups always focused on the needs of the youngest child.

"I suppose . . . ," Aunt Effie continued, seeing their disappointed faces. "You two could go on to the manor by yourselves. Would you like that? Right. It's not too far. I'll just walk you to the first stile."

A stile turned out to be two wooden boards that jutted out from the fence at the end of the pasture. The stile was next to a locked gate. *Just like funny stairs*, thought Meg, as she clambered up the boards. *People can climb out, even if the gate's locked, but sheep can't.* She decided she liked stiles, and climbed back and forth twice to get the hang of it.

"Mind you look out for Caesar," Aunt Effie called, as she tucked Ariel's arm in hers. "He's the ram. The ewes and lambs are fine, but don't turn your back on Caesar. Terror of the neighborhood. Why, just last week he knocked Mrs. Garthwaite flat on her bottomus. 'Know thy enemy and know thyself, and you shall win a hundred battles,' as Sun Tzu reminds us. He's an ancient Chinese general. He probably didn't mean sheep, but knowing Caesar means: Don't turn your back on him. Come along, Ariel."

"I wanna be with Megs and Will!" cried Ariel, suddenly realizing she was being left behind. "Why can't we all go? I wanna go too." She dragged her feet and tried to pull away from Aunt Effie.

Meg hurried over the stile and dropped into the next field. What if Aunt Effie changed her mind and made them take Ariel along? Better to pretend to be out of earshot. But as Meg watched, Aunt Effie firmly collected the dripping boots in her free hand and steered Ariel down the slope to the Griffinage, Uncle Ben trotting by their side.

Will clambered up the stile after Meg. "There's the manor!" he cried, from his perch at the top. "It looks like a castle."

It did indeed look like a castle. Ahead of them, across the sheep fields, rose four great stone towers. Mendip Manor loomed above the trees, each tower topped with a majestic point. If they didn't already know that Castle Cary's castle lay in ruins, it would be easy to assume that this magnificent building was Castle Cary.

"That's exactly where I would live if I were a ghost," cried Will, leaping from the top of the stile without using the steps. "Come on!" He charged across the next pasture at a run.

Meg followed more slowly. He must have forgotten about Caesar already. Meg kept a nervous eye on the sheep, who were standing bunched together on the crest of the hill. Was Caesar up there? She could almost feel his ram's horns barreling into her.

It was a short walk to reach the manor. When they arrived they found a tourist group clustered around a guide. The guide wore a black top hat, and nearby a folding easel announced: DAILY TOURS OF MENDIP MANOR 10 A.M. AND 1 P.M. ADULTS £5, CHILDREN UNDER 12 FREE. "That's us—we're free," said Meg.

"Good," said Will. "Because I didn't bring any money." They slipped in with the crowd, which was just moving toward the great entrance doors.

"Creepy," Will added as they entered the manor's hush. "Wouldn't want to live here."

Meg nodded. She'd felt dwarfed as soon as they'd passed between the manor's double wooden doors, each studded with metal spikes. The entrance was big enough to deserve a drawbridge. Inside was dark and vast. Spring wrens had been singing in the courtyard, but now their cheery song was swallowed up by thick stone walls. The only sound was the murmur of the crowd's shoes and the squeak of the children's rubber boots.

The tour led them through rooms with canopy beds, others with uncomfortable-looking stiff sofas, and everywhere tapestries and pillows with prancing lions embroidered on them. Then came a musty-smelling library with its own fleet of rolling ladders to reach the top shelves. "I wonder if they had their own private librarian, too," mused Meg. The next room was the grand ballroom, a space as big as their school gym, with mirrors stretching to the ceiling. Meg looked at her reflection. It was contorted and yellowish, and the mirrors were bent and coated in tarnish. Finally, the tour guide stopped at the bottom of a spiral staircase that disappeared up into the dark. "One at a time, please— mind the steps," he said.

"This must be the West Tower!" said Will. He'd been quiet during the tour of the bedrooms, sofas, and mirrors. Now he grew animated and darted up the narrow steps.

Meg followed, tracing her fingers along the stone. She had never been up a staircase like this before. Each step was dented in the middle, its stone worn away from centuries of footsteps. She took a step. Just think, with that tiny step, another bit of stone was wearing off. She climbed some more. They were ascending a cylinder. The walls were curved, and the steps shaped liked wedges: fat triangles at one end that grew skinnier at the other. At the skinny end, the steps stacked together to form a central column, like medieval Legos.

"One hundred and twenty-five steps," said Will, greeting her at the top.

"You counted them?"

They were standing in a round tower room. It was only about half the size of the Griffinage kitchen, and Meg and Will were forced to shuffle over as more bodies from the tour group pressed against them. Meg ended up near one of the tower's two windows. Above the trees and fields, she could see the Griffinage's distinctive thatched roof, with its fox weather vane. The tower smelled faintly of burned-out matches, and Meg wondered if sometimes the tour guide lit candles up here. Will began to hiccup.

"Do you think this is the tower Shep was talking about?" Meg said in a low voice.

"Shh," said Will.

"Shh yourself," said Meg, as Will's hiccups grew louder.

"Ladies and gentlemen," said the tour guide. "We are now standing in the most famous part of Mendip Manor, the West Tower, also called the Ghost Tower."

"See, it is," said Meg. Will hiccupped again.

"Ghosts! Cool," said a red-haired boy in the tour group.

"Mendip Manor is proud to have its very own ghost, a lady ghost. Elizabeth Carlisle lived in the manor until her premature death in 1860. She married Richard, baron of Mendip, and they had one child who was killed in an accident. After her daughter's death, Lady Mendip withdrew from society and often came to this lonely tower. She died soon after from a broken heart. Every spring, ghostly lights appear in this tower and people hear bells outside at night." The guide paused and cleared his throat. "They say it is Lady Mendip's ghost looking for her child."

"Why only spring?" asked the redheaded boy.

"Spring is when her daughter died. She died in early April."

"Why bells?" It was Will asking the question this time. He could always find a question to ask about music even in the middle of a ghost story.

"Church bells rang the night young Gillian died. Ringing the bells was like an alarm—it called out the search party to look for her. When they realized she was dead, they kept ringing the bells for three days in mourning."

Meg shivered. She ran her finger along the stone windowsill, imagining the poor girl dying so young and her stricken mother gazing out. This tower made her feel lonely, which was silly, because she was standing in a crowd of people. But she did feel lonely, the same sort of achy loneliness she'd felt this morning when she first woke up.

"Watch your step going down, please," said the guide, ushering them back down the staircase.

The tour group shuffled forward, but Meg and Will lingered near the back to be the last ones in the tower room.

"If there's a ghost here, you'd think we'd *feel* it," Will said, rubbing his ears. He still had the hiccups and the sound reverberated around the stone chamber.

"She must have stood right here," said Meg.

"Yeah," said Will. "More than a hundred and fifty years ago."

"Wouldn't you just love to see a ghost?" asked Meg. "Like her, I mean. A mother ghost. A nice, gentle one like that."

CHAPTER THREE

A Visit in the Attic

As Meg and Will descended the tower's spiral staircase, Ariel was on another set of stairs, at the Griffinage, climbing up.

"You can make the attic your playroom," Aunt Effie told her. "Just your size."

She was clean now, after her bath, and in her arms Ariel cradled a cardboard box. She didn't mind so much about missing Meg and Will now. Aunt Effie had just given her a present and she was eager to try it out. Uncle Ben padded after her, his great paws fumbling on the narrow steps. Ariel ran up them lightly until she came to a landing. There the staircase ended in a short ladder. Uncle Ben stopped beside her and whined. Ariel shook her head. A great big bulky dog couldn't balance on ladder rungs.

"You wait here, Uncle," she said, squeezing past

his furry body. "Don't worry. I'll be back and play with you." She made sure to say that. She didn't want him to feel bad. She knew what it felt like to be left out. Uncle Ben slumped on the landing and snuffed, his snout pointing at Ariel as if determined to follow her.

Ariel climbed up. At the top was the most enchanting room she'd ever seen. It was tiny, only about as big as a bed. It was high up, too, right among the thatched rooftop. One small window jutted out through the thatch and she could see the ends of the thatch stalks, their spiky tips bundled together. In an instant Ariel loved the little attic room. Child-sized. Good for secret games. The ceiling slanted so sharply even Ariel could only kneel at one side but could stand at the other. The room contained one window and was empty, except for a rug.

"Can't wear a hat in here," she announced, trying to sound like Aunt Effie.

She lifted the lid off the cardboard box. Inside was a china tea set. Six white teacups with pictures painted on them lay tucked inside cardboard dividers, plus saucers and a teapot in the middle. Ariel talked to herself as she set each piece out on the floor.

"One for you and one for you. Here's the teapot. You want some cake? We've got chocolate with vanilla fudge. Oh look, here's one with an angel face." She inspected the teacup and its miniature painting, which showed a chubby cherub ringing a bell.

"Hello," said a voice.

Ariel's hands jumped, and the angel cup landed in her lap. A girl was perched on the dormer window ledge. She was dressed in a midnight-blue dress with a white pinafore on top, just like the girls in Ariel's old-fashioned picture books. This little girl had only one shoe on, though. A black leather shoe hooked with many buttons, quite scuffed. On both feet she wore lumpy grey stockings.

It was the girl she'd glimpsed this morning. She could see more of her now. The one who'd held her hand when she first woke up and knew she was missing her mother. Her new friend.

Ariel smiled. The girl must have climbed through the window when she wasn't looking.

The girl smiled too, and slid down from her window perch to stand on the rug. She was taller than Ariel, and older than she was, but still definitely a little girl, not so big and busy as Meg or Will.

"I remember you," Ariel said. "Do you live here?"

"'Course I live here," said the girl. "I've always lived here."

"Does Aunt Effie know about you?"

"This is my house," answered the girl.

"Oh," said Ariel. If it was the girl's house, maybe Aunt Effie was just borrowing it or something—maybe "renting" was the right word. It didn't really matter. She was glad to see her new friend again.

"You have pretty eyes," said Ariel. She had never seen such beautiful eyes. The girl's eyes were silver. Shining silver, like a fairy, Ariel decided.

Down on the landing, Uncle Ben barked. The girl shrank back toward the window.

"Don't worry, that's just Uncle Ben," said Ariel. "He's a dog, not a real uncle, but he's a nice dog."

"Don't like dogs," the girl said.

Uncle Ben barked again, then his voice dropped to a steady rumbly growl.

"It's okay. He's too big to come up," said Ariel. "You wanna play? I'm playing tea party. You can have the angel cup."

She surprised herself when she said that. She'd been admiring the cherub face with wings and was planning to use that one herself, but the girl looked sad and she liked to cheer people up. The girl said nothing, simply accepted the angel teacup Ariel handed her.

"I'm Ariel."

"I'm Kay Kay," the girl answered.

The two girls sat cross-legged on either side of the rug and solemnly looked at each other. Besides the silver eyes, Kay Kay had stringy black hair and a locket around her neck. Her face was smudged, and Ariel could see her pinafore was streaked with mud, as if she'd spent her morning in rough play outside, the kind that would set a mother *tsk-tsk*ing and asking her to strip off her dirty things when she came in, perhaps even into an Emergency Bath.

"Your dress is dirty," said Ariel, who was still damp from her own bath and feeling unusually clean herself.

"They were chasing me," said the girl.

"Who was?"

"Everybody." Kay Kay shrugged. "They were all running and shouting. That's why I tripped." A tremor seemed to pass through the girl's body. She shivered and her hands shook.

"What's wrong?" asked Ariel.

"I don't like the dark!"

Ariel glanced around. A sunbeam was slanting through the window shining cheerful light across the attic. Ariel looked back at the girl, puzzled. Now she was rocking to and fro, clutching her face in her hands. Maybe she was remembering a nightmare. That happened to Ariel sometimes.

"You don't like dogs, you don't like the dark, what *do* you like?" asked Ariel.

The girl sat up, and fixed her gaze on Ariel, her silver eyes suddenly shining.

"I like you," she said.

≪⊙⊙≫

The first person Meg and Will saw when they approached the Griffinage garden was Shep. He was clipping hedges with an enormous pair of garden shears and showering bits of yew about his boots.

"Been up to the manor, have you?" he said, greeting them. "And what did you see?" Meg thought she saw a hint of suppressed excitement on his face.

"No ghost," reported Will.

"Well, not too likely, I suppose," said Shep. "Not with all those people tramping about," he added, giving the hedge a swift chop. "Keep your eyes out. You never know where ghosts may appear." He winked at them and looked around the garden, as though half expecting to see a ghost there, then beamed and raised his shears in greeting to Aunt Effie, who waved to them from the side window.

"Aunt Effie doesn't like ghosts, does she?" asked Meg.

"No," agreed Shep. "A fine woman otherwise. None finer." He coughed suddenly and moved round to the other side of the hedge. The children trailed after him, Will practicing his wink as he walked.

"Can you tell us more?" asked Will. "More about the manor ghost."

Shep paused and rested his shears beside him. They were behind the hedge now, and could no longer see Aunt Effie in the window. From the walnut tree, a robin sang and another robin answered from the thatch. Time seemed suspended.

"Well, the girl was called Gillian Elizabeth. I'd say

she was around your age, Meg. She was just ten—"

"I'm eleven," Meg interjected.

"Well, Gillian had just turned ten, and she died on her birthday."

"Oooh, that's horrible." Meg squirmed. She could think of nothing worse than dying on her own birthday.

"How did she die?" asked Will. "What kind of accident was it?"

"Horse riding. Very common accident in those days. Rather like car crashes we have today. Falls, kicks, trampling under foot. Not the horses' fault, mind, but it happened all the same, especially to children. Well, on the day of her tenth birthday, Miss Gillian went riding. They say it was late afternoon, with April mud as slick and slippery as today. She was out on her ride when a fog came up. Miss Gillian's horse headed down by Mendip Brook, slipped, and threw her. She landed on the rocks in the cold water and broke her neck."

The children huddled by the hedge in silence. The sunshine and robin's song seemed out of place. All Meg could picture was that rocky creek and the poor girl with a crumpled body. Walking back from the manor, she'd been hungry for lunch, but now she didn't feel like eating.

"As they say, the mother went wild. Of course, they found the body and held a proper funeral and all, but

Lady Mendip wouldn't stop searching for her daughter. Took to wearing a copper brooch and the same dress she'd worn the night her daughter died, a dress made of green velvet. She let her hair drape down all wild and tangled. She still looks for her." He picked up the shears again.

"Still wears it too," he added, almost as an afterthought.

"Wears what?" asked Will.

"The green velvet. And the brooch. Wears it over her heart."

Meg and Will looked at him, puzzled. Shep spoke with such authority, almost as if he'd seen the lady himself.

"But how do you know?" asked Will. "How could you know she still wears it?"

Shep shifted to the next part of the hedge and began clipping the highest branches with great whacks, but did not answer. Will pitched his next question loudly to make sure Shep could hear him above the *clack* of his shears.

"You don't really believe in ghosts. Do you, Shep? I mean, you can't *really*."

Shep turned his chapped face toward Will for a moment, then abruptly turned back to clipping the hedge. Scattered yew needles landed on Will's hair as the twigs flew.

"Now you've done it," Meg said, poking Will in the arm as they entered the Griffinage front door.

"What?" said Will.

"You made him feel dumb. He's all offended now."

"I never said he was dumb!"

"No, but that's the way he took it."

"So? I was just asking a question!" said Will. "Besides, most grown-ups don't take things like ghosts seriously."

Most grown-ups don't take kids seriously either, thought Meg. That's what made Shep so instantly likable. He treated everyone as equals: children, adults, and ghosts.

As the children washed their hands for lunch, the small ghost left the attic and drifted back to her spot near the walnut tree. Already she felt stronger. She rubbed her icy fingers and pressed them to her cheeks. They weren't so cold anymore. Oh, it was good to be back in the warmth of a human smile.

CHAPTER FOUR

The Creek

They didn't see any more of Shep that day. After lunch their parents called, and then Aunt Effie took them all into Shepton Mallet for a ride on the steam trains. That treat was followed by ice cream cones, proving, once again, that Aunt Effie was the best aunt of all. By the time they returned, the hedge clippers were hanging back in the toolshed and the bits of loose yew stems had been swept up.

Ariel was full of chatter during dinner, which was shepherd's pie with chocolate pudding for dessert. Will tuned her out. He was still thinking about ghosts, and wondering how they'd ever learn more if Shep was annoyed with them. Asking Aunt Effie was out of the question. There were some grown-ups you could ask for ice creams, and some grown-ups you could ask about ghosts; it was important to know which type of grown-up you were dealing with.

"I really, really like it here, Aun' Effie," Ariel was saying. "I have a friend and she's called Kay Kay, and Uncle Ben was too big to come up, but Kay Kay wasn't too big and she says she'll come back to play."

"Who's Kay Kay?" asked Meg.

"Well, she . . . Kay Kay just lives here an' plays with me."

"Another imaginary friend," said Will, rolling his eyes. "They always have kooky names."

"She's got a nice name," retorted Ariel. "And she's better than you, Will. She's got *lots* of time to play. And she said she'd play with me tomorrow."

"Lovely, dear," said Aunt Effie, before Will could answer. "Now about tomorrow. It's the school holiday here, so I don't teach classes, but I do have a spot of paperwork. I'll take you to Glastonbury in the afternoon. Full of history. King Arthur up on the tower hill, of course, and King Alfred down in the Levels, plus there's a museum with Iron Age artifacts." She laughed. "That's what you get with an aunt who's a history teacher! But in the morning I'm going to be boring as a brick, so you lot must amuse yourselves until lunchtime."

The next morning, Aunt Effie had already disappeared down the hall to her office with a mug of tea by the time the children came downstairs, and they soon heard the *tap-tap* typing of a keyboard. They helped themselves to breakfast, which was oatmeal.

Meg watched over Ariel. She helped her find a spoon, scoop the oatmeal, and pour the milk jug, which was too heavy for her skinny five-year-old arms. Being five wasn't easy, she thought. When she herself had been five, she would have been scared to even go on a trip like this. She would have missed her parents so much she probably would have cried. Meg began to feel bad about leaving Ariel yesterday when she and Will were off at the manor. After all, she always had Will, but Ariel didn't have anyone her age to play with.

"You're not listening," Ariel said.

"Uh. What?"

"I said Kay Kay likes blue best," Ariel repeated.

Meg nodded indulgently. "That's nice," she said. Ariel was always playing with imaginary friends. At home she would go on and on about her imaginary friend Mia, and before that, it was Gobi, or someone else.

"We both like blue, but I let her use the angel cup and it has a blue ribbon on it. There's a house, a lamb, a dog, a bear and a flower, but the angel's my favorite. Kay Kay's, too. Kay Kay says . . ."

"Wait. I thought Mia was the name of your invisible friend," Will interrupted. "What happened to her? Did you ditch her?"

Ariel was silent for a moment.

"Mia's still my friend," she said. "But right now I'm playing with Kay Kay."

⤸⤹

Aunt Effie stayed buried in her office through most of breakfast, but when Shep stopped by—entering, then knocking afterward, as usual—she emerged and came out to the entry hall. Will dropped his oatmeal spoon and got there first, hoping to corner Shep and ask him more about ghosts.

"Shep, I was wondering . . . ," began Will.

"Not now," said Shep, stepping past Will. "Good morning, Effie!" he boomed out.

Aunt Effie stood on the slate stones of the entry hall beaming at her visitor. Her hair was disarrayed and adorned with a stray piece of thatch.

"New lambs out in McBurney's pasture," Shep informed her. "Thought the kids might like to see them, since they're too worldly for ghosts." He gave Will a sidelong glance.

Will winced. Meg was right. He had offended Shep somehow. Meanwhile, Aunt Effie was bobbing, smiling, and exclaiming over the status of the lambs.

"Ah, Will," said Aunt Effie, a few moments later, suddenly noticing him. "What about a morning walk?"

"Looks as if you've been out this morning yourself," said Shep, with a shy grin. "How else did you manage to get thatch in your hair?" He leaned forward and plucked the stray piece from her curls.

Ariel was scooping out the last of the breakfast toppings when Will returned. Her bowl resembled a tower of raisins more than a serving of oatmeal. While Ariel balanced raisins on her spoon, Meg and Will made plans to go back to the manor. Will wanted to see the creek and explore the manor from the outside. Meg pointed out that Ariel had missed seeing the manor yesterday, inside or out, and the lambs would be fun to see on the way. Ariel didn't say anything, but looked dreamily out the window. So it was settled.

Will was the first to be ready. He pulled on his boots and stamped about on the slate stones in the entry hall. Meg went upstairs to the bedroom to check on Ariel. She expected to find her in the alcove playing with the stuffed animals she'd brought, but instead Ariel was standing by the window, gazing at the bare branches of the walnut tree.

"Come on, are you ready?" asked Meg. "You get to see the manor today."

"No," said Ariel, turning away from the window.

"What do you mean, no? You get to come with us."

"I want to stay here."

Meg stared at her sister in disbelief. She certainly *could* stay, since Aunt Effie was just downstairs, but . . .

"But Ariel, there's going to be lambs!" she protested. "Don't you want to see the lambs?"

Ariel shook her head.

"I want to play upstairs with Kay Kay," she said resolutely. Then she turned back to the window. Meg hesitated. Ariel turning down lambs was like Will turning down a piano. But it wasn't just the lambs; Ariel's refusal was also a strike against *her*. Most days Ariel was a nuisance, always begging to be with Meg and Will. Now here they were inviting her, and she stood looking at a tree.

"Come on," she said, reaching for Ariel's arm. "I know you want to come." Ariel shook her off and stepped away. Downstairs Meg heard the front door bang, and more stamping from Will's boots. She looked back at Ariel one last time.

"Are you *sure*?" she asked.

Ariel stood silent and Meg turned away.

As soon as Meg and Will left, Ariel slipped upstairs. She watched from Will's bedroom window until her brother and sister had cleared the first stile to McBurney's pasture. Meg did glance back toward the Griffinage several times, but each time Ariel ducked out of sight. Now they were too far away to see her. Meg and Will were way up the hill looking at the sheep. From Ariel's window, the lambs were bright white dots next to their mothers' yellowed coats. Ariel drew back from the window and ran up the attic stairs. Once again, Uncle Ben followed her as far as the landing. Already, a fluff of brown dog fur was collecting in the corner. Ariel climbed the ladder and pushed open the door. She smiled at what she saw.

"Hello," Ariel said. "You're back."

Kay Kay sat perched by the windowsill again. She wore the same white pinafore smudged with mud, and the same midnight-blue dress underneath. She dangled her feet off the floor, still with one shoe off and one shoe on. She was pulling her fingers in an agitated way and sat hunched, with her shoulders pinched together, but the moment she saw Ariel she slid down from the windowsill.

"There you are!" she said. "What took you so long? I've been waiting."

Without pausing for an answer, she turned to the tea set and began humming as she set the pieces out. Ariel said nothing, but watched her. It was a plaintive tune, made up of five notes. Before she knew it, Ariel also hummed along. La de de la da. La de de la da. Kay Kay's shoulders relaxed as the girls hummed together.

⊲⊱

Mendip Brook wound through woods and open fields for several miles near the manor before bubbling through a culvert under the A37 and heading south toward Yeovil. Meg and Will watched the lambs gamboling for a while, but it wasn't quite so fun without Ariel's usual exclamations. After the lambs, Will suggested a different route to the manor.

"If we go the same way each time, we'll never find clues," he said. "And with Shep not helping, we're on our own. Who knows, maybe we'll see something from a different angle. Besides, don't you want to see the woods where Gillian went riding?"

They turned east and struck out across a field dotted with cheerful yellow blossoms on spiky gorse bushes. As soon as they entered the woods, the air cooled and the ground grew muddier beneath their feet. The gorse gave way to sparse patches of bluebells. Outside the woods, the stream was tame, its waters gently murmuring through grassy, rounded banks. Here the brook gurgled in a commanding voice as it tumbled over stones strewn in its rocky bed.

"Look! There's the tower. You can see it from here," called Will.

Sure enough, the grey stone tower loomed between the tree trunks on the far bank. Will was keen to examine the tower from the outside. "You never know," he said. "They might have electrical wires rigged up somewhere to flash all those ghost lights."

Last night, though he hadn't told Meg, Will had

set his alarm for the middle of the night and peeked out his bedroom window at the manor tower. No lights. Everything ordinary, of course. It was what he'd expected, but still he'd felt a twinge of disappointment as he crawled back into bed.

"You really don't believe it, do you?" Meg was several paces behind him, picking her way slowly, stepping on roots to avoid the mud.

"Oh, I believe Gillian died all right, but believing the story doesn't mean I'm sure about the ghost part."

"You really think Shep's just . . . Oh!"

At that moment Meg fell. Her foot slipped off a particularly slick root, and she skidded down the muddy bank. As she fell, her boot heels dug into the stream bank, gouging a trail of mud and stones behind her. She came to a stop just before the water with her right hand buried in a thick clump of plants growing on the bank.

"Yowch! My hand." She cradled her hand, wincing in pain. Meg's hand was red and swelling rapidly, her skin pricked with many tiny white dots.

"Nettles," said Will. "You broke your fall in a stinging nettle patch. Good thing you didn't fall into the creek."

"Like Gillian," said Meg. She looked around in a panic. Maybe *this* was the spot. Of course, she wasn't riding a horse, so falling didn't have the same impact, but still. New shoots of pain made her wince. "Yow, these nettles hurt worse than ours back home."

"At least we know the creek's slippery," said Will. "That part of the story's true."

"Of course, it's slippery, Mr. Ghosthunter! Why do you think I fell?" Meg turned her back on Will. Her hand felt as if she'd been stung by ten bees. She crouched on a flat rock lodged midway in the creek and submerged her hand in the cool water to ease the painful swelling. Behind her, the bank where she'd fallen gave way, sending a small landslide of mud and stones into the creek.

Something silver glinted up from the mud. Will jumped down to the spot Meg had just vacated and scrabbled in the dirt with his fingers. "Found something," Will said. The object was deeply buried, just a corner sticking out. Will grabbed a stick and used it as a makeshift shovel.

Meg left her spot midstream and hopped back to the muddy bank. Will's body was blocking whatever it was, and she edged closer to see. "Let me help," she said. Meg picked up a sharp rock and chipped away at the bank next to Will, using her left hand to dig. In a few minutes, they tugged the silver object clear. Will dipped it in the stream to wash it off. It was a metal circle with some sort of handle or buckle loop on one side. Inside the silver circle was a prancing lion. A short bit of decomposed leather dangled from it.

"It's some sort of belt," said Will, looking at it dubiously. "I think." He rubbed it on his shirt to remove more mud.

"I've never seen a belt buckle like that before," said Meg. "But it's pretty, and I bet it's old. Probably Roman or something," she ventured, trying to sound erudite. At least she knew she was right that the ancient Romans used to live around here, since Aunt Effie was always talking about it.

"Are you nuts? Not that old. The leather would have rotted."

"Well, it has rotted."

"I mean all of it. Romans were here thousands of years ago."

"Look—there's writing, too," said Meg, eager to redeem herself and draw attention away from the not-quite-as-old-as-Roman leather.

They peered more closely at the strange circle. There were certainly marks next to the lion's paws, but they were faded and hard to decipher. It looked like a fancy *W*, or maybe Roman numerals. As they stared at it, a bit of the leather crumbled and dropped into the creek. Will shrugged and slipped the silver object into his pocket.

"Finders keepers," he said. "Let's go to the manor now. There must be something more we can find."

"I'm a lady from the manor," said Kay Kay solemnly as she poured the imaginary tea.

"I'm a lady from the manor too," echoed Ariel. "Let's pretend we're sisters." She'd always wanted a sister closer to her own age. An everyday playmate, like Will was to Meg.

"Oooh, would you like to?" asked Kay Kay. "You could come live with me and we'd be sisters always." She set the teapot down but held the angel cup in one hand. Then she slipped her free hand into Ariel's. Ariel pulled away. There was something about the girl's hands. So icy. Colder than her own hands felt on a January day waiting for the school bus. Kay Kay reached for her hand again, and this time Ariel let her hold it.

"Breathe on me," Kay Kay said.

Ariel looked at her new friend, puzzled. Kay Kay nodded and thrust her other hand toward her, so Ariel leaned over Kay Kay's frozen fingers and gave a few tentative puffs. Kay Kay rewarded her with a radiant smile. Ariel scooted closer then, and bent her head over Kay Kay's arm, cupping the girl's cold hands in both her own and gently blowing warm streams of air. As she blew, Ariel's hair swayed over their clasped hands, enshrouding them like a curtain. Kay Kay sat completely still, her silver eyes closed.

"Don't leave me," she whispered.

"All right."

"Don't leave me," Kay Kay said again.

"I'm not going to," said Ariel. "I'm not going anywhere. Well, not till vacation's done," she added. She sat up. The fingers wrapped around hers didn't seem quite so cold anymore, or was it her own fingers that were growing less warm? It was hard to tell.

Kay Kay screwed up her eyes and began to cry. Her body rocked rhythmically. Then she spoke again, her words sounding more like a chant, one she might have said hundreds of times before: "Don't leave me. Come find me. Stop the bells. Don't leave me. . . ."

"What's the matter?" Ariel said, withdrawing her hand. The little girl clutched her stomach, while still holding the china cup. She gave a low moan.

"Where are you?"

"I'm right here!" said Ariel, looking at Kay Kay in alarm. Kay Kay was the oddest girl she'd ever met. Was she sick? Maybe the best thing was to get Aunt Effie. Still Ariel didn't move, but stayed watching, fascinated.

The girl trembled. Then she flung out her arms with a jerk, as if to stop herself from falling. As she did, the teacup dropped. The angel one. It crashed to the floor, scattering broken bits of china. One shard landed near Ariel's foot. The angel was still ringing its bell, but a crack sliced through the angel child's cheek. Ariel stared at it. Why had she given Kay Kay her favorite cup? Why did Kay Kay have to break the angel?

A scream jolted her. From the landing, Uncle Ben began to bark, deep throaty barks. Ariel snapped her head up.

Kay Kay was gone. In the spot where she'd been, shards from the broken angel cup quivered.

Meg and Will circled the manor from the outside, looking for signs of secret wires that could be used for flashing lights, but they found nothing except an old boot lace and a startled toad, who hopped away. By the time they reached the front entrance, the ten o'clock crowd was gathering for a manor tour.

"Want to go again?" asked Meg. "Maybe the tour guide will say something different, or we could ask him."

"Too much old furniture," said Will. "All those sofas and chairs. I want to go straight to the tower, but they make you look at all the other stuff first."

"Okay, what about that place?" A sign had caught Meg's eye. Across from where they were standing in the manor courtyard was a row of downtown shops all joined together. She pointed to a narrow, crooked building with dark timbers crisscrossing white painted walls. The sign read: THE HAUNTED TOWER: TOYS, BOOKS, AND CURIOSITIES. The shop was so skinny it looked like a tower itself.

As they drew closer, Meg could see the sign was painted on a hanging wooden panel. Its hinges creaked

as the sign swayed back and forth over their heads.

"It's just a tourist shop," Will objected. "See all those plastic ghosts in the window? They're just trying to make a dollar—er, a pound—off people's interest in the manor ghost."

"Well, *we're* interested in the manor ghost," said Meg. "Come on."

The door clanked open. The store was full of bric-a-brac, but empty of customers, except for a girl and her grandfather, who were in the process of buying one of the plastic ghosts. The ghost had googly eyes and made a howling noise whenever the little girl pressed a button on its tummy. They navigated the narrow aisles, careful not to bump into stacks of ceramic ghosts, glass ghosts, or salt-and-pepper-shaker ghost sets.

"Can I help you?"

A short woman, no taller than Meg, stood behind them. Meg didn't hear her come up.

"Uh, no thanks . . . ," Will automatically began, but Meg was already asking a question.

"Do you have any books about the manor?"

The short woman pointed to a table in the back. "Architecture, Victorian furniture, tapestries, fashion of the day, legends and lore . . ."

"Legends and lore," said Meg promptly.

"The ghost, eh?"

The woman turned and led them to the back book

table. Meg followed silently. She didn't mind talking about ghosts with Will and Shep, but it was embarrassing with other adults. What would the woman think of her? The shop woman reached the table, rubbed dust off a pile of books with her fingers, and handed Meg a slim volume. Apparently, most people didn't come to this store for its literature.

"Here you are, dear," she said. "And if it's ghosts you like, have a look at our ghost window figurines. The ghost waves when sunlight strikes it, and we've got new ones in with LED lights that flash in nine colors. They're our most popular. Plus, they work all year. Don't have to wait for April."

"Oh, thanks," said Meg. *April, again. The ghost sure seemed to be tied to April. If there was ever a good time to see a ghost, this was it.* The woman walked back to the shop counter, and Meg settled down on the floor to examine the book. Will squatted next to her as she flipped the pages. The book was a general one about Somerset ghost stories, but it had a chapter on Mendip Manor.

"Let's see, here it is," said Meg. "Gillian Elizabeth, daughter of the last baron of Mendip."

"There's a picture of her, look," said Will.

Meg looked at the photograph. It was an early photograph, sepia-toned, showing a young girl, her hair pulled back with a prominent part down the middle.

She was holding the reins of a horse and dressed in a riding outfit. A lapdog danced at her feet, slightly blurry. Meg thought Gillian looked anxious to be off riding, too, as if impatient with the photographer.

"It says her horse's name was Spirit," said Meg, reading the caption.

"Spirit?"

"Well, the horse is sort of greyish white. Kind of like a ghost. Maybe that's why she named it Spirit."

"Or because the horse had a wild spirit," Will offered. "Maybe it ran too fast."

"Don't blame it on the horse," said Meg. "He looks sweet. Besides, Shep said horse accidents used to happen all the time."

Meg turned the page. It was filled with shields, swords, and coats of arms.

"Hey, look," said Will, pointing to a symbol of a dancing lion. Meg peered over his arm. The lion did seem familiar. She must have seen it before, but where? Oh yes, at the manor, on the beds and things, and somewhere else. Beside her, Will was busy fishing in his pocket. He pulled out the silver belt buckle they'd found in the creek bed. In his palm was a lion prancing just like the picture.

"It's the same symbol," said Will. "This buckle must have come from the manor."

"Yeah, and the *W* must be an *M*, after all. An *M* for

Mendip," said Meg. "I wonder what it was."

"Who knows? They had different things back then," said Will. "It could be anything."

"I wonder if it used to be Gillian's," said Meg. "Something she played with down by the creek."

"Or something she died with."

The little ghost shook herself and floated back to a branch of the walnut tree. Falling. Always falling. That final fall still scared her.

It was so pleasant with her new friend: holding hands, warm breath, smiles. If only she could keep that feeling forever. The warm contentment of company.

All the children who played with her went away.

It wasn't fair.

The last time a child had lived in the little cottage was a hundred years ago. The families always moved, and neighbor children who stumbled into the garden were entertaining for a few years but had an awful habit of growing up. Then she would be alone again.

If only she could keep one.

The little ghost dropped to a lower branch. Already she'd felt more stirrings. The cracks in time were opening. It happened every April. The earth heaving, groaning, and twisting with the strain of two worlds mixing, the living and the dead. She could feel herself grow stronger.

The ghost floated back to the cottage and peered

through the window at the cozy group gathered in the kitchen. Her playmate was seated among the living: chewing, laughing, eating food.

Yes, she could be the one.

How good it would feel to have this girl by her side.

Not just today.

But tomorrow and always.

A forever friend.

CHAPTER FIVE

Ghost Lessons

After lunch, they spent a windy afternoon at Glastonbury. It was a good thing Aunt Effie drove a Mini, Will decided. Some of the roads they took barely had room for anything else. It was strange enough to be driving on the left side of the road, but then there were prickly hedges and blind corners. Hedges towered like walls on the sides of some country roads, and at times the two-way road dropped to one lane. When the road narrowed at a corner, Aunt Effie tooted her horn and relied on mirrors mounted on the hedges to see if another car was about to crash into them.

Glastonbury Tor was a grassy hill with a ruined tower on top. It was so windy at the summit that Aunt Effie needed to shout as she told them stories about King Arthur and the ancient island of Avalon. The wind sliced through the tower's empty roof and windows, making a wild sound. They were glad to descend to the Levels. As they walked along the hedgerows, Aunt Effie introduced them to Gog and Magog, two ancient oak trees along the path. "These venerable old oaks are thought to be two thousand years old! Makes our walnut seem like a child, doesn't it? Just think of the history they've seen," she said in a wistful voice. Afterward, they stopped in Glastonbury for ice-cream cones, and Will tried a new flavor, raspberry ripple.

Uncle Ben greeted them back at the Griffinage. He nuzzled them all one by one, and wagged so hard that his great thumping tail nearly knocked Ariel over. Meg ducked out of the way. Her hand was still swollen from the nettle stings, and probably didn't want to be thumped. Will saw Aunt Effie mixing up another batch of baking soda paste.

"Why are you painting Meg's hand?" asked Ariel.

"Takes the sting out, dearie," answered Aunt Effie. "Nasty things, nettles," she continued. "Though I do know people who eat them. Nettle soup! With potatoes, of course. And nettle tea is supposed to be very good for arthritis and allergies: packed with iron, calcium, and magnesium. They say if you grasp a nettle firmly enough you don't get stung, but I must admit I've never had the gumption to try. Ladybirds love them and lay their eggs on nettle leaves. I suppose if you're an insect with an exoskeleton, nettles can't sting no matter how lightly you tread. There! That should feel better soon."

She patted Meg's arm and put the baking soda away. Meg examined her hand, which was freshly caked with white paste. *Like a ghost*, Will thought. He sighed. He didn't think he believed in ghosts, not really, but still it would be cool to see one. Here they were visiting in April, supposedly the best time, and Shep advised them to "keep your eye out," but no sign of anything mysterious yet. Meg cradled her hand and disappeared upstairs. Will fingered the silver lion in his pocket. At least they'd found something.

From the living room, he could hear Aunt Effie's voice as she began reading *Alice in Wonderland* to Ariel, Uncle Ben sprawled at their feet. They'd just reached the part in the story where Bill the lizard goes flying out the chimney. It was one of Will's favorite parts, but he didn't feel like listening. He wanted to know how to see a ghost. Will trailed up the stairs to Meg's room.

"What are we going to *do*?" he asked, flopping on her bed.

"About what?"

"Oh, Shep's mad at me, and he's the only one who knows about ghosts—*really* knows."

"Well," said Meg. "That's easy. You just have to get him un-mad."

"How am I supposed to do that?"

"You could apologize."

"But I didn't *do* anything. Not really. What do I say? 'I'm sorry I don't believe in ghosts'? People don't usually apologize for things like that."

Meg was silent. They both knew it would be good to have Shep back on their side and ready to talk. They had so many questions, and the book in the shop only offered vague phrases like "some say the tower is haunted."

"What about a peace offering?" Meg asked after a bit.

"You mean a white flag?"

"No, I was thinking of a present. Something to show we really like him."

"How about a chocolate bar?"

"That's perfect," said Meg. "Now we have to find some money."

"No, we don't," said Will.

"Well, how else are we going to get a chocolate bar?"

"From my sock," said Will, flashing his wide Griffin grin. "I saved one from the airport."

"He's home," Will reported a few minutes later. "I set it on the stoop, but I didn't go in."

Aunt Effie had pointed out Shep's house to them the day before. He was her nearest neighbor and the only visible house around, so it was easy to find.

"Good," said Meg, sitting down on the Griffinage

front step beside him. They'd decided to wait twenty minutes for Shep to find and eat the chocolate. Will had originally voted for half an hour, or even an hour, but Meg had pointed out that Shep might have to go out somewhere after that length of time, or a squirrel might eat it, so they settled on twenty minutes.

Twenty minutes later, Meg and Will approached Shep's house and found Shep himself standing in his doorway wearing his scuffed leather boots. Even with a regular-sized door, he almost had to bend his head to look out. There was no sign of the candy bar.

"Ah. Thought I might be seeing more of you two," Shep said.

"We've come . . . ," began Will.

"I know why you've come," said Shep, with a smile. "In you go, and shake your jackets off."

Meg struggled with her jacket one-handed, careful not to bump her nettle stings. She always felt shy entering someone's house for the first time. It was one thing to meet a person, but visiting where they lived was like meeting that person all over again. You got to glimpse inside of them somehow. Like seeing stray bits of soul they didn't know they'd left lying out. Shep's house smelled like coffee, fireplace smoke, and damp socks.

By the time Meg entered the living room, Will was already perched on a three-legged stool by the fireplace, tipping it up on two legs and talking animatedly to Shep. Meg settled back in a huge red wingback armchair and looked around Shep's living room. It was a jumble of centuries: old stone walls and musty books, plus computer cords and all kinds of devices strewn about.

"Care for a bit of chocolate?" Shep winked at Will when he said this. He dug in his vest pocket and produced a slightly squashed candy bar in an orange and purple wrapper.

"Double Decker, my favorite," said Shep. "Can't answer for its condition. Arrived mysteriously at my house this afternoon." Will blushed and righted the stool with a *thump*. Shep split the candy bar into three pieces, passing out sticky bits of nougaty chocolate to the children and popping the last bit in his mouth. They all licked their fingers in silence. Will perched on the edge of the three-legged stool and looked expectantly at Shep.

"So you want to know more about ghosts, do you?" Shep asked. The twinkle in his eye was back, and Meg settled into the armchair with a contented sigh. It was obvious Shep wasn't irritated with them anymore.

"Have you seen her?" Will asked.

"Not in years."

"But you did, once?" said Will. Will and Meg exchanged glances. So he did think they were real.

"Long ago," said Shep. "When I was younger than you. We all saw her for a while, us kids in the village. Saw her a couple of times, and other ghosts, too, before we stopped looking. Your aunt would hate it that I'm telling you all this." He paused and stared out the window, lost in thought.

"Why did you stop looking?" asked Meg.

"Eh?"

"Why did you stop looking for ghosts?"

"Got too old, you know," answered Shep. "It's young kids who mostly see ghosts. Starting around age two. That's when it starts, with nightmares and things. Parents think it's just a dream, but of course some of it's ghosts. I'd say it peaks between four and ten for most children. By the time I was twelve or so, maybe around eleven, I knew I wouldn't have much luck anymore, so I gave up. My brother, Pete, could see the ghosts, but I was done."

Meg and Will looked at each other. Both knew what the other was thinking: Shep must be telling them all this because he thought they were the right age. He'd probably seen a real ghost, maybe even lots of ghosts, and he hoped they'd see one too. *Around age twelve.* Will was ten and Meg was a year older. Were they young enough? Would they be able to see them?

"Of course, ghosts only show up when they want to. They've got their own agendas."

"Ghosts have agendas?" asked Meg. The word made her think about her agenda planner for school that listed all her class times.

"In a manner of speaking. Not to do with schedules and so on—no, that's for the living. Ghosts don't follow time, you see. They follow longings."

Shep looked directly at each child. Will, who'd been tipping the stool on its front legs to the outer limit since they'd arrived, righted it again on all three. Meg sat up straight in her armchair. The way Shep looked at her confirmed they were having a serious conversation. She'd never heard anyone talk about ghosts like this before. There was no sound except for the ticking of Shep's kitchen clock.

"A ghost longs for something most dreadfully," Shep went on. "We all long for things when we're alive—maybe for a puppy, or being popular at school—but a ghost longs for something so powerfully and so intensely that it just goes on longing even after its body dies. That's why only some people turn into ghosts. Most rest in peace. A ghost is an unfulfilled longing."

"And the manor ghost is longing for her child," said Will.

"That's right."

"So you sort of see their longing," said Meg.

"Right again," Shep continued. "When the longing is strong enough, the ghost becomes visible. Not to everyone. Grown-ups might see lights or nothing at all. But children can usually sense the longing and it looks like a real person."

The manor ghost's longing was obvious, thought Meg. But what about other ghosts? What were they all longing for so intently that it wouldn't let them be properly dead?

"Wait, how do you know all this?" asked Will. He sounded as if he'd been bursting to ask this question the whole time.

"A bit of personal study."

"You mean you went to ghost school?"

"Some of the best things in life you don't learn in school," Shep answered. "I discuss it with a friend of mine. He's a minister, in the business of souls you might say. But mainly I learned about ghosts as a boy by going right to the experts: conversations with the ghosts themselves."

Conversations with ghosts! Shep made it sound so friendly, Meg thought. What would she say to a ghost? She'd like to meet a ghost and try having a chat. *Hello, how does it feel to float?* she'd say. It would be like having an imaginary friend, like Ariel, but one you could really see.

"Now then," said Shep. "Must be getting close to your dinner time. I don't want to fall on Effie's bad side. Besides, if I fill up your heads with ghosts, she won't have any space left to heap on the history." He winked and ushered them to the door. "Keep your eyes open, see what you find."

On the way home, Will hopped from foot to foot in excitement and talked nonstop about ghosts. "He really saw one. More than one! And made friends with them. I hope we're here long enough." Meg only half listened. She was distracted by a mix of feelings. Excitement, yes, but learning about ghosts' longings had put her in a melancholy mood, and there was something else that was bothering her.

They reached the Griffinage garden. Above them, a sparrow perched on the thatch, tugged at a strand of straw, and then flew off with it proudly in its beak. From inside they could hear Ariel's small voice singing. It wasn't "Frère Jacques," her usual tune. It was something new, a rather mournful song.

"Do you think I'm too old?" asked Meg. She swallowed a lump that seemed to stick in her throat.

"We'll find out."

"Oh, Will, I couldn't bear it if eleven is too old. Just when things are getting exciting!"

CHAPTER SIX

St. Giles

Early the next morning, the music came again. From his bed, Will lay perfectly still, trying to catch the notes. It was the bell song, louder this time. The melody seemed to be surrounding the Griffinage. He strained to listen, moving in that drowsy half-awake state, but already the bells were fading.

"La de de la da," he hummed. "F, C-sharp, C, high F, C and then C-sharp, C, B-flat, F. La de de la da, la la de dun. La de de la da . . ."

That was it. That was the tune.

A sudden rush of energy swept through Will. He could feel his chest swell with happiness. He felt like this whenever a song came to him. A new one. A melody he liked to pursue and tap out at home on the piano. On mornings like this, his mother would come looking for him, leaning her head around the doorway, and find him still bent over the keys. "Will? You all right? You forgot to eat breakfast."

As if on cue, his stomach rumbled, but equally powerfully, his heart sang with the enchantment of this new melody. Usually, songs he heard in his sleep faded the instant he woke, but not this time. It lingered in his head, and he was pleased to realize it was the same tune he'd tried to remember the day before. Will tromped downstairs wishing again for a piano. The Griffinage didn't have one after all, though this was the first morning he'd really missed it.

"It's a little early to be singing," said Meg.

Will looked up. He hadn't noticed Meg come in. He was in the kitchen making toast, and playing with the cancel button that made the toast spring into the air. Meg stood in the kitchen doorway.

"I'm just humming."

"Well, that's loud humming," said Meg. "I heard it all the way upstairs. Woke me up."

"Did not."

"Did too. Ariel heard it also and started talking about Kay Kay again."

Will reached for his toast, which was now crisped dark brown from being toasted so many times. He must have been singing out loud without knowing it.

"Sorry. It just comes out sometimes," he said.

"Well, just don't sing at breakfast. I don't need an orchestra with my orange juice."

But music seemed to fill Will's head that morning. Try as he might, he couldn't stop humming or singing the new tune, even when Meg glared at him, even when Ariel knocked over her milk and soaked his second piece of toast, even an hour later, when Aunt Effie breezed in from the garden and started talking.

"Will! You haven't been listening," said Meg.

"What?"

"It might be a good chance to look for her."

"Who?" said Will absently.

"Who do you think?" asked Meg.

"Oh, the ghost," Will said. *La de de la da . . .* His mind was still on the song.

"So are you coming?"

"Where?"

"To the auction! It's at the manor," said Meg. "That's what Aunt Effie's been telling us, and they'll be letting people into special rooms that aren't usually open to the public, and . . . Oh, never mind. You're driving me crazy this morning."

Will groaned at the thought of auction crowds jamming up the manor. He'd be pressed and crushed. That was the last place he wanted to be right now. Besides, they would never see the ghost in all that mess.

"Go on if you want," said Will. "I'm going outside."

Meg scowled and stamped upstairs. He stepped over Ariel, who was lying on the threshold rubbing Uncle Ben, and found Aunt Effie to tell her his plans. Then, whistling, Will lifted the latch to the Griffinage door.

The truth was Will wanted to be alone. On days like this, when songs came, he liked to think and wander nowhere in particular. He was glad the manor auction was going on today. It would keep everyone busy while he went off on his own. From the corner of Bibsie's Woods, he watched Meg, Ariel, and Aunt Effie pile into the car, then he headed east and crossed over McBurney's stile.

By now he was whistling loudly. The ewes barely lifted their woolly heads, but the lambs twitched their ears and looked at him. *Nice song*, they seemed to say. *Stay and sing for us*. But Will walked on. He was headed in the direction of the village. He had half an idea of buying a sausage roll at the bakery and taking a long hike, but when he climbed up the second stile he saw something that made him stop. It was the little stone church in the village, St. Giles, with its rectangular bell tower. Bells meant music. The church should have a piano.

Will hurried down the last hill and entered the church door. Cool, silent air swept over him. It was a Wednesday. The church was silent. A hushed, expectant feeling pervaded the stone walls as Will's tennis shoes softly squeaked through the nave. To his left, a single candle flickered.

As he walked, something made Will pause and look down. There was writing under his feet. He could see letters and dates chiseled into giant slabs of what looked like limestone and slate. The church's stone floor, which he'd thought was simply paving stones, was made entirely of graves.

Ghosts and bodies everywhere, he thought. Back home it wasn't like that. They kept the dead safely removed in cemeteries, where no one was obliged to see them. He supposed it came from being in a country like England, where there was so much history. History kept piling up, so there wasn't room to separate past lives from the living.

Will bent down to read the nearest slab, peering closely since years of walking had polished away the letters. WILLIAM, it said. DIED JANUARY 15, 1753. Will shivered and stood up fast. Of course, William was a common name, but it was still eerie to see his name carved on a gravestone.

He stepped into a small chapel side room to take a breath. By the chapel entrance was a wooden carving of a robed man, cradling a deer in his lap, labeled SAINT GILES. The little alcove itself was cheery, glowing red and orange from its stained-glass windows. Directly under the main window stood an altar flanked by twin stone angels. The light coming through the window illuminated both angels, turning one cherub yellow and the other orange.

Will was about to move on when he looked down at his feet again: PETER, BELOVED SON, DIED 1803, AGED 10. *Ten like me,* thought Will. He gulped. More graves. Trying to ignore the graves at his feet and just look straight ahead, he inched toward the main church once more. But everywhere he saw names and dates: Katherine, age 8; Thomas, age 2 years 3 months; Eleanor, "in the 12th year of her Life." *All those kids,* thought Will. *I must be in a children's burial chamber.*

It was a relief to be back in the nave. Suddenly, Will wished there were other people in the church, people sneezing, scuffling their shoes, shushing their children, and generally making vibrant, human sounds. He looked up and down the side aisle, and that's when he saw a most friendly sight.

Tucked behind the stone pulpit was a piano. Just the view of it gave Will an unexpected jolt of pleasure. Warm and wooden in the middle of this silent, stone-cold place. Will drew closer. He was surprised by how much he missed playing. It had been several days since he'd touched his home piano.

His fingers twitched. He looked back over his shoulder. No one was around. What would it matter if he played? Just a few notes. The piano looked so inviting.

Will sidled up to the edge of the piano and lightly

trilled his fingers along the white keys. It was in perfect tune. Of course—they probably used it every Sunday. Before he knew it, Will pulled out the piano bench and started playing. Soon he was lost in the notes. Ten minutes went by, then twenty. He played the Star Wars theme first, then dreamily moved into Satie and a minuet by Mozart he'd been practicing back home. Then he sighed and gave in to the melody that was lodged in his mind and had distracted him all morning. Dream music. Bell music. His fingers eagerly chased each note. As he played, a swirl of sadness surrounded him.

"Hello there."

Will's hands shot off the keyboard. Someone was standing beside him, a man, just a few feet away, leaning against a stone column. The man smiled at Will as he came closer. He was dressed in jeans and a navy-blue sweater, and wore round wire-framed glasses.

"Sorry to startle you," the man said. "It's not often we get a pianist walking through our doors. Especially on a Wednesday. Harriet's day for choir practice is Thursday."

Will dropped his hands in his lap and blushed. "Sorry," he said. "I just saw it there, and . . ."

"No harm done," the man continued. "Warms up the place to have music. Harriet has a piano at home, so she doesn't practice here. This piano doesn't get much use—a shame really." He held out his hand to shake. "I'm Father Casey."

"You're a priest?" asked Will, staring at the man's blue jeans.

Father Casey smiled. "Well, actually, I'm the curate. That's a priest who's sort of an assistant to the parish priest."

Will relaxed. The man wasn't angry. He glanced at the curate again and realized he was quite a young man, not much older than his cousin Neil, who'd just finished university last year.

"What's your name?"

"William."

Will was a little surprised at his own answer. Only his great-aunt Hazel ever called him by his full name, and sometimes Aunt Effie. Maybe it was because he was talking to a priest, even an assistant, off-duty one.

"William," repeated the curate. "You're staying with your aunt, aren't you? Over at the Griffinage?" He smiled as Will's mouth hung open in surprise. "It's a small village, William. We tend to notice newcomers, and your aunt is a woman whose personality stands out, if you don't mind my saying so. Besides, I think I saw you and your sister yesterday over at the manor. Welcome to Castle Cary."

The mention of their visit to the manor made Will think of Meg. He suddenly felt bad about deserting her just because he wanted to play the piano. Plus, the auction was a rare opportunity. How could he have turned it down? Right now Meg might be digging up clues at the manor auction, and he was missing everything. But perhaps he could redeem himself. The priest might know something.

"Is the manor ghost buried here?" he asked.

Father Casey chuckled. "On a ghost hunt, are we?"

"Just curious," said Will, and tried not to look too interested.

"Of course you are," said the curate. "Who isn't? She's the one who puts Castle Cary on the map. Yes, she's buried here, William. Against her will, I might add. She demanded to be buried on the manor grounds, but the vicar at the time wouldn't have it. Insisted on consecrated grounds, you know. Maybe he was worried she'd come back to haunt things, which some say she did. In any case, the family vault's on the west aisle, right across from the Chapel of Innocents."

Chapel of Innocents, thought Will. That must be where all the children were buried. Maybe the manor ghost's daughter, too. He might have something to tell Meg after all. Will glanced down the nave toward the little chapel and saw a man's figure slip under its arched gates. Of course, grown-ups go in there, Will told himself, but this man's gait reminded him of Shep. He was itching to go now and see Meg, but Father Casey leaned on the piano in a comfortable way and was talking again.

"I never could get the hang of a piano keyboard

myself," the curate was saying. "Took lessons for years as a boy, and finally accepted the truth: I don't have it in me. But I am a keen listener. You have a gift, William. I can see you love music. Come and play the St. Giles piano anytime."

Will thanked him, then flashed his wide Griffin grin and pushed in the piano bench.

"Wait."

Father Casey put a hand on Will's shoulder. He spoke softly but with a note of urgency.

"Tell me, what were you playing just now? What tune was it?"

What tune? Will paused to think. The Mozart? No, that was earlier. Why, he'd been playing the snatch of music that had been stuck in his head all day.

"Dunno," he said. "Just a song I heard."

The priest looked at him sharply.

"Something you heard, William?" he said.

Will blinked. He'd heard it all right, first thing this morning. Was it a dream, or had it come from somewhere? Involuntarily, he looked up toward the ceiling. A web of Gothic stonework met his eyes, fanning out in intricate patterns. Up above was the bell tower. That was it. He'd heard church bells pealing. The song was like change ringing: the kind of music made by bells high up in a tower, played by a team of people tugging huge ropes. To create a melody, you tugged the ropes in a certain order. Of course, the bells must have come from here, from St. Giles.

"Yeah," he said. "I heard the bells playing. Then I just played the notes."

The curate looked at him closely again.

"The bells," he said finally. "The old bell song." Father Casey's hand dropped from Will's shoulder. He gazed off at the stained-glass windows, and for a moment seemed to forget Will was there. When he looked back, he said a curious thing. "You couldn't have heard the bells, William. Not unless you lived during my grandmother's time. She used to hum that same tune because she missed the old bells when St. Giles replaced them after the fire, but the bells haven't played that song for fifty years."

⊙✥⊚

The gold Mini was just pulling in when Will reached the Griffinage. He was hot and out of breath. He'd sprinted a good part of McBurney's pasture, wanting somehow to put distance between himself and the eerie bells. How could he hear bells that hadn't played for fifty years? It was creepy. Instead of seeing ghosts, he was *hearing* ghosts. If he stayed here much longer, who knows what he might start believing in.

Aunt Effie stuck her arm out the car window and waved to him over a cloud of dust. "Will! Give us a hand with this," she shouted.

In the back seat sat a black, bulky chest. It was caked with dust and mildew. So was Ariel. She'd obviously been drawing pictures on the chest's dusty sides with her finger on the ride home, and now dust decorated her shirt, hands, and the left side of her head. Will grabbed a corner of the chest next to Meg, and Aunt Effie took up the far end. Ariel yelled "Heave ho!" several times as she jumped up and down beside them.

The chest tipped precariously, and the three of them staggered under its weight. Will repositioned his grip to keep from dropping his end. This chest was heavier than anything he'd ever carried.

"Ouf!" said Aunt Effie, as they paused for a rest. "How can one box be so unearthly heavy? Good thing I've got you lot to help. Otherwise I'd have to drive the Mini right into the house."

Meg flashed Will a smile as they lurched forward once again with the chest. Will grinned gratefully back. All was well—she'd forgiven him for going off by himself this morning. That was good, because Will craved company now. He wanted nothing more than to be in a warm, lighted room with Uncle Ben, Meg, and the others. Ariel danced along in front of them, circling back every time they set down the chest on the short flagstone path up to the Griffinage door.

"Almost there!" sang out Aunt Effie. "In the living room. That's right."

⌒◯⌒

With a final *clunk*, they hefted the chest to the middle
of the living room rug. Clouds of dust billowed and
settled around their feet. Meg coughed and stared at
Aunt Effie. Their mother never would have allowed
such a dirty thing in the house. But Aunt Effie was
not looking at the grime. She was looking at the chest
with unabashed delight. Aunt Effie swiped the lid
with the back of her sleeve to dislodge a mass of dust
and grime. Then she stood back and admired her new
possession, her blue shirtsleeve gone grey, her face as
smudged as Ariel's, with cobwebs trailing from her
curly hair.

"From the manor," Aunt Effie said majestically. She
paused for a moment, plucked off a few strands of cob-
web from her eyes, then cried: "To business! Grab a
hammer from the hall closet, Meg. Let's crack her open."

"You mean you bought it and haven't even looked
inside?" said Will.

"Didn't need to," replied Aunt Effie. "It's heavy as
the dickens and came from the manor's library. Books,
the man said. The curator already looked it over and
said there was no need to keep it anymore."

Uncle Ben snuffed his way over to the dusty chest.
He sneezed twice then growled at the unexpected object
in the living room. Meg returned with the hammer.

"Quiet, Ben. No need to bark at books," said Aunt

Effie. "Thank you, Meg. Stand back, all of you. Ariel, over on the sofa."

Ariel took up a position behind the cushions and covered her ears. Aunt Effie grasped the hammer and gave the lock a mighty whack. The lid cracked. It exposed a hiss of air and a slit of black. The moment the hammer struck, Uncle Ben made a wild leap, barking madly, as dust spiraled up. He landed on Aunt Effie's reading lamp, which toppled off its table. Uncle Ben skidded across the floorboards, his nails screeching and collided into the armchair, still barking. Meg ducked. From the sofa, Ariel stood up and screamed. Will and Aunt Effie made a dash at Uncle Ben, but he was already bounding out the door as if pursuing a giant rabbit.

"Well, that's better," Aunt Effie said, a minute later when the din had died down. She righted the lamp and repositioned the armchair. From down the hall they could still hear a few low growls. "The disadvantages of having a large dog who gets excited about books. Now, then. Help me prise this up. Bound to be stiff after all these years."

With Aunt Effie on the left and Will and Meg on the right, they pushed and strained until the slit widened and cracked along the sides. A new plume of dust arose as Aunt Effie tugged the lid wide open. Will coughed, and Meg's eyes watered. Ariel sprang down from the sofa. All four peered into the chest at once.

The chest was filled with stacks of books, children's books, the sort Meg and Will had never seen before. Carefully, Meg lifted out the top volume. *Lessons for Children*, the title read. *That certainly looks dull*, Meg thought. Beneath it she saw *Pilgrim's Progress* and *A Child's History of England*. The pages were thick and crinkly. The covers smelled like musty leather boots.

"Ahh," said Aunt Effie with a long satisfied air. "What a treasure. Possibly some first editions in there."

She picked out each volume and stacked them on the floor next to the chest. Nursery rhymes, fairy tales, Aesop's fables, more books about being virtuous, and a child's Bible. But when she rested her hand under the fourth layer of books, her fingers scraped against a wooden box.

"A box inside a box," said Meg. "What is it?"

Without a word, Aunt Effie lifted out the smaller box. It had a small hinged latch, but no lock. Aunt Effie lifted the hasp. Nestled inside was a set of children's clothes: two tatted lace collars, a pinafore, and one indigo dress that shimmered in the afternoon light.

"Would you like some dress-up clothes, Ariel? A bit big for you, I think, but they might do," said Aunt Effie.

Meg expected Ariel to turn down the offer of lacy princess clothes. At home, she never wore sparkly dresses, just pants, but instead Ariel nodded solemnly. "Kay Kay would like that," she said.

Meg dug back in the chest again. She thought she'd seen another bundle of clothes in the space now vacated by the box, but instead her fingers hit upon something hard wrapped in a swath of green velvet.

"Wait, there's more." Meg lifted out the object and loosened one corner of the green cloth. Unblinking eyes stared back.

"It's a doll!" cried out Ariel.

"So it is," said Aunt Effie. "Must have been hidden under that box. Not all books after all. What a beauty!"

Meg unwrapped the doll swaddled in the velvet. It was a china doll with loose ringlets of black hair—real hair by the look of it—tumbling past her stiff shoulders. She had red-painted lips and rosy cheeks, somewhat chipped, on her hard face. Thin black eyebrows arched over the vacant blue eyes. Although the doll's head and hands were made of china, she had a cloth body. The doll was about as long as a loaf of bread, with two little white cloth legs sticking out from under a bundle of blue skirts and white petticoats. Looking at the blank blue eyes, something about the doll made Meg shiver, and she quickly passed it over to Aunt Effie.

"Oooh, can I hold her?" asked Ariel.

"'Course not," answered Meg. "It's real china. You can't play with a doll like this. It might break. People just set them on shelves—isn't that right, Aunt Effie?"

"Yeah," Will chimed in. "You can't have it. It's history. Like a museum thing." Meg looked at him. Did Will feel the same aversion to the doll that she did? She couldn't tell.

"Fiddlesticks," said Aunt Effie. "Dolls are meant to be played with. If a museum gets it, it *will* end up on a shelf. No great historical value lost, I'm sure. It's chipped, and there's no doll makers' mark. All the same, I'll ring the curator to make sure he meant to let it go with the books. Meanwhile, would you like the doll, dearie?"

"Kay Kay would like her," Ariel said, ignoring Will, who rolled his eyes.

"Then she's yours to play with," said Aunt Effie. "Take her."

Ariel reached out her arms for the doll and buried her nose in the doll's dark hair. "Thank you, Aun' Effie," she said. She gave her prize a protective hug and glared at Meg and Will. "I'm gonna show her to Kay Kay right now!" She headed up the staircase, her shoes spreading a trail of dust.

No one noticed what else had arrived in the chest of books. It glided down the hall, confused at the new location. This place looked like a peasant's cottage, not like home at all. It sniffed and drew its cloak around its ancient shoulders.

CHAPTER SEVEN

An Invitation

For the rest of the day, Ariel wouldn't leave the doll or the Griffinage. "Kay Kay likes it here," she said. "Kay Kay likes the attic room best. Kay Kay's bed is just like mine in the cubby." She dragged the doll to lunch, propping it on the wooden bench next to her, and cradled it in her arms, rocking. At least the doll was quiet, thought Will. He was getting mighty tired of Ariel's constant prattle: "Kay Kay likes blue. Kay Kay loves the doll. Kay Kay's scared of the well. Kay Kay's birthday is in April. . . ."

"If I hear one more word about Kay Kay, I'm going to throw her down the well myself," Will grumbled.

He was itching to get going. With his stomach comfortably full of cheese sandwiches and tomato soup, the worries of the morning were slipping away. The bell song might be strange, but the curate-priest fellow could also be wrong. It was easy for nonmusical people to mix up tunes; they did it all the time. Will shoved the thought of the bell song out of his mind. He was eager to show Meg the children's chapel at St. Giles and look for the tombs of Gillian and the manor ghost. The church would also put distance between his ears and Ariel's babble about Kay Kay. Aunt Effie seemed to sense his mood. "Ariel, you come help me in the garden after lunch. We'll let Meg and Will go off for a bit. Yes, yes, you can bring the doll."

The bells were ringing when Will and Meg reached the village. First they pealed, chiming a string of eight notes, then tolled the hour. Two dongs. Two o'clock. Will stood perfectly still, listening. He'd told Meg about his meeting with Father Casey, skipping the parts about the bell song. When the last reverberation died away, he shook his head.

"It's different."

"Sounds the same to me," said Meg.

"No, but it's different from the bell pattern I heard yesterday," said Will. "There's a C-sharp missing too. I didn't hear that bell at all."

"How can you tell if a bell plays C-sharp or not?"

"Well, I can. That's all."

They entered the church and the cold, sweet silence swept over them. *Wow*, Meg mouthed to Will. Will nodded. It was easy to feel a sense of awe in a place like this, with stone pillars arching up and giant grave flagstones covering the floor. Centuries of hushed footsteps filled the air, and Will half expected a medieval knight to enter and walk down the aisle beside them. It was the kind of place where you felt like whispering without being told.

"I can't believe you actually played Star Wars in here," said Meg, giggling.

Will glared at her. He hadn't exactly meant to play Star Wars; he'd just sat down at the piano and the music came out. There were times Meg couldn't understand. At home, Meg took piano lessons too, but she complained about practicing. Will grew agitated if he *didn't* play at least twice a day.

They circled the church in silence. Candles flickered from metal candleholders. Some were stubs, and others tall and recently lit. The candles were stacked in rows like bleachers, each row a step up. As Will watched, one of the flames snuffed out. He hurried to catch up with Meg.

She was standing near the altar looking into a small side chamber. The chamber glowed red and blue from its stained-glass window, and the mottled light touched a stone slab marked with a single name: MENDIP.

"The manor family tomb," whispered Meg.

In the middle of the chamber loomed a stone dais,

with a stone couple stretched stiffly side by side. One figure was a man, dressed in chain mail. Beside him was the stone effigy of a woman, a ruffed collar carved around her neck. They were lying down, as if on a stone bed, and even had two small stone pillows, complete with tassels. *Who'd want a stone pillow?* Will thought. Fancy stone clothes flowed around them, and their hands pointed up in prayer. Meg read the inscription aloud: "'James, Third Baron of Mendip, and Wife.' 1588. That's not the right one. Must be generations of Mendips buried here."

"Yeah, look at them all," said Will. "1588, 1630, 1752, what a lot. Let's see, 1860. That's it! There she is," said Will. He pointed to a monument mounted on the wall. Stone curtains draped over its edges, and in the monument's corner knelt a small figure, a stone girl. "'Here lies Richard, Fourteenth Baron of Mendip,'" read Will. "'Born March 12, 1815; died February 20, 1880. Also Elizabeth, his wife, born November 20, 1831; died December 2, 1860. Rest in peace.'"

"I guess they hoped she would," Will added, shivering a bit. It was eerie to stand next to a ghost's grave. Her stone monument looked securely mounted to the wall, not like some of these other Mendip tombs with stone lids that looked as if the people inside might pop out. He wondered if their skeletons were really in there. Still, those people were *dead* dead, not like a ghost who wandered about and could be anywhere. The thought made Will jump. He wanted to get out in the sunshine now, but Meg looked serene and in no hurry to go. He tugged her arm.

"You said we'd see the Chapel of Innocents," Meg reminded him. Will nodded, and they left the manor ghost's grave and crossed the nave to the east aisle.

The Chapel of Innocents was bathed in dappled orange, red, and gold light. Will smiled. Even though they were surrounded by children's gravestones, the sun's cheerful rays made this little chapel room much friendlier. Plus, none of these kids were ghosts.

Meg pointed to the little stone altar Will had seen earlier. It was flanked by two angels and decorated with stone roses. In the center were the words:

MENDIP
In loving memory of
Gillian Elizabeth
April 5, 1850
April 5, 1860
Lamb of God

"That's right," said Meg. "Shep said she died on her birthday."

"So?" said Will, still anxious to get outside. "It doesn't really matter. If you're dead, you're dead."

"But on your *birthday*." Meg shuddered.

"Makes it easy to count the years," said Will. "See? She was ten."

Meg examined the paving stones in the chapel. In the far corner was a small black stone on which someone had recently laid lilacs. "Look at this. It says: 'Katherine, daughter of Thomas and Anna Croft,'" read Meg. "'Born January 3, 1852, Missing April 5, 1860; age 8 years, 3 months, 2 days.' April fifth again. She died the exact same day as Gillian."

"But she didn't die. It says 'missing,'" Will pointed out.

"Yes, that's odd," agreed Meg. "Missing on April fifth. I wonder if they knew each other?"

Will felt a small chill. April fifth was two days from now. What if something terrible took place on that day? He didn't believe in bad omens, but still.

"I wonder what happened to her?" mused Meg. She gestured toward the plain black stone with MISSING carved on it. "Somebody around here might know. Somebody put fresh flowers on her grave."

Back at the Griffinage, the newly arrived visitor drifted into the kitchen. Heat still lingered from the morning's activity of coffee brewing and toast warming. This was the warmest room in the peasant cottage. The newcomer paused. Maybe it was here. It hunched

its ancient shoulders and poked at the stack of fire-
wood Shep had placed behind the wood stove, dislodg-
ing several sticks that toppled to the floor. Nothing. Its
heart ached. It cast about the cottage kitchen, angry,
irritated, then rose up the staircase to the rooms above.

Outside, Ariel scooped up a handful of fallen plum
blossoms. She was sitting in the orchard with Uncle
Ben, scattering petals like confetti on the great dog's
back. Beyond the plum trees, she could just see Aunt
Effie's bottom sticking up in the air as she bent over
a flower bed. Ariel let the blossoms run through her
hands, some landing on Gillian's head. That was what
they'd named the doll. It had been Kay Kay's sugges-
tion. Ariel wished Kay Kay would come back to play.
They'd met twice since she'd found the doll, always in
the attic. Ariel had looked up in the attic before coming outside with Aunt Effie, but the little room stood
empty. Where was her new friend?

At least she wasn't alone. Uncle Ben was here, and
Gillian, too. Uncle Ben was so delightfully furry, and
every time she held the doll she felt hugged in a warm
and delicious glow.

Beside her, Uncle Ben shifted and gave a low growl.
The vibrations rumbled through Ariel's legs where she
leaned against him. She looked up.

There was Kay Kay.

She was sitting on a branch of a nearby plum tree, one foot dangling from the branches. It was the foot with the shoe on it.

"Hello," said Ariel, scrambling to her feet. She darted around Uncle Ben, her face full of smiles. "I've been looking for you."

Kay Kay gave her a brilliant smile.

"I can't always come," answered Kay Kay. "But I can play now."

"Good! I brought Gillian." Ariel hurried back to where she'd left her, and shook the fallen petals off her dress. Soon the two girls were settled into a game, Kay Kay up on her branch and Ariel on the ground.

"You're sneaky," said Ariel, after a time. "How come you show up and go away so fast?"

The girl shrugged. "I'm good at that. I've always been fast. I can run fast too."

"But you're really fast! And quiet. You must be good at hide-and-seek."

Kay Kay nodded solemnly. "Nobody looks long enough."

All this time, Uncle Ben was rumbling a steady growl. Dogs made noise with new people sometimes, like the mailman, thought Ariel. Kay Kay wasn't exactly the mailman, and she wasn't even new, since she lived here, but she didn't like dogs, and maybe Uncle Ben could tell. Dogs were smart like that.

"Make him go away," said Kay Kay, pointing down at Uncle Ben, who now crouched at the base of her tree and was growling louder.

"Shoo, Uncle Ben!" called out Ariel. "Go away! Shoo!" Uncle Ben sat squarely on his haunches and cocked his head at Ariel. He looked as if he had no intention of shooing. Off in the distance, Aunt Effie finished weeding a tulip bed. She brushed away last fall's dried walnut leaves and moved on to the next flower bed, out of sight.

"Can I come up?"

"If you can."

Back home Ariel often climbed the crabapple tree in the side yard. This plum tree had nice, low branches, perfect for her height, and spread evenly around the trunk. She propped Gillian against the trunk, placed her hands on the tree's scaly bark, and swung up to the first notch.

Being up in the tree was like being in a snowy castle. Pure white petals surrounded her. The petals showered down like snow whenever she moved, adding to the ring of plum blossoms already carpeting the ground. Ariel laughed with delight.

Kay Kay laughed too. "Come to my birthday party!" she said. "You must come. You're my best friend."

"Okay," said Ariel, with a smile. She'd always wanted a best friend. "When is it?" she asked, a moment later.

"April fifth."

"Is that today?"

"No, but soon. I'll tell you."

Kay Kay climbed higher. Ariel looked longingly after Kay Kay, but did not follow. She knew better than to climb on tiny branches. The branches on these orchard trees thinned to mere slips of twigs, and Kay Kay was perched on a high one. Ariel watched a robin flutter in and land on an upper branch, causing a small shower of petals. It was funny. The little branch swayed under the weight of the robin, but Kay Kay's branch did not sag at all.

"Bring Gillian," said Kay Kay, talking about the party again. "You and Gillian will be my only guests, so you have to bring her."

"Just us?" Ariel loved parties. She might get extra treats being the only guest, since, of course, Gillian would only pretend to eat.

"And bring a present."

"You're not supposed to *ask* for presents," said Ariel, who knew her manners. "You're just supposed to say 'thank you' and smile even if you already have the exact same thing at home."

Kay Kay shrugged. "Presents are part of parties," she said, and Ariel knew this was true.

She left the highest branches and came down to Ariel's level so they were sitting side by side on the same branch. Then she scooted closer so their heads were touching. Ariel had never been this close to Kay Kay before.

"Hold still," whispered Kay Kay.

Ariel felt fingers touch her hair. Not like her mother's fingers. When her mother braided her hair, she could feel warm, knobby fingertips flick in and out from her scalp, moving with strength and confidence. These fingers were icy cold. Ariel sucked in her breath. The girl's fingers moved across her head with the lightest touch, caressing her hair. Kay Kay began to hum. It was the same high-pitched, wordless tune she hummed in the attic room, the song that was so sad. As Kay Kay hummed, the tune drew Ariel out of the sunny blossom-filled orchard and into a cold space where only she and the caressing fingers existed.

At the base of the tree, Uncle Ben whined.

The chill deepened. The fingers continued to ply her hair. Ariel longed to be back inside, back in the Griffinage with Aunt Effie, wrapped in a blanket, listening to *Alice in Wonderland* with Uncle Ben's big head in her lap. Or cuddled up with Mama, and Mama laughing and then saying, *How about hot chocolate?* At the thought of her mother, Ariel jerked away from Kay Kay's cold hands.

"I'm done playing," said Ariel.

Ariel dropped to the ground. She scraped her shin

on the rough bark, but didn't stop to see if it needed a Band-Aid. Instead, she threw her arms around Uncle Ben's enormous, comforting neck. The humming stopped, but a sound like a sob made her look back.

"Don't go," Kay Kay pleaded, her silver eyes rimmed with tears. "Stay with me. You're my only friend. My always friend."

◌◯◌

Meg and Will stood surrounded by flowering cherry trees in the St. Giles churchyard. It felt good to have left the stone silence of the church behind them. The afternoon sun shone down. A plump little English robin chirped and hopped nearby. Every now and then the wind sent a shower of pale pink petals tumbling down. Will brushed some off his hair. Things didn't seem eerie or mysterious now that they were outdoors.

Meg read a plaque and informed him that they were standing in what was called the "Reflection Garden." It was mostly a few benches amid beds of tulips and daffodils. Will relaxed. Maybe that's what you did in a reflection garden. Just then, a dark shape caught his eye. He pointed to a weeping willow, which stood in the corner, drooping its green fronds and yellow cat-kins to the ground. Something dark peered out from its edge. "What's that?"

"Looks like an old church bell," said Meg.

It was. Mounted on a stone pedestal hung a bell, a

huge metal one the size of a small boulder. Meg ran her finger along it. "Boy, it's big. Bells always look so tiny high up in their spires. Bet the noise is deafening if you're really up there."

Will wasn't listening. He ducked down and craned his head up inside the bell's belly. The bell was hanging from a wooden frame, so it was easy to poke his head inside.

"What are you doing?" asked Meg.

"Looking for information." Will's voice echoed from inside the great bell.

"Read the plaque, then." Meg stopped and read every plaque she saw, though Will wished he'd seen this one. "It says right here: 'Tenor bell from St. Giles church. Cast in 1804 by Mears and Son, from the Whitechapel foundry, London. Removed after the fire of 1968.'"

Will banged the side of his head on the bell as he crawled out. He groaned and waited for the pain to die away. As he lay still, he heard the slight reverberation of the bell itself. He'd played a note with his head. Suddenly, Will jumped up and grabbed a stick from under the willow tree. He whacked the bell hard. Meg jumped. A clear note sounded through the air.

"Come on, let's go," said Will.

"Wait! What's going on? What's the big hurry?" asked Meg.

Will ran to the churchyard gate. He did not look

back. He heard Meg swing the gate open, then a *bang* as the gate swung back on its hinges and slammed shut. He headed toward McBurney's pasture and the Griffinage. Meg ran after him.

"What's going on?" she asked again when she'd caught up.

"That's the bell I heard," said Will, panting and stopping to look at her. "It's a C-sharp. I heard that bell playing from fifty years ago when it shouldn't be playing." *So Father Casey was right*, he added to himself. Aloud, he said: "I'm going crazy. That's what's going on."

CHAPTER EIGHT

In the Night

At the Griffinage, they found Ariel cuddled up under a pile of wool blankets with Uncle Ben beside her. From the edge of the blankets, Meg could see a tuft of black hair from the china doll intertwined with Ariel's curls.

"Been there nearly since you left," said Aunt Effie, touching her hand to Ariel's forehead. "Wonder if she's coming down with something. I'll go fetch the thermometer." She disappeared down the hall. Will headed to the kitchen to get a drink of water. His hiccups were back.

Meg knelt beside Ariel and touched her forehead. It felt reassuringly warm, the right sort of warm, not sweaty or burning with fever. For the first time she wondered if Ariel could see ghosts. She was the right age, according to Shep. Should she ask her when she woke up, or would talking about ghosts scare her? Meg listened for a moment to Ariel's soft breathing mingled with Uncle Ben's low rumbles.

Suddenly, from the hallway came a splintering noise of shattered glass. Aunt Effie yelled. Ariel's legs twitched, but she did not wake. Meg sprang to her feet, but Uncle Ben was up before her. He pounded down the hall with Meg and Will after him. There, at the back of the house, stood Aunt Effie just outside her office door. She was staring in disbelief at the small bathroom across the hall, the one she called the loo.

"Are you all right?" asked Meg.

"Did something break?" asked Will. "What's all this glass?"

"What happened?" they both cried together.

The three of them stared into the little room. Jagged shards of glass clung to the window frame, and glass littered the floor. Aunt Effie pulled Uncle Ben back so he wouldn't cut his paws. A hole the size of Uncle Ben's head gaped in the center of the window.

"Like a bomb," said Will. "Holy mackerel!"

"Do you think it was a bird, Aunt Effie?" asked Meg.

"No bird that big around here," said Aunt Effie, shaking her head ruefully. "You would need an emu or an ostrich. Whatever it was had tremendous force. Better take a look outside. You lot stay here."

But when Aunt Effie returned, she was shaking her head.

"Nothing to be seen," she said. "That's more money out the window, quite literally. It will cost a pretty penny to replace that pane. Odd sizes always are, and this house is nothing if not odd." She grabbed a broom and began sweeping up.

Meg and Will helped Aunt Effie clean up the mess and tack heavy-duty plastic across the open window hole. All this time, Ariel continued to sleep. Uncle Ben prowled the hallway and poked his nose at the loo, then paced back to resume his position beside Ariel, ears alert and poised on his haunches as if ready to spring down the hall at any minute.

It was evening when Ariel finally stirred. She sat hunched in a rumple of blankets, yawning and looking dazed. "Well, at least we know *you* didn't do it, sleepy-head," said Aunt Effie. "Sleep is the perfect alibi."

"I'm warm now," said Ariel.

"Well, you had about a hundred blankets," said Will.

"Is Kay Kay gone?"

"I don't see her," said Aunt Effie, smiling. "Do you, Meg?" Meg politely shook her head.

Ariel hugged the doll fiercely. "When I hold her I feel like Mama's here," she said.

"We can do better than that," said Aunt Effie, giving her a hug. "Let's give your mother a quick call. Then it's supper and bed for you, missy. It's plain you're worn out." Aunt Effie ushered Ariel off the sofa and steered her into the kitchen. At the threshold, she turned to Will, who'd perked up at the mention of supper. "The three of us will eat later."

Ariel did not protest. She rubbed her eyes and followed Aunt Effie to the telephone, but clammed up after saying hello. "Too tired to talk," said Aunt Effie, taking the receiver. "Here, Meg, you have a chat." So Meg told her mother about the lambs and the manor and Glastonbury Tor. It was funny to talk about the manor without mentioning the ghost, but her mother was a practical sort, and ghosts didn't fit into the conversation. While Meg was talking, Ariel picked at her private supper. Then Aunt Effie bustled her upstairs and into her nightie.

"I'm cold, Aun' Effie," she whispered.

"There, now." Aunt Effie tucked a hot water bottle between the covers and added two wool blankets. "Now you'll be cozy as a campfire." Aunt Effie patted the blankets and tiptoed out of the room. Uncle Ben watched the proceedings. As soon as Aunt Effie was gone, he slipped into Ariel's room and settled down next to her bed.

An hour later, Will came into the kitchen hiccupping.

"Oh, Will. Go drink some water," said Meg.

"Tried that, hic," said Will, sliding onto the bench next to Aunt Effie. "Sorry." His eyes lit up as they always did at suppertime. His earlier fears that day about the bells, broken window, and curious gravestones seemed far away when he was surrounded by the comforting smells of fresh bread and roasted chicken.

"You were the strangest baby, Will," said Aunt Effie unexpectedly. "Born hiccupping."

"I was?"

"How do you know?" asked Meg.

"Oh, I was there," said Aunt Effie. "Helping to look after you, Meg. Things were hectic for your mum, what with Will coming along less than a year after you were born. You were just a tiny thing, Meg, always wanting to be held and hard to comfort." She paused. "I thought you'd never be born, Will. Do you know the story about your birth?"

"Mama's told us," said Meg. "Go on, though."

Will grinned and nodded. He always liked to hear the story about how he'd been born on Halloween night. He leaned on his elbows, trying to stifle his hiccups and ignore the whooshing sound in his ears. He pulled on his earlobe, but the sound wouldn't go away.

"We thought you might be a November baby," Aunt Effie continued. "Your mum went into labor early on October thirty-first, but you took your time coming out. She wanted a home birth, so there she was in one

room, and Meg and I were in the rocking chair in the
next. Wasn't until a moment before midnight that you
were finally born. All blue-faced you were, with little
fists balled up tightly. For a time there, we thought we
were going to lose you. You were just pale and limp, in
and out of this world and the next. Didn't take a breath
until November first. Then suddenly you came around,
and we knew everything would be all right. Hiccups,
Will. Started hiccupping like the dickens."

Will took a bite of chicken between hiccups. Meg
giggled.

"Remember that time you got the hiccups at the
Tower of London?" Meg asked.

"Hic," said Will, which meant "yes."

"That beefeater was so mad at us. He was being all
serious, and you kept letting out these great, huge hiccups."

Will nodded so he wouldn't let a new hiccup escape.
He remembered that day clearly. It had been during
the Griffin family's first trip to England, when Will
was only five and Meg was six. Ariel hadn't been born
yet. His hiccups had started by the portcullis water
gate, and they kept getting worse—great belchy ones—
until finally their guide, a bushy-browed beefeater,
strongly suggested they leave. "Never mind, Wills," his
dad had said. "Enough history for one day. Let's go get
ice creams." He'd picked chocolate marshmallow. How

nice it had been, sitting on a bench near the Thames River, licking his ice-cream cone, just the four of them.

"You looked so funny!" Meg said, dissolving into a fit of giggles. "We thought you might be thrown into the dungeon!"

Will grinned and exploded with another hiccup. It was cheerful in the Griffinage with the bright lights blazing. He loved storytelling evenings. There was something ever so satisfying about stories that were all about *you*. Maybe Aunt Effie would tell the one about how he'd fallen in the Cannon River when he was three. He was just about to ask when Aunt Effie turned her head and flicked her eyes to the window. Something was tapping.

"Wind's picking up," announced Aunt Effie. "That cherry tree always attacks the windows like that when the wind mounts. Makes a racket, doesn't it?" She stacked her dishes and stood up. "I better set a bucket under the upstairs thatch, and check that tarp over the back window, too," she said. "Sounds like a storm's brewing."

◌◯◌

Will was back in the Tower of London. He could see the beefeaters with their red suits and flat-topped hats, and high on the Tower's outer wall, a squadron of black ravens perched in a line. He was standing among the tour crowd, the guide's voice droning on, when a tremendous wind swept in. The force of it knocked Will over and pinned him to the ground. Around him, the other tourists stood unaffected, their coats merely flapping in a slight breeze, but the wind rushed on, targeting Will and spinning into a tempest. This wasn't right. He wanted his dad to call out for ice cream and get the wind to stop. But all he could hear was the wind's rage and the ravens calling.

Will woke up, hiccupping with relief to see he was in his bedroom at the Griffinage. Had he been hiccupping in his sleep? His father always said hiccups came in bunches: *If you get them in the morning, you'll get more throughout the day.* He never said throughout the night.

Outside, he could hear the wind rattling the branches. A faint smell of sulphur pervaded the room, like a match that just blew out. Light flashed, a green color. Did lightning ever burn green? He fumbled for his bedside light and clicked it on. Will hiccupped again, and the sound echoed in the shadowy room.

Now a great whooshing sound seemed to be worming deep into his ears. Loud and wild like wind. Like his dream. He didn't want to be alone. Will threw back the covers and ran the short distance to the girls' room.

"Meg!" said Will. He launched himself at Meg's bed, then paused and shook her arm.

"Meg, it's me. Wake up."

He waited impatiently as Meg blinked, sat up, and peered at him in the dim light.

"You okay?" Meg asked.

"Shift over," said Will. He climbed in next to Meg and pulled the blankets over both of them. Will rubbed his ears. The persistent whirring was gone, but his ears still tingled with the prickly feeling you get when your foot goes to sleep. *Except ears don't go to sleep*, he told himself.

"It's about my hiccups."

"You woke me up to talk about hiccups? Will, it's the middle of the night!"

"Shh!"

Will stiffened. He heard a sound in the hall. Then he sank back in the bed. It was only the soft jangle of dog tags as Uncle Ben reentered the room. He snuffed at Will, as if to say, *What, you here too?* then took up his post by Ariel in the alcove.

"No, it's important. Listen."

"Okay, but, 'shh' yourself. Ariel's sleeping right there." Will nodded. He could see the dark hump of Uncle Ben's body partially sticking out from the alcove. He lowered his voice.

"Look, I had the hiccups twice yesterday, plus just now, and before then too, remember, at Mendip Manor? And sometimes I hear this strange whooshing sound like the wind. Well, the same thing happened at the Tower of London. I just remembered."

"What do you mean?" asked Meg. She was fully

awake now. She sat up next to Will, her back propped against the wall, her arms clutched around her bent knees, pressing them to her chest.

"When I got the hiccups at the Tower, I heard this sound," Will went on. "And then it got really loud by the execution block."

"You mean where they beheaded all those people? Where the guard got mad?"

"That's where we were standing, remember?"

Meg nodded.

"Right," said Will. "My hiccups started when we were looking down at Traitor's Gate."

"Oh!" said Meg. "You mean where young Princess Elizabeth came in."

"Yeah, it was by the water gate."

"Oh yes, I remember. It was Queen Elizabeth I; she came in by boat and they threw her in prison when she was just a girl."

"Forget which queen it was, you're getting me off track," snapped Will. "Anyway, my hiccups got worse inside the White Tower, and then out in the courtyard they really got loud."

"Where the guide was telling us about Lady Jane Grey." Meg shuddered. "Poor Lady Jane! Only queen for nine days and then they beheaded her."

"Are you listening? The point is they beheaded her right there in that very spot. And I had the hiccups and the noise came that day. And it happened today, too. You know, I've been thinking, I don't get hiccups often, but when I do it's really bad and it's mixed up with this whooshing noise in my head and my ears get all tingly and stuff. I think it means something."

"You mean you think your body's trying to tell you something?" asked Meg, forgetting to whisper.

"Don't you see?" said Will. "Think about all the people they killed there. There are probably tons of ghosts in the Tower of London."

"Ghosts?

"At the Griffinage. And that's not all. I saw a green light, too."

"You mean—"

"I think she's here," said Will.

Dawn was just cracking the sky with a slit of red when two figures left the Griffinage.

"It's a mite early to be out visiting, isn't it?" Shep said. He was standing barefoot with an old overcoat wrapped around him. Meg and Will stood on his doorstep, heads close, hair touching. "Better come in," he said kindly.

Neither Meg nor Will had been able to sleep again. Of course, they'd been hoping to meet a ghost, but a middle-of-the-night ghost was much different than a daytime one, when you could sit down for a friendly chat. Meg drilled Will with questions. Why was he sure it was the manor ghost? Weren't there other ghosts around? Did it have the brooch? Will tried to answer, but the more they talked, the more things went in circles and they both grew agitated. "Look, there's never been a ghost in this house before," said Will. "Of course it's her! She's the one who's active."

After talking in Meg's room, they'd gone downstairs and huddled in the kitchen nibbling cold biscuits, while they waited for what Meg considered an appropriate time to bang on Shep's door. Now she realized it was still too early—the clock on Shep's wall said six thirty a.m.

"Something troubling you?" asked Shep.

Meg and Will both nodded.

"Right then, tea first. Won't be a minute." Shep plugged in the electric kettle and fished out mugs from the dish drainer. While the water heated, he shuffled down the hall and returned in less than two minutes dressed in his work pants and a plaid flannel shirt. "Time I was up anyway," he said. He set three steaming mugs of tea on the kitchen table, and they all sat down, cupping the warm mugs in their hands. "Now then, tell me what's on your minds."

"We were wondering . . . ," said Meg.

"We think she's here," Will blurted out.

"Eh?"

"Well, not here," Will said, "but at the Griffinage."

"The manor ghost," explained Meg. "Or some ghost." It still didn't make sense to her that the manor ghost would leave her tower.

"I got hiccups," said Will, "and when I was sleeping, I heard this wind—at least, I think I did. I was dreaming, but I heard it, though it might have been the storm, of course, and then I woke up and had hiccups." Meg listened as he stumbled through it. Explaining everything in daytime to a grown-up suddenly made the story sound flimsy. At night, in the darkness of their bedrooms, the ghost explanation seemed so clear.

"Well, that's what we thought, anyway," Meg said.

Shep set down his own mug. "Why don't you start over and tell me everything carefully," he said.

So they did. Will did most of the talking, and Meg chimed in when he forgot parts, like Lady Jane Grey. When he was done, Will gave his tea a fierce stir. When he looked up again, Shep was staring at him intently.

"Just you, Will?"

"What?"

"Meg didn't feel anything?"

Meg shook her head. Inside, she felt a hard knot in her stomach. Maybe it was all true about ghosts. Maybe she *was* too old for real ghost-finding. Shep nodded and turned back to Will.

"When's your birthday?" Shep asked abruptly.

"My birthday?" echoed Will. "I'm ten."

"No, the date, I mean."

"October thirty-first." This time it was Meg who answered. If she couldn't see ghosts, at least she could supply information. "At midnight."

"I see. A Samhain baby." But it didn't sound like that. He pronounced it "sow-in."

"A what?"

"Old holiday around here," said Shep. Meg was about to ask more when Will interrupted.

"What about my hiccups?" said Will.

"Looks to me as if that might be your sign," said Shep. "Your sign for detecting a ghost, that is. Some people feel them and some people don't. And with a birthday like that . . ." Shep shook his head. "As I said, it happens most with children. When a ghost is nearby, there're people who feel a tingle down their backs or their hair sticks up. In Will's case, it might be hiccups."

Meg's mind raced. She glanced at Will, whose mouth was drooping open. If he hiccupped now, it would be one of those great belchy ones. For a moment, she almost giggled, but that thought was chased away by a more unnerving one: When Will had bad attacks of the hiccups, she'd usually been right next to him feeling nothing.

"Do you think Will's right?" she blurted out. "Do you think his body really senses a ghost in the Griffinage?"

"People who don't sense ghosts are the ones who usually ask that, Meg," said Shep gently. "I don't hear Will asking."

Meg sank in her chair a little. She *was* too old. Will seemed to be the special one, not her. She felt tears welling up at the unfairness. With an effort, she pushed them down again. So what if she couldn't see ghosts. Will wasn't seeing one either, just hiccupping at one.

"Notice anything else, Will?"

"The lightning was strange. It was green, and everything smelled funny. Like matches."

"Sulphur," said Shep. "That would be her."

"The manor ghost?" asked Will. Shep nodded.

"But why would she suddenly *be* here?" asked Meg, exasperated. "She's supposed to haunt the manor, not the Griffinage."

"Can ghosts move?" Will asked. "I mean, to a new place, if they've haunted one place for years and years?"

"Take up a new residence?" said Shep. "I've heard it's possible. Have to follow something, though."

"What do you mean?"

"Remember what I told you," Shep answered. "Ghosts don't follow time and space the way we do. They follow longings. Usually, the longing is much greater in one place, so the ghost sticks around and we say the place is haunted."

"Like the West Tower," added Meg.

"Right," said Shep. "Like the West Tower. The lady of the manor died with a great longing unfulfilled, and that longing was strongest in the tower, so she hovers around there. I think it's because the tower overlooks the creek."

"A ghost can move if its longing moves?" Will said.

"That's it. The longing is usually attached to a place, but it can also be attached to an object."

"So if someone moves the object . . ." Meg was feeling excited. It made sense now. The ghost might actually be the manor ghost. A ghost at the Griffinage didn't feel like a nightmare anymore, not sitting here snugly with Shep. It felt more like an enchanted story.

"The ghost moves too," said Shep. "That's right."

"But what is the object?"

"I'm afraid I don't know," said Shep. "Has to be something she's attached to. Something she really cares about."

Will had been silent for some time. He stirred his tea, not drinking it, simply stirring.

"Shep, is there a way to make a ghost go away?" Will finally asked. "I mean completely away?"

"Only one way. Fulfill their longing."

Moving around following objects for hundreds of years seemed so lonely. Meg felt a sudden urge to help the ghost. What brought her here? What object was she following? What if she, Meg, could find her longing? Of course, that wasn't possible, because they all

knew she wanted her daughter. Still, there had to be a way to help.

"But if she's here—at the Griffinage, I mean," Meg said, resorting to logic, "why doesn't Will have hiccups all the time?"

"Gone dormant," said Shep.

"You mean sleeping?"

"In a sense. Ghosts are mostly dormant. That's why no one sees them much. Just once in a while they get stirred up, when their longing drives them to it. Not dangerous, mind you, just sort of restless. So Will here only senses when she's awake. That's when she's most powerful, driven by her longing."

"But not dangerous," repeated Meg.

"Only times I ever saw her as a kid she was just grumpy. Fact is, I've never heard of a dangerous ghost, except in fairy tales," said Shep. He stood up and collected the tea mugs. Meg saw him glance at the kitchen clock. They had been talking for some time. Aunt Effie might be up any minute and find them missing.

"You'd best be getting back," Shep said, echoing her thoughts. "I've got work in town, but I'll stop by later on and see about that window. Your aunt told me there was a freak wind yesterday that did some damage." He winked and walked them to the door. Will zipped his coat and stepped outside, but Meg lingered with another question.

"What about Gillian?" asked Meg, still thinking about the manor ghost's daughter. "Is she a ghost too? I mean, couldn't we just sort of reunite them?"

"No such luck," said Shep. "That child went peacefully to her grave. There have never been any hauntings by the manor child."

"Are you sure?" asked Meg.

"Pretty sure. Ghost children aren't like grown-up ghosts. Ghost children like to play, so they show themselves to age-mates, you know. No Castle Cary child has ever seen the manor child, not in 150 plus years. Just because she died, doesn't mean she died with longings. She was a happy girl, they say. Loved animals, especially her horse."

"Oh," said Meg.

Will was ahead of her on the short walk back to the Griffinage when Meg caught up.

"What'd you ask him?"

"Just if Gillian might be a ghost too," said Meg.

"And she's not?"

"She's not," said Meg. She purposefully walked ahead of Will and concentrated on not feeling bitter. It was a hard blow to learn Will was the only one who could sense ghosts. Just because he was younger and there was something special about his birthday. Why wasn't *she* the one born on Sow-in, or whatever it was called?

"Should we tell Aunt Effie there's a ghost in her house?" Will spoke in a low voice. They were standing in the entry hall shucking their boots as quietly as possible so they wouldn't wake Aunt Effie.

"Why bother? You know she'd never believe us," said Meg.

"Yes, but you know, what if something goes wrong?" he persisted. He had one boot on and one boot off and was looking anxiously at Meg. Meg reconsidered. Maybe being special like Will wasn't such a good thing. Perhaps a December birthday like hers was just fine. It was all very well for Shep to wink and tell stories. He was a grown-up and couldn't see ghosts anymore. Sometimes grown-ups forgot that being a kid was difficult, not all fun.

"Don't worry," she said. "Remember, ghosts aren't dangerous."

"Right," said Will, and gave her a smile. "Just grumpy. I'm sure glad Shep knows everything about ghosts."

CHAPTER NINE

Ghost at the Griffinage

Meg and Will padded upstairs, avoiding the seventh step that always squeaked, and slipped back into their rooms. Aunt Effie's light was on in her bedroom, but the door was still closed.

"Maybe she hasn't missed us," said Meg.

"Make some bumping around noises," advised Will. "You know, early morning sounds as if you're just waking up." Pretty soon Meg could hear loud thumps coming from Will's room and the sound of a drawer being banged in and out. Will reappeared in the hall the next instant stretching his arms and groaning in a series of exaggerated yawns.

"Uhhh . . . yiiuuuaa . . . Gosh, I'm tired," he exclaimed. "Good morning, Meg." He flashed her his signature Griffin grin.

"I think you're overdoing it," whispered Meg.

Will yawned again, this time a genuine yawn, and stomped down to the kitchen. From around the corner, Meg heard Ariel stir. No wonder she'd woken up with all that banging. Meg peeked in and saw she was sitting up in bed, her hair tousled and her cheeks flushed. Meg hoped she wasn't really getting sick. She'd been sick herself on vacation once when they went to Wisconsin, but of course, her mother and father had been there, which made it all right.

"Feeling better?" Meg asked.

Ariel didn't seem to hear. Her face remained blank as she stared out the window toward the walnut tree. Maybe she really was sick. Ariel usually dashed out of bed the instant she woke up. Uncle Ben was still beside her cot, fully awake, and nosing the covers by her waist. Noodles, her stuffed cat, lay facedown on the wide floorboards. Ariel didn't bend down to pick him up, and she didn't reach over to pet Uncle Ben. Instead, she reached for the doll and hugged it tightly to her chest. Meg watched. A slow smile spread across Ariel's face, and her eyes began to sparkle. That doll sure seemed to be a new favorite. Soon she hopped out of bed with the doll in her arms, looking bouncy and cheerful. Not sick at all. Maybe this was a good time to ask her what she knew.

"Have you ever seen a lady at the Griffinage?" Meg asked, trying to make the question sound casual. No need to mention ghosts. No need to alarm her.

"You mean like Aunt Effie?"

"No, a fancy lady with a big green gown."

Ariel was definitely the right age. What if Will and Ariel could both see ghosts? Then she'd be the only one left out. The ghost would still be here, but she wouldn't know where it was. Too creepy.

"No lady," said Ariel.

"Okay, good," said Meg, relieved. She only felt mildly better knowing Ariel hadn't seen a lady wearing a green dress. Will hadn't exactly either. A ghost for him was hiccups, whooshing, and bits of light. She might as well ask about that, too.

"Any funny lights, or, you know, something sort of weird and different since you got here?"

"Kay Kay's different!" said Ariel. "She's the most dif-ferentest girl I've ever seen."

"Oh, right," said Meg. "Never mind." She didn't need an earful about Kay Kay. But it was too late. Ariel's face broke into a radiant smile.

"Oh, Megsy," she cried. "Guess what? Kay Kay's having a birthday party and I'm the only guest!"

"A birthday party, how nice," said Meg. She yawned. She was sleepy after staying up half the night with Will, and it was hard to follow the gist of Ariel's chat-ter. Imaginary friends led such complicated lives.

"How old is she going to be?" Meg asked, trying to show interest.

"Kay Kay doesn't do numbers. She just has a party."

"Okay. Uh . . . have fun at the party today."

"Oh, it's not today," said Ariel, scrambling into the clothes she'd worn yesterday. "But it's soon. Kay Kay told me."

⁂

Meg was the last to come down to breakfast. Ariel had run downstairs after talking about the birthday party, and now Meg could hear voices drifting up from the kitchen. "Porridge is better than oatmeal," said Ariel's voice, followed by Will's. "You're nuts. It's the same food." "It's better." "You can't like one better; it's the same." "Kay Kay only likes porridge. . . ."

As she passed Aunt Effie's office, an enormous sigh made Meg stop. She poked her head in and saw Aunt Effie hunched over her desk. She was surrounded by piles of papers, her elbows propped on the desktop, her fingers buried deep in her tight curls.

"Ah, Meg. Good morning," said Aunt Effie. "Bit of a mess, isn't it? My office always looks like this, even when windows aren't blowing themselves up. . . ." She sighed again.

"Are you okay?"

"Oh, just the house, dearie," said Aunt Effie. She smiled. Meg recognized that smile, and didn't trust it. It was the sort of smile grown-ups put on when they're feeling troubled but don't want children to know. She said nothing but didn't move from the doorway. Aunt Effie looked up at her, and her face softened. "It's the house. The thatch needs repairing, the plaster's crumbling, there's a wall that wants propping up, and now there's the side window to fix. I'm trying to sort it all out. Old houses aren't easy. If I had any sense, I'd sell this place and move into a normal house with no thatch fluttering off the roof."

"But you can't sell the Griffinage!" said Meg. The words were out of her mouth before she knew it. Of course she could; Aunt Effie was the owner. But the very thought of selling the Griffinage made Meg's heart feel tight and sore. It didn't matter that a few days ago she'd never even been here. The Griffinage was more than a house. It seemed like part of the family.

"You love it too, don't you, dear?" said Aunt Effie. "I know. Still, one person in an old house that keeps breaking . . ." She stopped and swiveled her chair, looking directly at Meg as if a new thought had just occurred to her. "You were early risers this morning, you and Will."

Meg opened her mouth and closed it again. There was nothing she could say. It felt horrible to hide something as important as a ghost, but it would sound even sillier to talk about ghosts in front of Aunt Effie.

"Mmm," said Aunt Effie, still looking at Meg intently. "Next time, leave a note on the table. After all, it *is* my job to look after you. Your parents want you back safe and sound."

After breakfast, Meg and Will convened a meeting. They met on the stairs, a choice location where they could see Ariel who was playing in the living room, but not be overheard. Meg told Will what Ariel had said, that she'd never seen a green lady. "But I still think we should watch her," Meg said. "I know Aunt Effie's in charge of looking after her, but she's *our* sister."

They watched Ariel arrange her stuffed animals around Gillian from their vantage point on the landing.

"You know it wasn't a bird," said Will.

"The window? After you hiccupping all night long? Yeah, I know," said Meg.

"I wish we could get the manor ghost to go home," said Will. "Shep thinks ghosts are great, but maybe he's never had to live with one in his house. Or his bedroom."

Will was hiccupping again this morning. It was one thing to be staying in a seventeenth-century cottage and listening to ghost stories; it was another thing to be staying in the same cottage and living with a ghost who broke windows and kept everyone awake at night.

"We might *have* to make her go home," said Meg.

"What do you mean?"

Meg told him about her conversation with Aunt Effie, about how the Griffinage cost so much money to fix with the thatch roof and crooked walls, and how she'd even talked about selling it. "Will, we can't have a ghost here! If the manor ghost keeps breaking things, it'll cost even more, and she'll have to sell it!"

"Sell the Griffinage?"

Meg nodded. She thought of the bedrooms with their slanted ceilings and big black timbers. She thought of the swooping thatched roof, the little red door, the fox weather vane, and the stately walnut tree. If Aunt Effie moved and sold it, they'd never see any of it again.

"She can't sell," said Will. "She just can't. It won't even be the Griffinage anymore! The new people would have a different last name."

"Yeah. It'll just be a house," said Meg.

"A house with a ghost in it that destroys stuff."

Meg twirled a loop of hair around her finger. Shep was wrong. Ghosts were dangerous—at least this one was to the Griffinage. If the manor ghost kept wreaking havoc, and Aunt Effie moved, they would lose the cottage.

"Maybe we can get her a child," said Meg out loud.

"What? What are you talking about?"

"If the manor ghost had a child, she'd leave," said Meg.

"Get her a child? Are you loony? What are we going to do—snatch one off the street in London? 'Oh, her mother won't mind. It'll make the manor ghost happy.'"

Meg looked hurt. "Of course not. Nobody's snatching kids off the street."

"Well, then . . ."

"I'm just saying," said Meg, her voice mollified. "That's the only way she'll go away. Remember what Shep said? She has to fulfill her longing, or follow something. We don't even know what the object was that brought her here."

"I bet I know," said Will.

"What?"

"It was the chest."

"You mean the chest itself?" Meg felt a flicker of hope rise inside her.

"Yeah, it's big enough. And my hiccups got louder after the chest arrived, and more crazy stuff started happening. Remember how Uncle Ben went nuts when we took off the lid? I bet she came inside the chest from the manor."

But when they went downstairs to ask Aunt Effie where the chest was, they found her striding out of her office room at a clipped pace, looking distracted. "The chest? Yes, it's here. No time to show you where it is now. I've just had a phone call. In here for a minute, all of you."

Meg and Will followed her into the living room.

Ariel looked up from her spot on the floor and placed the doll in her lap.

"Now, I know I promised you an outing to Wells today to see the cathedral and watch the swans ring the bell in the moat, but I'm afraid we'll have to put it off, dearies. I've just learned some people are coming to tour the Griffinage this afternoon. Rather important visitors. It's just been arranged."

"You mean a house tour?" Meg stiffened. She knew people generally didn't tour other people's houses unless they were house buyers. Surely Aunt Effie wasn't thinking of selling the Griffinage already?

"Yes, they'll want to tour the cottage and the gardens. I'll need you lot to help out. . . ." Aunt Effie went on asking them to tidy up their rooms, sweep the hall, and stay outside while the visitors were here.

Will leaned over to Meg and said in a harsh whisper, "I bet they're *buyers!*"

"Of course! Shhh!" Meg whispered back.

"You can play in the garden. Oh, the garden! That's right. I haven't finished mulching the roses or pruning the lavender. Need to tidy that up before they come. And bake. Let me see. Scones. Nothing like fresh buttered scones to sway the human heart, and today the Griffinage will certainly need to sway some hearts." She paused as Will made a choking sound.

"You all right, Will? You don't mind about the swans, do you? We can go tomorrow. This just came up suddenly. Could be a very good chance."

"Okay about the swans," Will croaked out.

Meg swallowed hard. If Aunt Effie was trying to bribe people with food, she must be really serious. Meg couldn't stand the thought of watching strangers tromping around the Griffinage, poking into each bedroom and talking about prices and sales contracts. Aunt Effie had already vanished into the kitchen. Will trailed after her, and Uncle Ben immediately followed, growling at the woodpile.

"What about the chest? Can we see the chest now?" Will asked.

"Good gracious! I'm not getting that dirty thing out today, not with visitors coming. Later, Will. The chest can wait. Now, Uncle Ben, what's wrong with you?" She tapped his dog dish with her foot, where his breakfast lay untouched. A dust ball of fur whirled up as she tapped. "Lost your appetite, have you? If it's not one thing, it's another."

⁂

Aunt Effie spent the rest of the morning tidying things up about the cottage and mixing flour and butter. The children could hear snatches of song drifting from the Griffinage kitchen as she worked:

She wheeled her wheelbarrow,
Through streets broad and narrow,
Singing cockles and mussels,
Alive, alive, oh!

"She sure seems happy about selling the Griffinage," said Will in a dark voice. They were upstairs cleaning their rooms, which for Will meant stuffing a mix of socks and music books under his bed, then sauntering down to the girls' room, and for Meg it meant helping Ariel make her bed properly and tuck the tea set, pinafore, and other toys away in the cabinet by the window.

"What next? We can't *do* anything until we move the chest," said Will. "And by the time these stupid people go home, it'll be late, and we probably can't move it until morning."

"Well, the manor ghost has lived a hundred years in the manor. I guess one more night in the Griffinage is all right," said Meg.

"That's easy for you to say," retorted Will. "You try sleeping with her in the house."

Meg reconsidered. He was right. She had no idea what it was like to sleep with a ghost when your body could sense it. Probably like a bad dream that wouldn't go away when you woke up.

"Okay," said Meg. "Then we'll find it ourselves. The

Griffinage isn't that big. We'll move the chest before tonight."

⸎

A hush settled over the house. Ariel looked about her. Will and Meg had finally gone away. They'd been hovering around the stairway and bedrooms all morning. That was why Kay Kay hadn't come. Ariel only ever saw her when she was alone. She heard Aunt Effie in the kitchen, pushing Uncle Ben out the back door. "You and those great paws can muck about outside," she said. Then the back door slammed, and a few minutes later the front door banged behind Meg and Will.

Normally, Ariel would have run after her brother and sister, but today she'd been waiting for this moment. Hoping to be alone.

Ariel propped Gillian, the doll, next to her on the floor by the sofa. She looked around expectantly, willing Kay Kay to come. She knew she didn't have to go to the attic to see Kay Kay now. Yesterday, Kay Kay showed up in the orchard. Ariel traced her finger around Gillian's nose and wondered what to give Kay Kay for a present.

"Don't forget my birthday."

Ariel looked up. There was Kay Kay herself, standing by the fireplace smiling with her beautiful silver eyes. Aunt Effie crashed a pan in the kitchen, and Kay Kay jumped. She flicked her eyes back to Ariel, and they seemed clouded, not so beautiful.

"I can't stay. But don't forget. The party's tomorrow."

Ariel bounced on her knees. She loved parties, especially ones with balloons and candy prizes. She hoped there'd be a red balloon. Then a thought occurred to her.

"Where do I go? Where's your party?" Usually Mama took care of that, the driving and getting there.

"Outside," said Kay Kay.

"Where outside?" asked Ariel. She liked backyard parties too. One party she'd been to even had an obstacle course.

"Outside by the well."

"The well!" said Ariel. "That's a funny place for a party. I thought you were afraid of the well."

"I am," said Kay Kay. "But it has to be there."

"But I don't know where it is," said Ariel, pouting and trying to imagine a wishing well with a little roof on top. "There is no well."

"'Course there is," said Kay Kay. "I'll take you there. I'll show you. Just come and meet me by the walnut tree. You know where that is."

Ariel nodded. Aunt Effie crashed another pan and Kay Kay jumped again. From the hall they could hear the clock chiming eleven.

"Tomorrow, remember," said Kay Kay. "Listen for the church bells. Come when you hear the bells chime three."

Ariel blinked. She was alone in the living room. Kay Kay must have run away again. She was always doing that, so she wasn't surprised. She squeezed Gillian in an excited hug. A private party! She'd go find Meg now and ask her about a birthday present.

Ariel found Meg by the garden shed. She was watching Will dig through piles of burlap sacks inside the shed, so Ariel stood and watched too.

"Whatcha doing?"

"Looking for something," said Meg.

Will emerged with burlap dust in his hair and shook it off, which made Meg sneeze. "Not here," he said, discouraged. "You'd think something as big as the chest would be easy to find."

"Let's look inside again," said Meg. "Maybe we missed something." They'd already looked in the broom closet, Aunt Effie's bedroom, and her office. Will had also checked the Mini.

"I've seen it," said Ariel.

"The chest from the manor? You know where it is?" asked Will. His eyes looked eager, and he smiled at Ariel.

"In the basement," she said.

"Don't be silly. The Griffinage doesn't have a basement," said Will. His eager look disappeared, and he turned away from her, slapping his pants to shake the burlap fibers off.

"It's in the basement, and I seen it when Aunt Effie took me there to get pickles."

"Show us," said Meg.

Ariel proudly led them around the back of the Griffinage kitchen to a slanted trapdoor in the ground. There were two doors with handles, and after that a set of stone steps leading down under the house. Ariel showed them where the light was, and Will flipped it on, then they all trooped down. The air was cool and smelled like apples and sawdust. They were standing on an earthen floor in a small room lined with wooden shelves. Most were empty, but some had rows of glass jars and there was a tub of potatoes on the bottom shelf. Ariel looked and saw more pickle jars.

"A root cellar," said Meg.

"See, lots of pickles," said Ariel.

"There's the chest," said Will, and he grinned.

Will and Meg hurried over to the chest and began to talk. They seemed to have forgotten her. Ariel eyed the pickles and wondered if Aunt Effie would notice if one of the jars had a pickle missing, but when she tried the lid it was sealed too tightly to open. Then she remembered the reason she'd come to find Meg. She walked over to the chest and tugged at Meg's arm.

"I need a present," she said. "For Kay Kay. Something special for her birthday."

"Why don't you draw her one of your pictures?"

asked Meg. "Those make good presents."

"No, something *really* special," said Ariel.

"Here, take this." It was Will. He was fishing around in his pocket. He put something heavy in her hand, and Ariel gasped with delight. It was silver and old-fashioned, the sort of thing Kay Kay would love. She looked at the silver circle with its dancing lion.

"What is it?"

"Dunno. We think it's a piece of a belt. Came from the manor long ago. Meg and I found it down by the creek."

Ariel took the treasure and fastened it around Gillian's waist with her hair ribbon. It looked like a shield or huge royal belt, and it made Gillian appear extra fancy and important. She hugged Gillian tightly, and again the warm, comforting feeling spread over her. Gillian was unlike any doll she'd held. She was *special*. Whenever Ariel loved her, she could feel the hollow-missing-mother places inside her disappear. She could feel the doll loving her back.

At the other end of the root cellar, Will and Meg were lugging the chest over to the steps. When they got to the foot of the steps, they stopped. A sound was coming from the open trapdoor that sounded like the rumble of a car engine.

"Shoot, that's the buyers," said Will. "They'll be crawling around everywhere in a minute."

"At least we know where the chest is," said Meg. "We can get it later."

"What buyers?" asked Ariel. Nobody answered her, so Ariel stuffed Gillian down her shirt in case the strange people might want to buy dolls. The silver circle felt cold against her tummy. She poked her head down her shirt's neckline to check on Gillian. "You'll be safe in there," she whispered in the doll's china ear. "Okay? Now go to sleep. There's a big party tomorrow."

The ghost stirred, newly energized. There it was at last. A clear and strong signal calling her. That's why she hadn't been able to feel a well-defined direction before. There'd always been two directions, muddling their signals, crossing them, keeping her aimless and worried in this peasant house. Now she knew exactly where she must go. She glided toward her target.

CHAPTER TEN

House and Garden

Meg peered around the hedge as footsteps crunched up the Griffinage walk. A branch obscured her full vision, but she could see a pair of legs appearing, then another, then a third. She felt Will's elbow knock her knee. Ariel's shoe pressed into her back. They were squatting behind the hedge outside the kitchen.

"Can you see anything?"

Meg poked her head farther out. There was Aunt Effie waving and calling out cheerful hallos and welcomes. Her back was to Meg, but a moment later she turned and came striding back to the house, straight toward the hedge. Meg ducked and bumped into Ariel, who'd stood up next to her. Ariel squealed.

"Shh," said Meg at once. "Get down."

"You stepped on me!" protested Ariel, still standing.

Will yanked Ariel out of sight. She scowled and scooted into a girl-sized cavity in the yew bush next to Meg. Meg glanced down at her sister, wishing she could explain what was going on. Ariel probably thought this was a simple hide-from-the-grown-ups game. But the stakes were higher. If Aunt Effie wanted to sell the Griffinage to these people, it was up to her and Will to try to stop it from happening.

Meg studied the cluster of grown-ups at the Griffinage stoop. There were three of them, an odd assortment for a family. First came a tall, balding man holding a tweed cap in one hand. He stood on the front walk, eyeing the child-sized red door as if calculating how far he'd have to bend to enter. The other two were women. One a squat, square shape. The other a tiny birdlike figure, hardly taller than Meg. The two women held notepads and were busily writing. The tall man was turning in every direction, snapping photos. The children froze as he pointed his black lens directly at the hedge.

"From 1660," Aunt Effie was saying. "Originally a shepherd's cottage. The family raised sheep, and later the women used to cook up at the manor. Cook's Cottage, they called it then. . . . Mind your head, yes, come in, come in."

"Let's go," said Will. Meg nodded and tugged Ariel to follow as the last legs disappeared inside. There was another good hiding spot by the living room window.

❧❧❧

Meg and Will retreated to the garden wall. They'd learned nothing from their hideout under the window. Only a murmur of voices. Just enough to know the visitors sounded pleased. That was the opposite of what they'd hoped. Meg imagined exclamations of delight as the interlopers poked around upstairs and into the alcove. It made everything seem hopeless.

Ariel was crouched by a clump of heather, talking to her doll. She'd lost interest in the spy game. Meg twisted her hair around her fingers. She let it spring back and twisted it again. Will scraped a rock against the stone wall. They sat waiting. Then the voices grew louder and a beaming Aunt Effie opened the back door and led the unwanted visitors into the garden.

"Stone wall from the Fosse Way built at the time of the original cottage, and near it you'll see the pride of the garden. Our walnut tree is at least two hundred and fifty years old."

"Incredible!"

"Simon, take a picture of that tree."

"Look at the size of it."

"Yes," said Aunt Effie, obviously pleased. "It's been part of the Griffinage since the time of George II. Ah, Meg, there you are. Can you and Will take our visitors round the garden a moment? I'm just going to pop in and see about those scones."

Meg slid down from the wall and plastered on her polite smile. It was the smile she used for grown-ups she was forced to be nice to, but didn't like. Will hung back and did not join her. *Fine*, she thought. *Don't come. Don't think I want to do this either.* The visitors were standing at the base of the walnut tree, *ooh*ing and *aah*ing, running their hands up and down the trunk. Meg tried to ignore the tight knot in her stomach. It clenched each time one of the strangers touched the grand walnut. *Hands off our tree!* she wanted to cry. Instead she opened her mouth to say hello.

Her mouth stayed open.

Instead of "hello," she gasped.

Uncle Ben was tearing out of the house, barking deep throaty cries. He flung himself at the walnut tree. The birdlike lady screamed. The squat woman jumped back and swung at Uncle Ben with her clipboard. The tall man yelled, lost his balance, and his hat flew off as he tipped over into a prickly holly hedge.

"Beast!" he cried. "Call off your beast!"

Uncle Ben charged around the tree again. The next instant, he changed course. He sprinted toward the garden toolshed. The shed leaned against the back stone wall, far back, near the walnut, its door partly open. A blur of fur went by. Ariel stood stock-still. Will made a lunge for Ben as he flew past.

"Uncle Ben!" Meg called, but no one heard her, especially not Uncle Ben, who'd reached the toolshed. He wedged himself through the doorway, and the door swung fully open. Inside, they could see Ben collide with a rake and tools crash down. The impact dislodged a row of flowerpots from a shelf. The pots smashed to the ground.

Out of the din and damage, Uncle Ben sprinted away. Fragments of broken flowerpots clung to his fur. Clay shards skittered in his wake. Bits of pots scattered into the gardens, and some struck the visitors' feet. The birdlike lady paused, took a breath, and renewed her scream. Uncle Ben answered with a bark. Then he barged at the back door and ran smack into Aunt Effie, who was hurrying out with a tray of blackcurrant jam and hot scones.

Uncle Ben's furry mass hit her at full force. Aunt Effie fell, and the plateful of scones—jam side down— tumbled into the dirt.

Suddenly, everything was still.

Uncle Ben vanished inside. The kitchen door vibrated from its final slam. The birdlike woman shut her mouth midscream and pressed her lips in a tight line. The stout woman retrieved her clipboard. The tall man carefully replaced his hat. They all looked at Aunt Effie, who lay sprawled in a patch of tulips and lily of the valley. In those awkward, awful moments, Meg noticed Will was hiccupping fiercely, one huge belchy hiccup followed by another.

"That dog," Aunt Effie said with a forced smile as she struggled to sit up. "Always underfoot."

The tall man coughed and inspected his camera. From her spot close to the house, Aunt Effie sighed and picked up a scone that had rolled in the tulips. She brushed the dirt off with her sleeve, then reached for another scone among the jonquils.

Will skirted past the scene of the crash and walked to the far side of the garden, approaching the group by the walnut tree.

"It was actually a ghost," said Will, in a low voice. "The manor ghost. We kind of share her here."

"A ghost, you say?" The tall man cocked an eyebrow at Will.

"Yeah, the manor ghost. She comes here when she's not hanging out at the manor."

Meg stared. What on earth was he doing? Then it dawned on her. This was what they'd been hoping for. The perfect chance to scare buyers away from the Griffinage. Will was telling the truth. Whether or not these grown-ups believed it, right now they were definitely shaken up enough to be disturbed by a ghost story.

"That's right," she said, stepping forward. "The ghost must have spooked the dog. You know, dogs can sense things like that." It sounded good, anyway. She flashed her best polite smile. "Not everyone could take living here."

"My aunt didn't want to tell you," Will said. "She's not big on ghosts." He filled in a few more details, punctuating the end with a loud hiccup.

The stout woman nodded and scribbled something on her clipboard. The other visitors exchanged looks. Then all three of them marched up to Aunt Effie, who was kneeling in the garden bed, a scone in each hand.

"Thank you for your time today, Ms. Griffin. I believe we've seen enough."

"Is there . . . won't you . . . ?" began Aunt Effie.

"Thank you, no," said the tall man, who came up rubbing his shoulders.

"We have another house to see," said the birdlike woman.

"All very interesting . . ." The stout lady stopped and cleared her throat as Aunt Effie extended a slick, jam-slimed hand to shake. "Yes," the lady said, stepping back. "Splendid," she said, gripping her notepad with both hands. "A pleasure, I'm sure."

The next minute, the car door slammed and the visitors' car jounced down the Griffinage driveway.

"Well!" said Aunt Effie. "That was a disaster."

She stood up from the flower bed, shaking off dirt and dabbing at her butter- and jam-streaked forehead.

A cloying scent like a bottle of spilled perfume spread over the garden from the crushed lily of the valley. "I wonder what startled Ben? I've never seen him go berserk like that before. And he's off his food. Oh, Uncle."

Ariel had stayed rooted to her spot during the commotion, but now she walked up to Aunt Effie and took her hand. Meg and Will were still back at the walnut tree. Gillian the doll was out of her shirt hiding place, and she hugged her close. She didn't know exactly what had just happened in the garden, but her tummy felt funny and she knew she had to tell a grown-up.

"It was the lady, Aun' Effie," said Ariel quietly. "Uncle Ben didn't like her."

"What's that, dearie? I must call the vet. I'm sure I haven't missed one of his booster shots; maybe it's his thyroid or his hips again. . . . Oh, look at this mess!" She kicked a scone with her toe and watched it tumble down the garden path.

"The lady was here," Ariel said again, tugging on her sleeve.

"Yes, I know, two ladies and a gentleman. They've gone." Aunt Effie patted Ariel's head distractedly.

"We're sorry, Aunt Effie," said Meg, rushing up a minute later with Will beside her. She meant it, though she wasn't exactly sure how guilty she should feel. After all, they hadn't moved the ghost into the house on purpose.

It was true they'd wanted the buyers to run away, but all the ruckus started before she and Will said anything to scare them. She was sorry simply because Aunt Effie's face looked so stricken and bewildered.

"Oh, it's just me and my great galumph of a dog," Aunt Effie said, and sank heavily down on the back steps. Her body sagged with a mixture of grief, embarrassment, and defeat. Meg looked down at her shoes.

"I don't understand it," Aunt Effie continued. "Everything was going along fine indoors. They seemed to really like the Griffinage. And then . . . Chaos, Disaster, and Consternation. Not even a good-bye," she added.

"Don't worry, Aunt Effie," offered Will. "With those buyers gone, you get to keep the Griffinage."

"Buyers! Will, those people weren't trying to *buy* the Griffinage. They were my best chance of *saving* it! Mrs. Carmichael is president of the Somerset Heritage Society. The society gives out grants to homeowners to help repair historic buildings! Of course, with the number of historic buildings here in Somerset, there's scads of competition. Foolish me, I thought I could tip the balance in my favor if they left full of hot, buttered scones, but I didn't count on that dog of mine. Now what have we got? Complete calamity. Well, I hope garden slugs like jam."

With that, Aunt Effie turned and walked inside.

"The Heritage Society!" said Will. "We've ruined it."

"The ghost ruined it."

"Who cares? There goes our chance of saving the Griffinage."

They sat glumly for a moment, watching the ants discover the spilled blackcurrant jam.

"Why didn't she tell us? said Will. "Now we've really got to move the chest. That ghost is stirred up. The Griffinage doesn't stand a chance unless we clear it out."

"I don't feel good."

Neither of them had noticed as Ariel came up and stood beside them. She held her stomach with one arm. The doll hung loosely by her side. She looked pale and swayed a little as she spoke.

"Oh, Ariel!"

Meg put her arm around her and helped her inside, while Will ran to fetch Aunt Effie. Aunt Effie took one look at Ariel and bundled her into an armchair.

"There now, missy. You probably just overdid it after yesterday. I need a rest too, after all that," said Aunt Effie. Ariel moaned. "Come, I'll read to you, if you like." Aunt Effie still had dark jam streaks across her forehead, but she plopped Ariel on her lap, pulled a tumble of blankets around them both, and opened *Alice in Wonderland*. She started in on the chapter where the baby sneezes and finally turns into a pig. Meg and Will slipped out of the room.

CHAPTER ELEVEN

The Storm

It was a dismal evening at the Griffinage. No one much felt like talking except Ariel. She had emerged from her story time looking flushed but improved, and jabbered on about Kay Kay during dinner, until Will snapped at her and said he was sick of hearing about nonexistent people's birthdays. Ariel pouted, then dissolved into a fit of tears when she realized she couldn't find Gillian the doll.

"I can't sleep without her, Aun' Effie! I neeeeeeed her!"

Aunt Effie shot Will a look as she carried the protesting Ariel upstairs.

"Make yourself useful, Will, and clean up those blankets in the living room. One goes in my room, one in yours."

Will grabbed the pile of blankets from the

"Time to get rid of that thing," said Will.

"Do you think the chest is making Ariel sick?"

"Let's get rid of it now and find out later," said Will. He was trying to shake the feeling that he'd seen a flash of green when Uncle Ben crashed into the toolshed. When he'd looked again, there'd been nothing there.

"Do you think she saw the ghost?" asked Meg, her voice sounding shaky.

"Who, Ariel?" Will gulped. Ariel did look weird. Maybe Ariel could see green flashes too.

"I asked her before and she said no," said Meg. "But maybe today it was stronger. You know, more obvious or something. We better ask again."

"Well, we can't now," said Will. "Not with Aunt Effie sitting right there. And we need to get the chest, remember? Once that's gone, it won't matter. Ariel won't see anything."

The chest was leaning exactly where they'd left it: at the base of the root cellar steps. The lid was slightly open. Meg saw Ariel's finger marks still visible from swirling the dust on the chest's outside panels. She stared at the bulky thing, then eyed the stairs. There were only eight steps, but they angled up sharply.

"Maybe we should go get Shep," she said. "Remember how heavy it was?"

"That's when it was full of books. It's empty now."

"I know, but the chest itself must be heavy. Books can't weigh that much."

Will didn't answer. He'd already begun to shove. His sneakers sent up puffs of dirt as he scrambled for a toe-hold. The chest slid easily, a few inches up the steps. Meg came around and pushed too. It was much lighter. The chest slid more, and to their delight they were able to stumble up the steps heaving the chest in front. It teetered at the top. Meg feared it was going to come crashing down on top of her and Will, but the far end finally tipped and settled on the grass. The chest was up. Outside in the open air.

It took them the rest of the afternoon to haul it as far as they could away from the Griffinage. Although the chest was lighter than before, it was still bulky and awkward. They made it to the edge of Bibsie's Woods, which Will declared good for now.

"What if Aunt Effie wants it again?" asked Meg.

"Then she can have it," said Will. "I don't mind a ghost in Bibsie's Woods for the night. We can always tell Aunt Effie where it is and she can drive it back to the manor tomorrow."

"Yes, but what if Aunt Effie doesn't want to give it back to the manor? She might like it, that's what I mean. She'll be mad and we'll get in trouble."

"She'll just have to be mad! We'll get Shep to drive

it, and we won't tell her. Come on, Meg. You know we have to. It might help Ariel. And save the Griffinage." *And save me, too*, he almost added. Meg wouldn't understand because she couldn't sense things. But getting hiccups in the middle of the night was no joke. Hiccups used to be kind of fun. But not now. Not knowing a ghost was knocking around nearby.

Will grew more skittish as the day drew close to evening. Already the daylight was weakening, and the sun had dipped below McBurney's hill. Will stuffed his hands in his pockets and bit his lip. They watched as dusk enveloped the Griffinage. Will's bedroom window was bathed in a honey-colored glow as the thatch caught the day's last light. Then the glow disappeared, the thatch flattened to grey, and the shadows crept forward.

armchair where Ariel had been snuggling, and tromped up the stairs, the blankets dragging behind him like a ragged king's train. Upstairs, he could hear Ariel's gulps and sobs still going full force. There'd still been no chance to ask Ariel about the manor ghost. Aunt Effie was always hovering around. He heard the sound of nose blowing, then more sobs. It wasn't *his* fault Ariel was crying. As if he knew where the stupid doll was.

Half an hour later, Aunt Effie emerged from Ariel's room and announced she was going to bed herself. "Head-ache," she said. "You'll manage without me for one evening, I hope."

"What's 'Sow-in'?" asked Will as she turned to go.

"Samhain? An old Celtic holiday, observed for thousands of years, sort of a ghost or spirit day. You'd know it as Halloween. Whatever made you ask that, Will?" Then she stooped and nuzzled her face with Uncle Ben's. "Oh, Ben! You haven't touched your sup-per. What am I going to do about you?"

Without Aunt Effie bustling around and laughing, playing cards, and generally keeping them company, the Griffinage seemed extra dark and full of creak-ing noises that evening. "Let's go to bed early too; then we won't notice," suggested Meg. She yawned. Will immediately agreed. They were both tired, and if you're waiting for something, he knew, sleeping is the fastest way to make time pass. As he yanked on his pajama bottoms, he willed the night to speed along.

That night, it took Will a long time to fall asleep, even though he was tired. He kept thinking about the black chest abandoned in the dark in Bibsie's Woods. Every time his eyelids drooped, he pictured something lifting the lid and coming out of the chest. Something creeping toward the Griffinage, cracking branches in the wood. Then he realized the cracking noises he was hearing were real and close by. The wind had picked up. It sounded like tree branches thrashing around. Maybe it was another storm. Will buried his head under the covers and forced himself to calm down by tracing the pattern of one of Beethoven's bagatelles. Somehow the notes mixed with the bell song after a while, and when he tried to unravel them, he couldn't. He'd fallen asleep.

Two hours later, Will woke with a start. Thunder rumbled. Something banged against the window, and outside the wind reached a fierce peak. Another April rainstorm. That's what had woken him.

In the dark, he began to hiccup. *It can't be*, he thought. *We've moved the chest. These are just regular hiccups.* But his words were not convincing. A wave of cold air washed over him, and Will heard a familiar whooshing sound.

She's awake.

Will trembled. He opened his eyes into slits and

peered out into the darkness. Downstairs, the hall clock whirred as its mechanism stirred to life and began to strike midnight. Will listened to each reverberation echo through the Griffinage and die away. It chimed in G, a bit flat. Outside, the wind mounted and branches rapped against his bedroom window. Inside, Will's hiccups punctuated the night.

Will drew the covers up to his chin. Maybe he should bunk with the girls again tonight. Meg had a big bed. And Uncle Ben would be there; he always slept by Ariel's bed in the alcove. All he'd have to do was run down the hallway to join them. Better than being in this room full of shadows. Outside, the storm suddenly opened up and rain poured down in sheets. He heard it pound the roof and clatter against the flagstones on the front walk.

Will slipped out of bed. He pulled one of Aunt Effie's blankets around him like a cloak and padded across the room. The cold floorboards made his feet prickle. He was halfway across when he realized his bare feet were more than cold. His toes and heel were tingling like pins and needles, and the whooshing sound was growing louder. He stiffened as he heard a bang on the banister. Then a squeak on the stair. Was it the seventh step, and was it just Aunt Effie headed for the loo in the middle of the night? Oh, why wasn't he already down the hall, curled up in Meg's warm bed?

Will ran. He reached the bedroom door. His hand fumbled for the knob. He stopped. The sound was coming from the doorway.

Will froze. He held his breath. Tiny sparks raced up from his feet and scaled his spine. He could feel his scalp covered in a wash of hot pinpricks. He took a step backward.

Something pushed the door open a crack. Will shrank back, then stumbled to the far side of the room, where his bed stood, his feet tangled in a blanket. *Oh, let it be Uncle Ben! Please just let it be Uncle Ben.*

But the next instant, he knew it wasn't. Something was poking around the door's edge. Clothing. The door gap widened. He saw more as the door slowly creaked open. A shoe. The folds of a gown. Will pressed into the shadows by his bed. Even in the room's dim light, he could see what was entering: green velvet.

The whole creature stood before him. A figure, not a person. People didn't glow, and this grown-up-sized figure shimmered ever so slightly. Long black hair draped her face; strands partially covered her eyes and swayed across her mouth. Her hair was matted and disheveled, part of it still in a single braid slung over her shoulder, the rest unraveled. A dark green dress swept down to her ankles, and a copper-colored brooch glinted at her collar. There was no doubt who she was. He was finally seeing the manor ghost. And she was absolutely terrifying.

The ghost swayed to the center of the room, paused, then moved away from Will. *She's looking for something,* thought Will. *Maybe she can't see me. Maybe she doesn't even want me, she's just in here, kind of visiting, just regular haunting.* He tried to hold his breath to prevent the next hiccup from coming, then realized the hiccups had stopped on their own the moment he saw her.

There were still ten feet between him and the door, and the ghost was in the middle. He couldn't possibly reach the door, but maybe he could disappear like a field mouse outwitting a hunting owl. He slid down the wall and bedpost, trying to stay as still as possible, and pulled more blankets over his head. He held his breath again. It felt safer down here. He shifted the blanket slightly to peer out with one eye.

The ghost turned. Will saw her eyes for the first time. The spirit had two piercing specks of light in each eye, the pupils shining silver. The silver eyes roamed the room, traveling over the dresser, the stool, the bookshelf. The green dress swished as she swayed from side to side. Then the ghost grew rigid. Her silver eyes swiveled and landed on him.

The instant their eyes locked, Will's forehead exploded in pain. He tried to scream but could only gasp. The Griffinage bedroom disappeared and he saw . . . *Trees. A lightning flash. A bleeding horse. Slick rocks, something silver, a blue hair ribbon pressed in the mud.* And noises: *Shouts, squeals, and bells, bells.* Will forgot about screaming. He clutched his head and moaned.

The pale shimmer of the ghost's body flared to a blaze, and the silver eyes bore straight into him. With a happy cry, the manor ghost lunged toward Will, arms outstretched.

"My child!"

The voice sounded crackly, like static on an ancient record player. Will scrambled to his feet, trying to dodge her, and knocked into the nightstand and the bedroom wall.

"There you are! Where have you been? You naughty child! Worrying your poor mother!"

With each staccato sentence, the ghost lurched toward Will. He dodged again, but couldn't get closer to the door. His legs were trembling, his eyes riveted to her bright light. It was growing brighter, wilder, like a fireworks sparkler gone mad. Sparks flew off her copper brooch and velvet dress as the ghost shot across the floor in bursts of electric energy. Will choked on another scream. He was nearly cornered. He dropped on his stomach and tried to wriggle under the bed.

"Gilly, it's Mama! Mama's here. You've had a fall. Come, don't hide. I'll take you home. Gilly . . . Gilly!"

"Will! My name's Will" was all Will could think to say. He'd only managed to get one and a half legs under the bed. The rest of his body was sticking out in full view.

"Of course it is," said the ghost mother soothingly. "Gilly, darling child, come to Mama."

She reached out both arms and her body pitched forward until it blazed a few inches from Will and his pile of blankets. Will felt his forehead raging with pain.

"Will Griffin!" yelled Will, as a thunderclap shook the house. "I'm not Gilly! It's a mistake! I'm Will Griffin, not your child!"

The panes rattled in the windows, and Will's teeth rattled too. He shrank against the floor, feeling the cold, solid surface as he pressed his side to it. This was the twenty-first century. Aunt Effie's house. Somerset. His parents were both professors, attending a geology conference in Yorkshire. He'd eaten oatmeal for breakfast. Surely nothing could happen to a modern boy like him. It would just go away if he stopped believing in it. Ghosts weren't supposed to exist. And if they did, ghosts couldn't hurt people—or could they?

Will shut his eyes. He forced his brain to think, to think hard and push the ghost away with logical thoughts, but his mind was slow and jumbled and didn't obey him. His forehead prickled, then throbbed. A piercing pain shot through his skull as the ghost reached out her arms to embrace him.

"My child, my child!" cried the manor ghost.

Will slid instinctively to the left, and as he did, the ghost mirrored his movement. He was out from under the bed now. The bed no longer felt safe, more like a trap. He inched along the baseboard, trying to gain a clear path and bolt for the door. His instincts screamed: *Run!* He leapt to his feet, but her fingers touched his shoulder. Searing cold stopped him. He yelled, again and again, but his yells were swallowed up by thunder.

This was real.

The place where the ghost's fingers touched him stung fiercely. He felt a chill surging through his body, electrifying each artery and tracing each living blood vessel's path. Will dropped to the floor and screamed as the cold spread out: from his shoulder to his arm, his arm to his chest. Edging closer to his heart.

Coarse, prickly velvet brushed his face. She loomed before him, so close he could have felt her breath, except no breath came. He blinked. The manor ghost was kneeling, surrounded by a plume of green velvet, her silver eyes boring into him. His vision blurred from the intense green light. The last thing he saw was a look of rapture on her face.

"Mama's here," the ghost said. And she leaned forward to kiss him.

CHAPTER TWELVE

April Fifth

Green light blinded Will. He tried to focus, to keep his wits about him, but the glare was too intense. He could only squint and gasp as shock waves radiated through his legs, arms, neck, and spine.

From a distant part of his mind, he heard a scream followed by a great *crash*. The next moment, a tremendous blow landed on his chest and his body skidded into the bedpost.

Will lay in a heap on the floor. The bright glare in the room was gone. Tentatively, he raised his head. No sign of green velvet. Will heaved a breath in relief but choked instead. The blow had taken the air out of his lungs. He struggled to his knees gasping, desperate for air, and tried not to panic. He couldn't breathe. *He couldn't breathe!* He was saved from the ghost but about to suffocate. He tried to gasp again.

No air. Like soccer when the ball knocked the wind out of him. *Easy, now*, he told himself, the way his coach always did. It seemed like eternity until the first ragged breath came, but it came, and he sobbed in gratitude.

Then something licked him. A warm muzzle prodded his cheek, and he looked up into the shaggy brown face of Uncle Ben.

"It was you," whispered Will. "You saved me."

He sobbed again and clutched Uncle Ben's fur in a tight grip. The room smelled strongly of burned sticks mixed with wet dog. At that moment, Will noticed how wet he was. His pajama sleeves flapped like wet washcloths. Why was he suddenly wet? And getting wetter, too. It felt as if he were inside a waterfall. Will looked up. A cold cascade of water splashed his face and sluiced down his neck.

Directly above, a hole gaped open to the night sky. The ceiling, rafters, and thatch had been blown off. Scorched thatch blackened the hole's edges. Will was sitting in a puddle with rain drumming on his head.

"William Moraine! Are you all right?"

Aunt Effie burst into the room, followed by Meg and Ariel. Both girls looked dry and perfectly normal.

"Oh, Will!" said Meg. "I heard the noise. I was so scared!"

"Well, thank heavens!" said Aunt Effie. "Gave us a real fright."

In an instant, she'd scooped up Will and settled him on top of his dry bed. She inspected the hole, sent Meg for a bucket, then turned back to Will. Peering into his eyes, she felt his pulse, stripped his pajama top, and pulled up the crumpled bedding. Then she wrapped a dry blanket around Will's shivering shoulders.

"There now! That's better," she said. "First step in getting dry is to get out of the rain, I always say. What on earth were you doing on the floor—right in the worst part of it?"

Aunt Effie shook out another blanket and wrapped it around Will's still-trembling form. Something fell from the blanket and clattered to the floor. Ariel's eyes grew wide and her face exploded into a smile. She ran across the room and plucked the object from the tangled blankets.

"There you are!" she said, clutching her lost doll to her chest. "Ooh, you're all wet," she added, climbing onto Will's bed. She wiped the doll's face with the corner of a blanket, then cleaned water droplets off the silver lion that still hung from the doll's waist. Uncle Ben nosed onto the bed, and Will opened his arms to welcome the great furry head.

"He's the one who saved me," he said, patting Uncle Ben's back and rubbing his ears vigorously to say thank you.

"That or good luck," said Aunt Effie. "You were

inches away. Must have given you a real jolt."

"Not inches. She was right there," said Will. "All light and energy. And so bright I couldn't see."

"Not surprising," said Aunt Effie. "Look at the roof! You were smack-dab in the middle of that lightning strike."

⊰⊱

Will bunked the rest of the night with Meg in the girls' room. No one slept well at first except Ariel. After watching the excitement of Aunt Effie setting up buckets to catch rainwater under the hole in Will's room, Ariel returned to her cot, fiercely hugging Gillian, and slipped into a deep, still slumber.

"It wasn't lightning," said Will. He'd changed into dry clothes—a T-shirt and sweatpants—since his pajamas were soaked. Now he and Meg were lying in her big bed, propped up by pillows. "It wasn't lightning," he said again. He'd tried to tell her before, but she kept shushing him until they could hear Ariel's steady breathing.

Meg swallowed hard. "I knew you'd say that. And I wish you wouldn't."

"Meg, I saw her this time."

"You *saw* her?" Meg's eyes widened. "Like a person? What'd she look like?"

"Horrible." Will buried his head in his hands and wouldn't say more. When he tried to explain, green velvet and aching cold flooded back, and he could feel those silver eyes boring into him again.

"Forget it. Doesn't matter," said Meg. "We've got to tell Aunt Effie."

"Are you crazy?" said Will. "She'd never believe us. She thinks it's lightning! She doesn't believe in ghosts, remember?"

"The police?"

"You think the police are going to come out for a ghost story?" asked Will.

"Tell me what happened."

So Will told his story, skipping the physical description of the ghost, and Meg fidgeted with her curls as he talked.

"But the roof . . . ," Meg said when he finished.

"Must have gone out that way," said Will. "When Uncle Ben hit her. Or rather, when he hit *me*. I think he knocked her off somehow and the energy just sort of went up. That's not a lightning hole, that's a fast exit for a ghost."

"Oh!" Meg shuddered and tightened the blankets around her chest. "It's strange, though. She was nothing like Shep said, a chatty ghost having conversations. And she didn't care that you're a boy. The child she lost was a girl. Even the clothes you're wearing didn't bother her. She couldn't tell the difference between a boy in plaid pajamas and her own child wearing a dress from one hundred and fifty years ago."

"Or didn't want to."

"What do you mean?" asked Meg.

"Maybe she'll go after any of us. You might be safe—you might be old enough—we don't know. But Ariel definitely isn't, and we know I'm not."

Will slept late into the next morning, despite thinking he'd never close his eyes at all. He woke groggy, with a blistering headache. The others were in the kitchen. Aunt Effie jumped up when he came in and hovered about him, smoothing the hair on his forehead and saying, "Thank goodness!" every two minutes.

"I've already called your parents," Aunt Effie said, patting his head again. "Told them about the storm. Left a message that you're safe and sound."

All this head patting made Will feel worse. He ate a few spoons of oatmeal, poked at his egg, and left his toast getting cold on the side of his plate. It was one thing to be lucky and thankful about a near miss with a lightning strike, it was another to know it wasn't a lightning strike, but something much worse.

"Rain's clearing up," said Aunt Effie. "That's a relief, anyway. I've already emptied those buckets three times." She looked at the children, patted Will's head and kissed it this time, then moved on to

Uncle Ben, who was prowling about the kitchen and had barely nibbled his breakfast. Aunt Effie gently cupped Uncle Ben's cheeks in her hands and gazed into his eyes.

"Oh, Ben," she said. "You and this house together are going to be the death of me. I've got a broken window, a hole in the roof, an ill child, and now a dog who's poorly."

"I'm not sick anymore, Aun' Effie," said Ariel. She was cheerfully spooning brown sugar–slathered oatmeal into her mouth. The raisin box was empty, but the brown sugar jar wasn't. She'd been up first and had her breakfast long ago, but decided she needed a "second breakfast" when she saw Will eating. Aunt Effie ran her hand over Ariel's forehead to check for fever, and smiled.

"I believe you're right," said Aunt Effie. "That's one cheerful thing about today. You're the picture of health and rest. Good, we don't have to worry about you." Aunt Effie kissed her, then disappeared down the hallway. A short time later they heard snatches of conversation like "oh, this house!" and "splendid, splendid, three o'clock." Will poked his egg again. If Aunt Effie was making more plans for the Griffinage, he couldn't worry about it. There was a ghost to get rid of. A ghost intent on loving him to death.

"You're taking forever!" cried Meg, pulling his plate away. "Come on, we've got to go to Shep's. Shep will believe us. He'll know what to do."

Will nodded, his head still aching, and tugged on his boots. Ariel was safe for the moment. She was coloring outside Aunt Effie's office, with Gillian propped beside her and Uncle Ben lying at her feet. What could happen? It was daylight, and she had a dog and a grown-up.

⌒⌒

The little ghost danced above them in the branches of the walnut tree. Today was the day. *Her* day. Her special birthday—or was it deathday?—she always got those two mixed up. Both involved going in and out of the earthly world.

She waved as she saw the older two children walk off across the fields, and hopped to another branch. The walnut was tipped at an odd angle today, not quite the same as usual. She studied it, then shrugged and turned her attention to the house. The little one must be inside somewhere. She'd wait. Oh, yes. It wouldn't be long now. After enduring so many Aprils, it was easy to be patient until three o'clock. She skipped a bit, and then fluttered down to peek in the east room's window. Where was she? Not there. She laughed and dropped down to spy in a lower window. There she was. Her friend. Ariel was holding some sort of waxy blue pencil and drawing a picture. How much fun they'd have. Always together. Already, she could feel the dark weight on her soul lightening. Soon it would lift right off. She flew to the top of the walnut tree. After today, she'd never be lonely again.

Shep's house was dark. The door stayed shut and locked no matter how much they pounded. They checked behind the house, where Shep usually parked his Jeep. It was gone.

"Don't worry, he'll be back," said Meg. "We just have to wait till he returns."

"Who knows when that will be!" groaned Will. He kicked the dirt in the driveway and nervously glanced toward the Griffinage.

"We can leave a note. Or come back—it's not far. Maybe Aunt Effie can call him."

"What does he really know?" said Will, exasperated. "He seems to know a lot about ghosts, but he thinks they're only grumpy! He doesn't know anything about a ghost that pulls people out of their beds and tries to kill them!"

"Why was she even at the Griffinage?" asked Meg, as they trudged back home. "We moved the chest."

"We must have moved the wrong thing."

They were both silent. There was no need to say the obvious truth: If the chest wasn't right, they'd have to discover the right object before the ghost came back.

The first thing they saw as they reached the Griffinage was Aunt Effie standing outside staring at the walnut tree. The giant tree had split. One branch was snapped, bent double and hanging half suspended along the stone wall. A fresh line of splintered bark traveled from high in the top branches, snaking its way down until it disappeared into the ground. Besides the gash, the entire tree tilted on its side.

"Now the walnut!" Aunt Effie cried as they came running up. "My beautiful old tree. She's alive, but damaged. Quite unbelievable that lightning struck twice, so close together last night."

Meg and Will exchanged glances. Had there also been a lightning strike? It looked like the kind of scar lightning made, but maybe it was a ghost track. Shep would know. Or might know, Will corrected himself.

The three of them walked closer to inspect the tree damage, but before they'd reached the tree's canopy, Aunt Effie stuck out her arm to ward them off.

"Not too close. Stay away from the tree today, my dears," Aunt Effie went on. "Not safe to be around. Branches might fall, or the ground could be unstable. See how it's tipping. Who knows what the tree roots could unearth after a jolt like that. Old ruins. Roman lead mines. Buried wells. I'll have to get the tree trimmers in. Oh, my. Another expense. What a week we're having here at the old Griffinage." She wiped her hands on her pants. "Only thing to do is soldier on." She ushered them toward the house.

"Aunt Effie, do you know where Shep works?" asked Meg.

"Shep? He's always out and about. Goes where the computer bugs are. But today I know where he is."

"Where?" Both Meg and Will spoke at once.

"Why, he's in town getting a new glass pane and roof supplies for me. I called him this morning and told him about our rainstorm."

"That means he'll be back soon?" asked Meg.

"I certainly hope so. Might be more rain tonight, and I do want to get that hole patched. The Griffinage feels its age with a gaping hole in its head."

Meg cornered Ariel in the bathroom to ask her about the manor ghost, but Ariel spoke before she could open her mouth.

"I saw her," said Ariel. "The lady you said."

"You really saw her?" asked Meg. She caught her breath. Of course, she knew there'd been a ghost in the Griffinage, the way Uncle Ben had pounced and gone crazy, and Will's terror last night and all the damage to the house. She knew it logically, but it was another thing to have your little sister matter-of-factly state that she'd seen a ghost.

"When did you see her? Today?"

"No, yesterday, when all those people were here. She was outside by the big tree."

"What did she look like?"

"Just like you said. A lady wearing a green dress."

"Was she . . . scary?"

"No, but she's no fun. I like Uncle Ben and Kay Kay better."

"Me too," Meg assured her. "If you see her again, come tell us right away, okay? Don't wait. It's important."

She hurried off to find Will and reported the news to him. "But I don't think it changes anything," Meg concluded. "We know we have a ghost to get rid of. It's just that you two are the only ones who can see her."

Will had slept so late that the rest of the morning was short. Aunt Effie took them for a walk, but Uncle Ben growled when she fetched her coat and refused to chase the squirrels. Lunch was egg sandwiches and water, accompanied by Aunt Effie sighing a lot. After lunch, she announced she was taking Uncle Ben to the vet.

"I've never seen him like this. Agitated, aggressive, no appetite. I hope it's nothing serious. Lucky the vet can fit us in today." She cradled Uncle Ben's furry head in her hands and rubbed his ears. "Oh, Ben, I'd rather have you than a thousand Mrs. Carmichaels."

Waiting by the gold Mini, Meg and Will shuffled their feet and tried not to look as uncomfortable as they felt inside. Will kept glancing at his watch and staring helplessly at Meg as the day inched by, ever closer to nightfall. Meg swallowed her own growing fear. If only Shep would come home. Maybe they could even sleep over at Shep's for the night, or get a hotel or something. There was sure to be a hotel in town near the vet's. The tricky part was how they could convince Aunt Effie that they needed to spend the night away from the Griffinage. Meg pictured herself saying, *It's a ghost emergency, Aunt Effie. We need to rent a hotel room.*

But she said nothing and watched glumly as Aunt Effie loaded Uncle Ben's dog bed in the Mini's back seat, then added his water bowl and leash. The next moment, her despair deepened.

"There's only room for Ariel, one driver, and one dog, I'm afraid," said Aunt Effie.

"We're not coming?"

"Not you two. A Mini can beat world records, but not where Newfoundland dogs are concerned. A Newfie's not like an umbrella, you know. He won't fold up." She smiled, but Meg and Will didn't smile back. They trailed after her as she returned to the house and reappeared shaking a box of Bowzer's Bones.

"He never can resist these," she said. "Fish sticks for dogs."

But it seemed today he could. Uncle Ben did not budge. Instead, he backed up and gazed at Ariel, who was skipping rope on the flagstone walk.

"I think he doesn't want to leave Ariel," said Meg. "Or

what I mean is, leave any of us." If only Aunt Effie would change her mind and take them all. Or if Uncle Ben wouldn't get in the car, then they could all stay home.

"Ah, that's a good idea," said Aunt Effie. "He does love that little girl. Must think she's his puppy. Right, then, Ariel, you pop in first." Ariel stopped skipping and climbed in the Mini. Once Ariel was tucked in, Uncle Ben obligingly walked into the Mini and lay down. Aunt Effie shut the door behind his great shaggy rump with a *click*.

"Right. Won't be long." said Aunt Effie. "Sorry, dears, this isn't much of a vacation for you, is it? We'll go to Wells tomorrow, I promise. It's just Ben's got me worried, and the vet only had one appointment left—I've got to take it—and I do love the old fellow...."

Suddenly Meg felt an urge to tell Aunt Effie everything. It didn't matter if she believed them or not. What if Aunt Effie didn't return until late? What if her car broke down and they had to spend the night at the Griffinage alone? What if ...

"Aunt Effie ...," she began.

"What is it, Meg? You look pale. You can't be taking ill too, I hope."

"No, I'm fine. It's just that . . ." She started again. "Well, we've been . . ."

"What she means is, is the vet close by?" asked Will, helping her out.

"The vet? The vet's in Yeovil. What's on your mind, William Moraine?"

"When will you be back?"

"Oh, that's it!" said Aunt Effie. "You're thinking about supper. You'll find apples and cake in the larder to start. I'm picking up lamb chops for supper."

"So you'll be back before dark?" asked Meg.

"Sure to be back long before dark. Now I must be off—the vet won't wait. Is that all you wanted to know?"

"Yes," said Meg. She wanted to say no. She wanted more answers, lots of answers. How do you make a ghost go dormant? How do you find the object a ghost's attached to? What should they do if the ghost comes again? Meg wanted to cry out: *Don't go! There's nothing wrong with Ben except a ghost! The vet can't fix him! Stay with us.*

Instead, she found herself waving good-bye to Aunt Effie and Ariel. At least Ariel would be out of harm's way, Meg thought. She watched with a sinking heart as the Mini started down the drive.

CHAPTER THIRTEEN

Prelude to a Party

The Mini had rolled only a short distance when Ariel sat bolt upright and cried out. "What time is it, Aunt Effie? What time is it?"

"Half past two or thereabouts."

"Is that close to three o'clock?" asked Ariel.

"Yes, dear. Quite close to three."

"Will we get home for three o'clock?"

"No, we'll be at the vet's then."

"Then I can't go!" cried Ariel, grabbing the door handle and opening the Mini door. They were still on the long Griffinage driveway. They hadn't gone far. "Kay Kay's birthday party is at three. She said so."

Aunt Effie, however, didn't want to let her go. She kept talking about responsibility, and how old everyone was. Ariel was getting impatient. Meg and Will often looked after her at home; why not here? Finally,

Aunt Effie took out her cell phone and called Shep.

"There," she said. "Shep's just around the corner at the hardware store. He'll stop by."

"So I can stay?"

"You can stay, dearie. Mind Meg and Will, and Shep will be there in a jiff. Now I'm lucky to get Ben to the vet before she closes."

Ariel bounced out of her seat and waved to Meg, who was standing by the red Griffinage door, and seemed to be waving to her with great big waves. Meg would help her know when it was three o'clock. It was confusing which hand was supposed to point at the numbers. Then she remembered: She didn't have to. Kay Kay had told her to listen for the bells.

"Bye, Uncle," she said, as she slipped from the car and ran back down the drive to the Griffinage. Inside the car, Uncle Ben heaved to his feet, clunking his head against the roof. He turned in circles, frantically barking. The Mini lurched as Aunt Effie restarted the engine. His enormous body rocked the Mini as the car pulled away to Yeovil.

At the Griffinage, the cottage was bathed in fresh sunshine, the kind of spring sky that breaks out after a big storm has gone. Water dribbled off the eaves. Daffodils nodded from a light breeze by the rain barrel. The plum portion of the orchard was at its peak of new life, bursting forth with a radiant display of white blossoms.

"Seems safe now, doesn't it?" said Meg, looking around. She and Will were standing on the slate front walk. Ariel had her jump rope and was skipping again, hopping from stone to stone. She sang:

> *Miss Lucy had a baby.*
> *She named him Tiny Tim.*
> *She put him in the bathtub, to see if he could swim.*

"The trouble is we don't *know*," Will said. "We know the manor ghost is looking for a child. We know she goes dormant, so most of the time she's not a threat. What we don't know is what wakes her up."

"You're right," said Meg miserably. "We'll always have to watch and always be watching Ariel."

> *Miss Kitty had a dolly.*
> *She named her Gillian.*
> *She put her in the well, to see if she could swim.*

"What time is it?" Ariel left off singing.

"Let's go see," said Meg. "Shep should be here any minute." She smiled as she said this. She'd been shocked at the sight of Ariel skipping back down the Griffinage driveway, but Ariel's reappearance was quickly tempered with the news that Shep was on his way. At last!

Meg and Will followed Ariel indoors. The hall clock read 2:38. Ariel plunked down in front of it.

"Play with me, Meg?"

So Meg joined her on the floor and they played Hickory Dickory Dock, with Ariel being the mouse, running her fingers up and down Meg's back, then switching who was the mouse and who was the clock. After that, Ariel put on the dress-up pinafore and played with Gillian, while Meg and Will sat silently and stared at the time ticking by. Eleven minutes since Aunt Effie had left. Now fifteen. Where was Shep?

"I'll go check his house," offered Will, reading her thoughts. "Maybe he forgot and showed up there or something." Will disappeared, but returned soon.

"What time did Aunt Effie say he'd be here?" he asked.

"She didn't say," replied Meg. "Just that he was around the corner and would be here in a jiff."

"Well, it's a long jiff," groaned Will, and he flopped on the sofa.

The minutes ticked by. Meg and Will agreed to stick together, all three of them, except for quick runs to Shep's house to grab him the minute he got home. "We'll take turns going to check," said Meg.

At five minutes to three, Meg set out to look for Shep. She left Will lying on the sofa with Ariel beside him on the floor. He was half listening to Ariel, half batting a sofa pillow in the air. Outside, robins sang and pulled stalks from the thatch. A bumblebee buzzed by. Everything looked so calm and normal, it seemed strange to believe they were battling a ghost.

Will sprawled on the sofa as he watched Ariel line up her stuffed animals. She was playing "party" again, and delighted to have all the attention from her brother. Ariel chatted incessantly, prattling on about Kay Kay and her birthday party.

"Mmm-hmm," he said to Ariel. He yawned.

The sun was pouring through the window. Will squinted his eyes to shade them from the bright patch of sunlight, as Ariel chattered on. He yawned again. His headache was coming back. The effects of the warm sun and two harrowing nights with broken sleep crept up on Will. He did something he shouldn't have done.

Will fell asleep.

Ariel looked up. Her brother wasn't talking to her anymore. In the silence, she heard three distinct *bong*s from the St. Giles bell tower. Then the hall clock whirred and struck its chimes. One-two-three: three o'clock. Both clocks said three.

She smoothed out the white pinafore she'd put on for the party and tucked a lace collar around the doll's neck. For a moment, she sat still and enjoyed the surge of loving warmth she felt whenever she held Gillian. It was a delightful feeling, like the way your tummy feels when you were surrounded by blankets and cozy fireplaces and hot chocolate. It was almost like being with her Mama. She gave Gillian a tight squeeze. Then she stood up, and gathering Gillian in the crook of her arm, slipped on her outdoor shoes over her bare feet. As she lifted the latch to the Griffinage door, she remembered what Mama always said: tell someone where you're going before you leave the house. Ariel turned and came back.

Will's mouth was open, and his left arm was tossed over his eyes. A red sofa cushion covered part of his face, and his bangs splayed out on the pillow. He didn't move when she spoke.

"I hafta go to the party now, Willy," she said. "Bye."

"Where's Ariel?!"

Will sprang awake the moment Meg came barging in.

"She's here. She's right here!" he protested. Then, with a sickening twist in his chest, he realized she was not. A patch of sunlight illuminated the floorboards where Ariel had been sitting, but Ariel and her doll were gone.

Meg gave him a disgusted look, but didn't waste an instant. She dashed upstairs, calling Ariel's name. Will scrambled off the sofa, flinging the sofa cushion to the floor.

They checked the east room first. Ariel's crayon box stood at the foot of her bed in the alcove. Its lid was closed. Scattered pictures were strewn about the floor, but not her usual pictures of animals. These were pictures of girls and bells and dark holes, made starkly black by pressing hard with the crayon.

"Nothing here," said Meg. She spun around, knocking into Will who was a few paces behind her.

"The attic." They both said it at once. There was something odd about that little room perched so high up in the house. And wasn't there something she'd said about playing birthday party today? That was it! She'd probably brought the tea set up to the attic for her "party."

"I'll go!" said Will, desperately wanting to find Ariel and redeem himself for losing her in the first place. "You check downstairs." They split up. Will dashed upstairs, scrabbling up the little ladder, but one glance told him the attic was empty. He clattered down the steps again, two at a time, and bumped into Meg in the hall. Will stood on the slate paving stones in the entryway for a moment, undecided. Which way would she go? Kitchen? Root cellar? Then he looked down.

"Her shoes are gone!" cried Will.

"Okay, she's outside," said Meg, "Quick! She could be anywhere! Oh, where is Shep?"

❦

The orchard looked the same as when Meg had passed it a few short minutes ago. Limbs dipped and bowed in the breeze. A few plum blossoms fluttered to the ground. But now the sunlight felt harsh, the stark white blossoms mocking, menacing. The blossoms themselves blocked their view. Meg felt a tight knot of fear growing in her stomach. She wanted to call her parents, wanted Shep to appear, wanted someone to step in and take over. Beyond the stone garden wall, a robin chirped and the wind rustled the orchard branches.

"How long were you asleep?"

"I don't know!" said Will miserably. "Only a minute, I think."

"A minute? She can't be far, then."

"It could've been a minute, or could've been longer," said Will. "I have no idea."

Ariel's jump rope lay discarded on a front walk paving slate. Meg forced herself to focus and scanned the garden. The Griffinage grounds sprawled before her, full of corners, hedges, and hiding places. How could she have disappeared so fast? Maybe she was in the enormous block of orchard trees. The apples weren't blooming yet, so it was easy to see through the bare branches, but the plum trees were thick with blossoms. She knew Ariel played there to make it "snow."

"Ariel!" she called. The robin stopped singing, and only the wind blew. Meg dashed around the first hedge and glanced at the back garden. No one there, but it was riven with nooks and foliage where a five-year-old could hide. Maybe the toolshed or the chicken coop, or out in the pastures.

"You don't think she'd go see the lambs, do you?"

"Let's check the orchard first," said Will. "She could be on the swing."

Meg tried to imagine Ariel playing on the swing and waving to them. She'd be pumping her legs and begging for an underdog push. But in her heart, she knew it wasn't the swing that had drawn Ariel out of the house. She was sure of that, and more sure when Will began to hiccup.

They said nothing, but broke into a run, calling Ariel's name. Meg raced down one row of orchard trees and Will the next, agreeing to split up without saying it. The blossoms had an infuriating way of blocking her view and playing tricks on her eyes. Every time she looked up, she thought she caught a glimpse of a girl dressed in a white pinafore. Then the wind blew and the image vanished into snowy blossoms.

She caught up to Will at the end of the orchard row, where he stopped and stood hiccupping.

"Shhh!" said Meg. "What's that?"

"What?"

"I hear something." She held her breath to hear better. Will was trying to do the same, partly to stop his hiccups, but only succeeded in muffling them. They both strained to listen.

"It's singing."

A high-pitched melody was drifting through the air. It sounded like a child's voice, though plaintive and slow, not the sort of tune a young child might sing. Then the tune changed to a song Meg knew, and the voice grew louder. The sound was coming from behind the Griffinage, way back at the end of the garden, from the direction of the old walnut tree.

"Over there!"

Will led the way, and they both pelted toward the Griffinage. When they rounded the corner hedge, they saw her. It was Ariel who was singing. She had her back to them, the pinafore string tied in a lopsided bow around her waist, one loop drooping behind her like a tail. She was walking directly toward the spreading branches of the ancient walnut tree. The storm-damaged area, where the ground was newly churned up and unstable.

Ariel was holding something. The next moment, she stretched out her arms as if to give a present to someone.

Meg gasped and tried to double her speed. Beside her Will's feet pounded. Ariel wasn't alone. Someone else was there. The stone wall and Ariel's pinafore string and the walnut tree all jumbled together as Meg ran, bouncing up and down in a blur. Despite running hard, a chill enveloped her. She was much closer now. Suddenly, Meg could see it clearly. Her eyes bugged wide. It was a figure with a slight blue glow and something odd about the eyes.

Ariel was walking straight toward a ghost.

CHAPTER FOURTEEN

An Unusual Party

Kay Kay was waiting by the trunk of the walnut tree when Ariel arrived for the party. She looked exactly the same: She wore the same midnight blue dress and dirty pinafore she'd worn every day before, one shoe was still missing and her hair was hopelessly mussed.

Ariel frowned. At home, she always dressed up for parties. Mama would clip on her best hair ribbons and let her wear her shiny black buckle shoes. Today, she was wearing her regular red Crocs because Mama hadn't packed her party shoes, but still she'd dressed up. This morning she'd added two bows to her hair and put on the white ruffled pinafore while she was waiting by the clock.

"Don't you want to look pretty for your party?"

Kay Kay tossed her head. Ariel thought for a moment. "Here. Put this on."

She slid one of the bows out of her hair and handed the hair clip to Kay Kay. It was pink and red, one of her nicest, with a stripe of silver running down the center so it sparkled. Silver to match her eyes.

"Ooh!" said Kay Kay, stroking it. "So pretty! Is it from the manor?"

"It's from my suitcase."

Kay Kay clipped it by her left ear and twirled around, trying to catch a glimpse of the bow as she spun. Satisfied, she plopped on the ground next to Ariel.

"Did you bring my present?"

"Yes, but we have to have the party first," said Ariel.

Kay Kay sniffed, then led the way past the walnut tree. She ducked under the tree's damaged branch. Ariel followed. Kay Kay stopped not far away by a rock. She pointed to several round biscuits laid out on the rock's surface. "Real scones," said Kay Kay, with a grand wave of her hand.

Ariel stepped over a mound of dirt and came closer. They were scones all right, but funny-looking ones. She could see currants sticking out of them, untidy jam streaks, and specks of dirt trapped in congealed butter.

"Those are Aunt Effie's!" she cried. "The dirty ones she dropped in the garden."

Kay Kay sniffed again. "Doesn't matter where I got them," she said. "They're still real."

Suddenly, it occurred to Ariel that her new friend

might be poor. Eating thrown-away scones for her birthday, wearing the same dirty dress, and always playing by herself. Her parents must be at work all day, working far away screwing lids on tubes of toothpaste, like Charlie Bucket's family in *Charlie and the Chocolate Factory*. Or maybe they were sick and couldn't get out of bed. Maybe they even forgot Kay Kay's birthday. That was probably it. As the only guest she'd have to be extra nice.

"I love scones and jam," Ariel said. "And look, the dirt comes off."

Ariel made a big show of brushing off the dirt, then wiped the scone on her pinafore and took a bite. The crust was hard and took a lot of gnawing, but the buttery flavor still flooded her mouth and tasted good. She smiled at Kay Kay to show how much she liked the party food, then gagged on the next mouthful when a clod of dirt she hadn't noticed hit her tongue. Her eyes watered, but she swallowed it down, dirt and all.

Kay Kay's scone lay in her lap untouched. Her silver eyes followed Ariel's hand as it traveled to her mouth and also lingered on the doll. Ariel obligingly kept eating. Kay Kay kept watching. After a little while, Kay Kay began to hum. It was a familiar tune, the one Kay Kay always hummed, and by now Ariel knew it well. Just a few notes repeated over and over. She joined in the humming, crumbs of scone stuck to her lower lip.

Kay Kay stood up abruptly and shook her dress. The

uneaten scone fell to her feet. She ran lightly over to the garden wall and sprang up. Her jump looked so graceful. A soft leap, and there she was, perched on top of the stone wall, dangling her legs. Ariel stared at the spot where Kay Kay had jumped. Kay Kay was a funny girl. Now she seemed to be waiting.

Ariel stuffed the rest of her scone in her mouth and looked expectantly at her.

"What next, games?"

"Presents," Kay Kay announced.

"All right."

From her seat on the ground, Ariel started to unfasten the silver knob from the doll. Kay Kay's silver eyes tracked her fingers as they moved. The metal circle slipped off, and Ariel wiped away a splodge of blackcurrant jam from the lion's mane. It would be nice to keep the funny silver circle. It looked good on Gillian. But then she would have no real present. The hair clip didn't count; it was a small, everyday thing. Kay Kay was expecting a special gift. Ariel had nothing else except the doll, and she certainly wasn't going to give Gillian herself away. The very thought made Ariel give the doll a fierce hug. It would have to be the silver lion. She took a breath and launched into the birthday song before she changed her mind.

"What's that song?" asked Kay Kay, still perched on the stone wall.

"'Happy Birthday,' of course," said Ariel. "Don't you know anything?"

She sang a little louder. Kay Kay was smiling as if she'd never heard the song before. Ariel stood up and held the silver circle outstretched. Kay Kay laughed and clapped her hands.

The ground under her feet was bumpy. Sort of like a garden where someone had been digging. Soft and turned up. Ariel stepped over a mound of dirt and a blown-down stick. Kay Kay beckoned to her with great wild arm motions. To her left, Ariel saw what looked like an old footpath, a faint line of trodden earth that still held its shape. Kay Kay flapped her hands in joyful anticipation. Ariel smiled and waved back.

Then she stepped on the old footpath with her red rubbery shoes and walked forward.

"It's the manor ghost!" cried Will. "Ariel's headed right for her!"

Meg stumbled as she ran. In her fear, she'd forgotten to be surprised that she could actually *see* the ghost. She wasn't too old after all. The ghost's body was as clear as Ariel's: arms, legs, hair, and clothes. Why now? Why not before? She'd been jealous of Will, wishing she could see the ghost herself, but now she panicked. Her neck chilled, and she choked on her next breath. A real ghost.

"Can she see it?" she panted.

"She's *singing* to it," said Will.

Will was right. Ariel was singing to the ghost and didn't seem afraid at all. In fact, she was walking right toward it. *Of course*, thought Meg—*she's young; the view's clearer. It probably looks like a real person to her.*

"It's smaller!" gasped Will. "It was bigger last night!"

Meg stared at the ghost figure as she ran. It *was* small, hardly bigger than Ariel. And there was no green velvet; it was dressed in blue. She was closer now, close enough to see a bright ribbon clipped in the ghost's hair, one that looked exactly like her sister's.

"It's a girl," said Meg, with sudden realization. "It's not a woman. It's a little girl!"

"What?"

"Two ghosts! The Griffinage is full of ghosts! Ariel! Arielll!"

Ariel did not turn. Was she bewitched? As Ariel and the ghost drew closer, the ghost radiated a fierce blue-white light. The ghost leapt off the stone wall and advanced to meet Ariel. Will picked up a rock and hurled it. It fell short. The ghost glanced up and glared but did not stop.

Meg had a stitch in her side, sharp, under her ribs. She ignored the pain. They were still five car lengths away. Three. They'd never get there in time. She tried to call Ariel's name again, but her throat was parched from running. She could only croak. Meg willed Ariel to look. *Stop! Oh, please stop and turn around.* But Ariel walked steadily forward, singing. The ghost girl stood with both hands outstretched. Waiting.

Ariel took another step. Her red Croc tipped and dangled for a moment.

Then . . .

They couldn't see her anymore.

Ariel had disappeared.

CHAPTER FIFTEEN

The Walnut

Deep inside, the walnut tree trembled. Another time, long ago, it had reached out and stopped a child. Then its roots were young. Flexible, but not long enough or strong enough to cushion the child's fall. Last night the ground shifted. It could flex its ancient roots in this new space. A crack had opened and the tree remembered.

It stretched its tendrils deep into the earth in all directions. The weight it caught now was heavy, and the tree strained to hold its grip. Soil crumbled away.

The walnut rustled its upper branches, then sighed into the wind as pain stabbed through its trunk and flowed along the newly ripped gash in its side. Down below, its bare roots stiffened, exposed to the chill air after centuries nestled under cover. Deep in the earth the weight slipped. The tree strained forward to cradle the child. Leaning, bracing the child's weight, the tree groaned and shifted to rest its roots on the old stone ledge. More soil crumbled. Not much time now, not much time.

CHAPTER SIXTEEN

The Well

"She's gone!" cried Meg. "She's just *gone!*"

One moment Ariel was walking in front of them. The next second she'd dropped from sight. Vanished. A tuft of grass quivered in the spot.

The ghost girl left the wall. She flew this time, buzzing in a direct line, and hovered over the exact spot where Ariel had been. The ghost girl crouched, hanging in the air, and peered down intently.

Then she clapped her hands and, with a swoop, dove into the earth.

Will choked on a fading hiccup and put out his arm to stop Meg. They'd reached the walnut tree, quite close to the spot where Ariel had disappeared. Meg grabbed his arm and stood panting beside him. "Shh!" said Will.

They both froze and listened. It was a cry. Small

and muffled, as if coming from a great depth.

"A hole!" cried Will.

"That's her! I heard her!" screamed Meg. "Ariel!" She tried to rush forward, but Will grabbed her back. If one sister could disappear, another could too. The land must be highly unstable. They'd have to spread out their weight. Will dropped to his stomach and crawled forward.

"Hold my legs!" he called. He inched forward and was relieved to feel Meg grip his ankles. Just ahead, soil began to drop and disappear. Will slowed. His belly bounced as he hiccupped again, though he could tell his hiccups were subsiding. They were smaller and spaced farther apart. Then his hands touched something. Solid stone. His fingers had found a hard edge. Past the stone border, there was only air. He was at the brink of the hole.

He scrabbled at the rim to pull away grass and brush to define the edge. If he knew where the edge was, he couldn't fall in it. Will waved to Meg and she crept beside him. Together they stared into the pit. Below them yawned a deep, stone-lined shaft that reached into utter darkness. There was no sign of Ariel.

"Ariel! It's Meg! Can you hear us?"

"It's an old well, or something," said Will. Where had it come from? He'd never noticed it before out by the walnut tree.

"She fell down a well?! What if she drowns? Arielll!" Meg yelled.

Her voice echoed. But no other sound came from the pit.

This was the area the storm had churned up. The area Aunt Effie had told them to stay away from. The dirt was soft and raw, pushed up as if a giant mole had burrowed underneath and upset the quiet underground world. The pit was about three feet across, dank and earthy smelling.

Will gripped the stone edge and squinted into the blackness. The darkness seemed complete: stones going down in an endless circle, losing all color, vanishing to black.

"We need a light," said Meg. "Any light."

"Look." Will pointed, his arm trembling.

Down the well shaft, a light was glowing. A shimmery sort of white with tinges of blue that illuminated the walls and slowly cast shadows into the stone crevices.

"That's good," said Meg. "Now we can see."

"No, that's bad," said Will. "Very bad."

The light grew brighter. He knew exactly what it was. The ghost child was down there, and if she was like the manor ghost, getting brighter meant she was touching Ariel.

"There she is!" Will grabbed Meg's arm in excitement.

They could see Ariel. She hadn't fallen far at all. Her body lay partway down, out of reach, but resting on a ledge of some sort. Or partially. Her torso lay on the ledge. Her right arm dangled off it, and worse, her right leg hung precariously, swaying over the pit's emptiness. The ghost girl hovered next to her, her glowing fingers interlaced in Ariel's hair.

Will couldn't see anymore. He blinked. He was crying. *Okay*, he told himself sternly, wiping away tears. *We don't know yet. We don't know if she's alive.* He took a shaky breath.

"How deep do you think it is?" asked Meg. She wasn't crying. Her voice was tight but steady.

At least someone was still thinking straight. Not like him. How could he have stupidly fallen asleep when he was supposed to be watching Ariel? Whatever happened to Ariel, it would always be his fault. He heard Meg's voice again.

"Wells are deep, right?" she said. "Could be a hundred feet. Maybe three hundred."

"Deep," he croaked.

"Too deep."

They both knew what that meant. If Ariel fell off the ledge, she could not survive the next fall. Uncle Pierre in Quebec had fallen off a ladder and died, and that ladder was only sixteen feet high. The thought of his uncle, however, steadied Will and helped push his fear away. Falls were regular things. Not magical. They could get help for a fall.

"We'll call 911!" said Will. "This is definitely an emergency. A real one with a well that grown-ups can understand."

"911. Yes! That's it. Oh! No, we can't," Meg said. "We're not home, remember? 911 won't work. It's a different country! With a different number."

"What number?"

"I don't know," said Meg, miserably. "Ahhh! The ghost's right on her. We have to do something!"

As they watched, the ghost child wrapped her body over Ariel and stroked her arms. Or was she tugging on them? Will looked again. Yes, she was definitely pulling now. It was almost as if the ghost child wanted her to fall, though luckily the ghost's tugs weren't strong. *That's it. She wanted her to fall because she wanted her . . . dead. Dead like her.* The thought shot through Will with a sickening jolt. He scrambled to his feet.

"Where are you going?"

Will didn't answer. He sped to the garden toolshed. He knew there was rope there, and also a ladder. If ladders worked for ice-skating rescues on Minnesotan ponds, they'd work for a well rescue in England.

Will snatched a coil of rope, slung it over his shoulder, and hoped it was long enough. It would have to be. He gritted his teeth and grabbed the ladder. Meg joined him. They ran with the ladder bonking their knees, then laid the ladder across the well's opening like a bridge. It clattered as it hit the stone rim and more dirt fell. The ladder's clatter echoed down the well. Deep inside the shaft, the light flickered. It seemed to be rising. Will's stomach clenched. Did that mean the ghost had won and Ariel was a goner, or . . . His stomach dropped. Or was it coming to get him and Meg?

The ghost was rising toward them. Will veered back as the ghost rose right out of the well. Will threw up his arms to defend himself, and beside him Meg's body trembled. Will braced himself for a repeat of last night and felt a wash of intense cold pass through his veins and arteries.

"Will! Open your eyes."

He cracked his eyes open, not realizing he'd snapped them shut. The ghost had floated past him and Meg and kept going. His heart surged at this piece of luck. Maybe it wasn't trying to attack them. Only Ariel. Not exactly lucky, but it made things easier. Ariel was alone now.

"Ariel!" yelled Meg, sticking her face into the pit.

A faint moan came from the well.

"She's alive!" Now it was Meg close to sobs. "Oh, Will, hurry! The ghost's gone, and Ariel's hurt. We have to get her out."

Will said nothing. The ghost girl hadn't gone. She

was sitting in plain view. He could see her blue-white glow among the tree branches. Meg must not be able to see her anymore. The girl was kicking her shoes together, or rather one shoe and one stockinged foot. He didn't have any hiccups. *Maybe I don't hiccup when the ghost is visible*, thought Will. *She's not dormant, though. Just nervous. Something spooked her. Maybe the ladder noise. Something spooked the spook.*

He swallowed hard and turned back to the well. Meg was busy with the rope, running it around the walnut's trunk and tying a bowline on the ladder rail.

Will stood by helplessly. He was rotten at knots. His knots always came out weak and sloppy and usually slipped. Meg's knots were good, tight ones. She'd learned from their dad, who said everyone ought to be able to tie a bowline behind their back with their eyes closed. Meg took him seriously and practiced. Will still couldn't do it with his eyes open. He waited, trying to be patient. At least he could climb down the well pit. He could do that part. He was good at climbing.

"I'm ready," he said.

"Don't be crazy," retorted Meg. "How do you expect to tie a knot around Ariel when you get down there?" Her voice began to shake. "I've got to be the one."

Will looked at Meg. She hated dark places. She even hated hiding in the hall closet for hide-and-seek. But now her eyes were hard and her chin jutted with fierce determination. He'd been about to ask, "Are you sure?" but the words dried up in his mouth.

Meg stared down the dark pit and shuddered. Without the ghost, the well shaft was pitch dark. Of course, she preferred an impenetrably dark well shaft without a ghost to one with a ghost, but still.

She concentrated on tying the rope. She tried to remember how a harness for the climbing wall worked at the school gym. Under the legs somehow, plus around the waist. She looped and tied the rope around each thigh, then made a waist loop and cinched everything tight. She yanked and tested the knots. They all held. She forced a wan smile in Will's direction.

"Ready?" said Will. "I'll lower you down."

He was standing near the well pit with the rope braced around the walnut tree to take off some of the weight. If their plan worked, he'd be able to inch her down by degrees, keeping tension on the rope and paying it out bit by bit. If he dropped it . . . Meg shook the thought out of her head. If he dropped it, the knot on the ladder would just have to hold.

"Ready," said Meg. She didn't feel ready at all. She felt like climbing into bed and putting her head under ten pillows. She forced herself to sit on the edge of the well shaft. *Steady, Meg*, she told herself. Then she grabbed the ladder with both hands, closed her eyes, and swung out into the darkness.

The knots around Meg's waist and legs squeaked as they tightened under the strain. Will had a firm grip on the rope. She kept one hand on the ladder's rail, groped for the rope with the other hand, then leaned back in a diagonal position until her feet bumped the stones on the shaft's opposite side.

"I can reach the wall," she called up.

"I've got you!" answered Will.

Here goes. Meg sucked in her breath and let go of the ladder's safety. Instantly, she dropped. The rope cut into her skin. Her body jerked, and she fell her own body length. Then she jerked again and fell more. The rope tightened around her stomach, then . . . blessedly held.

She let out her breath. She'd stopped falling. Will must have gained control of the line above. Meg took a tentative breath and looked about.

She was hanging suspended in blackness. Where was the ledge? How far had she dropped? Up above she could see a starkly bright patch of sky at the top of the shaft. She blinked and looked down again. Looking at the sky would not help her eyes adjust to the dark. She couldn't do that again. She needed to focus in the well. Gingerly, Meg reached her hand into the inky darkness. Stone walls, slightly moist. There was nothing above her, so the ledge must still be below.

"Lower me down some more!" Meg called up.

He did. Slowly, this time, to Meg's great relief. He must be getting used to the rope's pull. Her foot touched something solid. She jerked back. She'd have to be careful not to tip Ariel off the ledge. If her foot nudged her the wrong way . . .

"Stop!"

Will stopped the rope. Meg swayed gently. She was level with Ariel, she knew it. The pit felt warmer, more alive, definitely different. It even smelled different. The air was earthworm-y and gave off a strong scent of soil, surprisingly mixed with something that made her think of kitchens, the soft scent of butter and jam. Her fingertips explored the ledge, whatever it was Ariel had landed on. There was stone, almost a stone shelf of sorts. That's what Ariel was lying on. But how had she landed so perfectly? Why hadn't she cracked her head on its harsh stone? Or missed it altogether? Then Meg's hand touched something round, rough, and sinewy. Instinctively, she grasped it with a trembling hand. It held steady. Not only steady, but warm and encouraging, as if she had a friend down here in the pit. Meg heaved a sigh and instantly felt better. She was still in the dark, still suspended above a pit, still with an injured sister and a ghost hovering around, but now she had a firm handhold, not just a rope, and that simple fact made a huge difference.

Meg tightened her grip and wriggled up next to Ariel. As she did so, she knocked against Ariel's foot. For a moment, she felt the familiar rubbery sole of Ariel's Croc. Then it wobbled, dropped, and after a short delay she heard a splash. Ariel's shoe. The other one was already gone. She could feel her bare feet.

Meg moved more carefully now. The ledge wasn't big enough for both of them, but she could stand with her body straddling Ariel's. It was an odd ledge, part flat stone, part twisted and earthy. Wood. What was wood doing down here? Ariel's weight seemed to be resting on a stone outcropping, but on top of the stone she was cradled in a gnarled nest of wood.

"I'm at the ledge!" Meg called up the shaft. "I'm standing on a tree root or something!"

Meg ran her fingers over Ariel's face. Ariel was breathing. Her forehead felt wet, and her eyes were closed. Meg slid her fingers around the side of her sister's head and loud-whispered in her ear once she located it. "Ariel!"

"Oh, it's you Meg," said Ariel, in a drifty, dreamy sort of way. Then she stopped talking and Meg couldn't rouse her.

Meg took a deep breath. She tried not to think about the drop below them, or the splash the shoe made when it fell. They only had one rope. She would have to untie her own rope in order to put it on Ariel.

That was the horrible part. Then she'd have to keep her balance while Will hauled Ariel out. And wait. Alone in the dark well.

It's only for a minute, she told herself. *I'll just be alone for a minute.* If only there had been more than one rope in the toolshed. Meg felt in the darkness for something to brace herself with. A sturdy tree root grew along the shaft wall, and she wrapped one arm around it, entwining the root in an awkward embrace. She could still use both hands this way, with her arm wedged behind the root. She hoped the tree was steady. It must be the old walnut up above. It was certainly big, but had looked tippy after the storm. Maybe under the bark it was rotten. Meg pushed that thought from her mind and picked at the knot keeping her safe until the cord around her own waist loosened. Then she slipped it off and fastened the rope around Ariel.

An ache of deep loneliness suddenly filled Meg's heart. She tugged on the new knots to tighten them. By now she had Ariel tied in three places—waist, legs, and armpits. Ariel was lighter than she was; the knots would surely hold. But as she thought this, the loneliness and despair grew stronger. It invaded the pit, sweeping forward in a great rush. Meg froze and leaned against the stone wall to steady herself.

She wasn't alone. Besides Ariel, there was something else in the pit.

Meg craned her neck to look up and trembled. The top of the well shaft was brightening to blue. The ghost was back. There was nowhere to hide. She shrank against the ledge, precariously balancing and trying to shield Ariel. The light plunged down toward them.

The gold Mini passed Hembridge and Huxham Green, and was heading toward the River Brue on the A37, when Uncle Ben threw back his head and howled. He could sense the girl, her mark still lingering on the car seat. The scent drove him into a panic.

"Now, Ben!" called Aunt Effie from the driver's seat. "Quiet! Nobody's in danger. Just behave yourself back there."

Uncle Ben barked and lunged at the side of the Mini. The car rocked. He whined, then lunged again, sending the Mini skittering in its lane. Aunt Effie yelped and clutched the steering wheel in both hands, then pulled over to the side of the road in exasperation. She flung open the door.

"Ben . . ."

With a blaze of brown fur, Uncle Ben leapt from the back seat and landed with a *thud* on the road's shoulder. Behind him he heard Aunt Effie yelling, calling his name. Uncle Ben barked in reply. Then he left the road and struck out across the pastures, running at full tilt.

Meg cowered on the ledge. The light descended until it shone directly across from her. The glare was blinding after the enveloping darkness.

The ghost was floating next to the ledge. She could see it: mostly blue light, but also the human shape of a girl. It put out its arm and reached for Ariel's hand.

"No!" Meg cried, trying to bat it away.

The ghost paused. Then it shifted.

It dropped Ariel's hand and reached for Meg.

Meg felt a chill spread across her skin. Fingers, flesh-less but firm, gripping her arm. Time suspended when they touched. Meg was swimming in time, swimming in loneliness.

She couldn't see the ghost, the well, or her sister any-more. She could only feel. She was lost in deep, unend-ing waves of despair and isolation. She felt the cool touch on her hand spread to her shoulder. She shivered. She wanted her mother. She wanted someone's arms to wrap around and comfort her.

What happened next, she couldn't explain. She was still in the well, but she wasn't Meg anymore. *The bells were sounding. Above, she could hear more shouts. They were all looking, looking, but never looking for her. The lonely feeling deepened. How much longer? How much lon-ger until they found her? Until they realized their little girl was missing? She called out: "Down here! I'm in here! Look down the well!" Only the bells answered. Time passed. Her voice was raw from shouting. She was thirsty. The bells rang. The pain in her head throbbed. She thought of Cook's Cottage and her bed in the alcove. How good it would feel to be tucked up under the blankets there. The bells sounded again. Something tugged and wanted her to lift away, to glide away and leave the well, but she shrank back. "I don't want to be alone. Please, come. Someone be with me." The bells rang back, chanting, mocking: no one is coming, no one is coming, no one cares . . .*

A tug jerked Meg. It was the rope she'd tied around Ariel, which she was still holding in her hands. Meg heard more shouting, but this time it was Will calling from above. The feeling of loneliness lingered, but it wasn't inside her anymore. Next to her, the ghost girl hung suspended, clear down to the detail of sagging stockings and smudged pinafore.

"You're a lonely little girl," murmured Meg, with sudden understanding. "Just lonely and scared." Her voice came out soft and soothing. The ghost glowed more brightly, making the stone walls radiate blue, and for an instant Meg thought the loneliness in the pit began to ease. The girl stared at Meg and they locked eyes—Meg's green-brown ones and the girl's stark silver ones.

"You don't want her," Meg began. The ghost cocked its head, listening.

"She won't make you happy. She doesn't belong here."

The ghost did not stir. *If I can only keep her attention away from Ariel*, Meg thought.

"I'm sorry you died. I know it's awful in here. . . ."

The ghost's silver eyes flashed. Ariel let out a ragged breath, and the ghost slid to her side. The tenuous connection Meg shared with the little ghost was broken. Now the ghost flashed cobalt blue and touched Ariel's hand. Ariel cried out.

Meg's own fingers flew fast, tugging the knots in one final test. She shouted for Will to pull up.

"I don't care how lonely you are," she said. "You can't take my sister."

⟡

For several eternal minutes, Ariel's body hung between the ledge and the ladder. Then Will gave a final heave and Ariel's body bumped against the well's rim. She was up! Now to get her fully out. He wished he had a second person to help him. It was hard to hold the rope taut and grab Ariel at the same time, but he'd just have to do it. He reached across the ladder, gripped Ariel by the arm, and hauled. She moved, then slipped. Will heaved again, and this time her legs scraped against the stone rim, and she was out. Out of the well. He'd done it.

Despite the ropes and bumpy ride, Ariel was not awake. She was breathing, though, and amazingly, still had the doll clenched in an iron grip under one arm.

How was that possible? He tried to push it out of the way, but it wouldn't budge. It would have to stay. Will set to work untying Meg's knots. At least he was good at untying, and knew how to do it: bend the knot back to loosen it. But untying knots took time. He chafed at how slowly his fingers worked. He wished he could check Ariel for broken bones, but that would have to wait. Meg needed the rope. He needed to take care of the knots first.

The final knot came free. Now for Meg. Will's neck prickled, causing him to look up. He was just in time to see the ghost girl shoot out of the hole. Will froze.

She moved in a jerky fashion, and appeared highly agitated. She didn't rise up to the walnut tree this time. Her unnerving eyes glared at him, shining more brightly than her body, as she advanced to where Will crouched next to Ariel.

It's just a girl, he tried to tell himself. So small, so young, so much like Ariel. Could she really mean to harm them? The silver eyes glinted at him and his hands began to shake. His encounter with the manor ghost flooded back. *Yes, she could.*

From a muffled distance, Will heard Meg shouting for him. He wanted to go to her. He wanted to run. Instead, he stood up, grabbed the rope, and whirled the end like a lasso toward the ghost. It was all he could think of. The ghost ignored the flying rope. She dodged around it, glided forward, and stretched out her hands. Will backed up and tripped on the rest of the rope jumbled in a pile. He hit the ground and covered his head with his hands. *I'm sorry, Meg. I couldn't do it. We're all stuck now. She's coming for me. First me. Then Ariel. Then you.* Will pressed his head to the ground and waited for the inevitable cold touch. But none came. The ghost girl bypassed him and moved directly to Ariel. Then the ghost took Ariel's head in both hands and began to hum.

La de de la da.

F, C-sharp, C, high F, C.

Will sprang up. That was his tune, at least the beginning of it. The ghost was singing the old bell song. The ghost had given him that song. A strange pounding mixed in with the song. The pounding grew louder. It didn't seem to be coming from the ghost, it was coming from the pastures. Will turned. From McBurney's fields, a blur of brown fur streaked toward him. The pounding was a giant dog running at full speed.

Uncle Ben! In a mass of fur, he lunged at the ghost girl. The girl shot off Ariel before he landed, and Uncle Ben, who couldn't stop in time, rammed into Will.

They slammed into the ground, dog and boy. Uncle Ben was barking, covered in burrs, his underbelly slathered in mud. Will didn't care. He flung his arms around the dog's broad neck and cried "Oh, Ben, Ben."

The ghost girl retreated up the walnut tree in a fast float. Will's relief was so great he didn't notice at first what Uncle Ben was doing. Ben had crawled off Will and was nosing Ariel's body.

Ariel's face had turned a ghastly white. Her eyes rolled back, open, and now they stared at nothing. Sweat beaded her forehead. She needed help. Medical help. Grown-up help—at once. He'd never seen a face look like that before. He'd have to go for help. Leave Meg. Hope Uncle Ben could keep the ghosts at bay. Meg would have to hold on.

"Stay!" he ordered Uncle Ben. Will set off at a run.

CHAPTER SEVENTEEN

Officer Targent

Meg stared up at the top of the hole. She called out again.

"Will! Will!!"

She strained to hear his answering shout. Even a cough, or the murmur of Will's voice comforting Ariel, but Will didn't answer. Her own voice echoed eerily about the pit.

Meg squatted on the subterranean tree root. No rope. No cheerful Will voice telling her it would be okay, to just hang on. She'd been so focused on getting Ariel out of the pit and avoiding the ghost that she hadn't noticed the dark so much. Now she was alone. The darkness collected about her, thick and terrifying.

Meg's ankles wobbled as she crouched. She sat down quickly and gripped the tree root with both hands. *Steady, steady.* Far below she heard a soft splash as more dirt fell. If she slipped, she'd plunge into the waiting, menacing inky water.

Meg closed her eyes. It was dark either way, and she preferred blocking out the well. Will wasn't coming. Not *yet*, she corrected herself. If Will couldn't come at all, someone else would find her. They'd have to look down here eventually. When she heard the rescuers, she'd yell and they'd hear her. Of course, that was only sensible. She'd had plenty to eat for lunch. All she had to do was wait. Someone would come.

Meg shifted her position, careful to stay on the ledge. As she did, her hand touched something. Not wood like the rest. The object was hard and curved. She shrank back. *Of course.* Many years ago another girl had waited here. Another girl had called and cried and waited for someone to come.

High above, the church bells began to ring.

The bells tolled four and stopped. In Meg's mind, the bells kept playing, bonging mournfully off the stone walls of the well pit, swirling around her. Alone with the bells. Far overhead, the sun-drenched, living world had disappeared. Meg curled into the smallest bundle she could and pressed her eyes tightly closed, trying to shut out both the bells and the darkness.

A new sound entered the pit. A regular rhythm. Meg sat up. Could it be? Yes, amazingly, it was. A blaring, blasting, honking sound. She clutched the ledge and stared at the circle of light above. Sirens were screeching toward the Griffinage.

The next minute, two heads poked over the well hole and blocked the sky.

"There she is! Hello, Meg!" cried the head that was Will's.

"All right. No worries, we'll get you out," said the new head.

The new head lowered down a rope and a harness—a real nylon harness with a padded waist belt and clips for carabiners—not a toolshed rope. This was like climbing-wall harnesses she knew from school. Meg wrapped her arm around the sturdy tree root again for balance, automatically stepped into the harness, and adjusted the straps. She tugged on the line to indicate she was ready. Then, marvelously, she was rising. Rising up the shaft, secure and snug and safe at last.

At the top, Meg stood blinking in the bright afternoon daylight as her eyes adjusted from the dark pit. She could make out a bright yellow-and-green ambulance parked on Aunt Effie's grass and a police car beside it. Two emergency workers were fussing over something in a stretcher and shifting it on to a wheeled hospital bed. *Ariel*, thought Meg. The body was still and covered with a sheet. She stumbled toward the ambulance, but a strong arm stopped her.

"Whoa, girl." Meg was face-to-face with her rescuer, a man dressed in dark green with embroidered medical patches on his uniform. He gripped her shoulders with both hands.

"Easy there, slow down, I've got you," said the medic. "Your sister will be all right. Looks as if she has a broken ankle and certainly a bit of a shock. They'll get her sorted out at the hospital."

"She's alive," stammered Meg.

"Yes, she's very much alive."

Meg relaxed in his grip, and the medic eased her down to sit next to a tangle of rope that lay pitched on the grass. She was glad to sit. Her stomach felt queasy. Meg noticed Uncle Ben was there too. If Uncle Ben was home, maybe that meant Aunt Effie was home, but no, that didn't make sense. If Aunt Effie were here, she'd be darting all over, talking about Roman well construction and fussing over everyone. There was no one darting around except Will, who was dancing from foot to foot trying to talk to Meg.

"Let me get this straight, young lady," said the man. "You didn't fall?"

"No, I went down on a rope."

"This rope." He held up the toolshed rope. It was grey and thin and noticeably frayed.

Meg blinked. She hadn't noticed the rope's condition when they'd grabbed it from the toolshed. Some strands were newly frayed, maybe from rubbing against the walnut bark.

"Right. You're a brave girl, but mostly a very lucky one. Abandoned wells are nothing to play around with. Ever. They're death traps." He paused and stared at Meg and Will hard, then gently began examining Meg's hands, legs, and torso. "Seems you've got by with nothing but some slight rope burns. Those will heal up. Lucky, as I said." He stood up and called to his colleague. "Right, Jack! This one's checking out fine." He gave Meg a quick playful salute, then turned to join the other rescue workers.

Will took his place the moment the medic turned away. He poked her in the ribs.

"Ouch—don't. Where is she?"

"Over there. In the ambulance already."

"No, the girl."

"Up the walnut tree. I think. Or maybe gone dormant. I can't see her," said Will. "Uncle Ben scared her off and now I'm sure the sirens really freaked her. Maybe she's hiding. I don't sense any sign of her."

"You sure freaked me out too." Meg's lip trembled. She felt more like crying now that she was safely out of the well. She couldn't throw off the ache of darkness and despair when no one answered her calls. Down among the moist stones, lost in the dank pit with nothing but the bells ringing. In those few minutes, she'd glimpsed the ghost girl's everlasting loneliness.

She tried to shake off the feeling. She turned, and her eyes landed on the ambulance sitting there on the Griffinage grass, squat and blaze yellow, with checkered green squares painted on the side.

"The ambulance," Meg said. "How did it get here?"

Will smiled his great goofy, Griffin grin. "I phoned. Just dialed 911 and it automatically rerouted the call to the right emergency number. It's 999, by the way."

As they watched, the ambulance back doors slammed shut, showing neon orange stripes. Meg startled into action.

"They're leaving!" she yelled, and scrambled up, dashing toward the vehicle. Her rescuer was in the driver's seat, but Meg ran up beside him. She grabbed his sleeve through the window.

"Wait! Where are you going?" she cried.

"South Mendip Community Hospital," said the man. "Don't worry, the constable will take care of you." He pointed to the police car, where a tall, overly freckled policeman stood. Then the siren pierced the air and the yellow ambulance drove off.

"Whew. I'm sure glad Ariel's getting far away from the well," said Will, as they walked over to the police officer. "I think that's where the ghost is strongest. It's like her power center or something. I've never seen a ghost so bright."

"And how many ghosts have you seen?" countered Meg.

"Two."

After the storm, the manor ghost had holed up in her tower. The tower had been her home for so long. It usually brought comfort, but now she was restless. The pull was too strong. She'd have to return to the peasant cottage. She glided out the West Tower window, slid down the tower's curved stone, then sidled through the trees near Mendip Brook, finally drifting over the fields toward Cook's Cottage. She could already see its thatched roof.

Then she stopped midfloat. Something was different. It wasn't there. The powerful tug came from another location now, farther away, and moving fast. She changed direction and sped up.

"Can you take us to the hospital? We've got to stay right with our sister when she wakes up!"

The police officer bent down and smiled, spreading out his freckles.

"You're the boy who called. Will Griffin, am I right? I'm PC Targent. And you must be another Griffin," he said, turning to Meg. "I can always spot a Griffin. Look just like your aunt." Meg didn't flinch at the reference to her hair.

"I'm Meg," she said simply.

"Will you take us?" persisted Will. "It's very important."

"Jump in the back. I've already called your aunt. Might as well have you all together in one spot when she comes to get you."

"Thanks!" said Will. He immediately crawled in the back seat. The police car looked different than the ones at home. This one was white with giant yellow and blue squares decorating the sides like a checkerboard. Up top, the lights were bright blue, not red.

Meg didn't follow. "Will!" she whispered. "We've got to bring Uncle Ben! We don't know what might happen."

Will swallowed hard. The excitement of riding in a real police car had temporarily made him forget about the ghosts. Of course, Meg was right. Even in the hospital, Ariel could still be in danger.

"Oh no, you don't," said Officer Targent, seeing them bring Ben over. "No room for muddy dogs."

Meg burst into tears. "He's just *got* to come, Officer! Oh, you've just *got* to let Uncle Ben come," she sobbed.

It was false crying, Will could tell at once. A real blubbering, whining show. But Officer Targent didn't seem to notice. He blinked his eyes and shuffled his feet. He probably didn't have kids, Will decided.

Meg kept blubbing: "I've never been so scared in

my life, and he's part of the family—oh, *please!*"

The policeman's face softened. Meg shot Will a conspiratorial look through her tears. Will hissed, "Come on, boy," under his breath, and Uncle Ben leapt into the cruiser.

"Oi! Got me clean seats all muddy. And the windows!" Officer Targent protested. He flicked ineffectively at the mud prints with a paper napkin. Uncle Ben wagged his tail and spattered more mud as he turned around, then dropped a long strand of dog slobber that fell on the policeman's neck. Officer Targent crumpled up the napkin, mopped his neck, and stared at his unwanted back seat passenger.

"You've made your mess now," he said. "Might as well stay for the ride." He paused and his face crinkled into a smile. "To tell the truth, I always liked dogs. Would love to be a handler on the dog unit," said Officer Targent, swinging his shoulders back to the steering wheel. "We'll put the siren on, shall we?"

Will grinned in delight. Wait until he told his friends back home about riding in a cop car. With the sirens on.

"Not far to South Mendip," the officer said, raising his voice as the sirens kicked on. "Just the other side of McBurney's west pastures. By road it's twenty minutes, but it's a straight shot through the pastures; you could walk in half the time." He stepped on the gas. "Off we go! Make way for the Griffinage dog."

Will felt a flush of excitement as the siren blared. It wasn't as loud as he'd expected from inside, but much more exhilarating. Again, he momentarily forgot about the ghosts as Officer Targent swung the patrol car up the Griffinage driveway, honking the horn for good measure. They were turning onto Queensway Road when Meg tugged Will's arm and leaned over to cup her hands over his ear.

"I saw bones down there, Will. I'm sure I did. I felt them on that ledge. A skeleton. I'm sure it was a real human skeleton."

CHAPTER EIGHTEEN

South Mendip Hospital

When the squad car turned into South Mendip Community Hospital's drive, the ambulance was just pulling away, slowly, with its lights off. Officer Targent clicked off his siren.

"They've taken her in already. I'll help you find the room," he said as the children tumbled out of the back seat with Uncle Ben. "Oh no, you don't. You stay outside," he added, addressing Uncle Ben. Uncle Ben promptly sat on Officer Targent's foot and looked accusingly at the police officer.

Officer Targent folded his arms and jerked his head at the glass entrance doors. There was a NO SMOKING sign next to a prominent NO DOGS sign. Will groaned.

"Can't you say he's your police dog?" asked Will.

Officer Targent shook his head.

"German shepherd, Belgian Malinois, Dutch herder, maybe a Doberman or springer spaniel . . ." Officer Targent ticked the names off with his fingers. "Those are police dogs. I've never heard of one of these fuzzy-headed, giant-pawed dogs being on a police dog unit. Especially not a muddy one with a tongue like that."

Meg looked at Uncle Ben. His tongue was as long as her forearm. Right now it was sticking out and dribbling dog drool on Officer Targent's pant leg.

"How about over there?" said Meg, as Officer Targent tried to extract his foot from under Uncle Ben's bulk. She pointed to a patch of grass and bushes marked MEMORIAL GARDEN to the side of the hospital doors. There was a row of azaleas and a motorcycle parked nearby.

"Nice and shady," she added.

"Right. Fine," said Officer Targent, still wiggling his trapped foot. "Put the dog in the shade." He gave a sigh as Uncle Ben lifted his rump and followed Meg and Will to the memorial garden.

"Do you think he'll stay?" asked Will. They didn't have a leash to tie him with.

"He'll stay," said Meg. "He knows we're going in there. Didn't he run all the way from Yeovil to get here? He wants to be with us."

"With Ariel," Will corrected.

Meg cupped Uncle Ben's ears in her hands and

peered into the dog's great brown eyes. "Ariel's inside, Uncle," she said. "We need you here. We'll get you inside somehow, I promise. Now: Stay. Good boy."

Ariel was lying on a white-sheeted hospital bed upstairs in the children's ward, still holding the doll, when Meg and Will came in. It was a private room, marked ROOM 3. A nurse dressed in a teal tunic stood by, checking her chart and adjusting a bag of clear liquid, which hung on a hook beside the bed. Beside them, a young doctor wearing blue scrubs and a stethoscope was leaning over Ariel and massaging her left ankle. She looked up when she saw Will and Meg.

"Your sister's going to be fine," she said. "She sustained a sprained ankle in the fall, but nothing to worry about. No broken bones. The ankle will be sore for a while, so she needs to rest. Because of the fall, we'll probably keep her overnight just to watch her."

The doctor finished her examination, patted Ariel's leg, and after a brief chat with the nurse went out.

"If it's just her leg, why is she sleeping?" asked Meg.

"Had a bit of a fright, didn't she?" said the nurse. "Falling down an old well. You kids should know better than to play around one of those. Loads of them around the hills, here, but they should all be capped. Anyway, it's quite normal for someone to pass out like this after a nasty accident, especially a little maid like your sister. Poor thing," continued the nurse. "White as the sheets when they first brought her in. Looked as if she'd seen a ghost!"

Meg gasped and tried to pretend she had coughed. Will began coughing too.

"Cover your mouth," admonished the nurse. "We keep things sterile around here, if you please."

"Oh yes, we will," said Meg, dutifully coughing into her elbow. She smiled at the nurse.

"Mmm," said the nurse. "She's resting now, just leave her in peace. Vitals all good—she's stable. No worries about shock. I'll be back in a mo' to check on her."

The minute the nurse was gone, Meg and Will rushed up to the bed. Ariel's hair was plastered to the hospital pillow, her face warm and the right color again, her breathing soft and mellow. At first, Meg worried it was too soft. She leaned forward and put her cheek against Ariel's mouth and was rewarded with a steady whisper of air.

"She's breathing," said Meg.

"Of course she's breathing!" said Will. "'Vitals all good,' remember? You think the nurse would have left her if she weren't breathing?" The hospital atmosphere was reassuring. All these uniformed professionals going their rounds in red, navy, and teal tunics. Everything was bright lights and modern technology. Nothing at all like the Griffinage, or the manor's ancient towers.

He looked around Ariel's room: all gleaming, computerized, and twenty-first century. Not a likely habitat for a ghost. For the first time that day, Will relaxed.

"Where do you think the nurse went?" asked Meg.

"Probably for her afternoon tea. It's that time of day." He paused and looked embarrassed.

"Oh, Will, not now!" groaned Meg.

"It's not me; it's my stomach," said Will. "I can't help it if ghosts make me hungry. All that hiccupping, and I haven't eaten since lunch." He paused again. "I'll just check on Uncle Ben, okay? And if there's a vending machine nearby, I'll bring you something."

"Oh, all right," said Meg, turning her back on him. She took up vigil next to Ariel.

Will stepped out into the linoleum hallway. The hall was lined with private patient rooms like Ariel's, plus some bigger ones with multiple beds and curtains separating them. A row of windows stretched along one side, and Will noticed the windows looked out on the memorial garden. He thought he heard the hum of a vending machine around the corner, but first ran over to the windows and peered down. There was the great brown furry body of Uncle Ben next to the azaleas. He was sniffing the tires on someone's motorcycle.

"Hello, William."

Will spun around. There stood Father Casey,

dressed as before in his blue jeans and sneakers, but this time he also wore a formal black shirt and white clerical collar on top of his jeans. It was strange to see the curate outside St. Giles church. *Of course*, thought Will, *ministers always visit people in hospitals. It's one of their jobs.*

To Will's astonishment, Father Casey did not seem at all surprised to see him there.

"Visiting, are we?" asked Father Casey.

"Yes," said Will. How did he know about Ariel already?

"Very kind of you. Know which room?"

"Um . . ." Will nodded vaguely toward Ariel's door.

"No, it's around the corner. Cadbury Ward, bed two. I'm sure he'll be glad to see you. Now I'll say good-bye. I've got two more visits myself." Father Casey moved on with a cheery wave.

"Who will?" called Will.

"Down the hall. Around the corner!" called Father Casey. He waved again, but Will did not see. He was already running down the hospital hallway.

Will skidded to a stop outside Cadbury Ward, a room with several beds and curtain dividers. Bed two was right by the door. The patient had one leg strung up in a purple cast, and lay awkwardly in a green-and pink-dotted hospital gown. His sturdy arms sprouted red hair that looked out of place on the starched white sheets. The man looked up and whistled.

"Well, here's a turn of things," he said, struggling to prop himself up by the elbow. "Here I am supposed to be looking after you, and now you come along to look after me."

"Shep!" cried Will.

It was Shep all right. From his curly red hair to his bearlike frame. Will couldn't help sighing with relief. It was good to see Shep at last, even if he was wearing pink and green polka dots with his leg strung up in the air. "What happened? We've been looking for you everywhere!"

"Well, you should have looked under the woodpile at the timber yard," said Shep, shaking his head ruefully. "Had a bit of an accident there. My leg, timbers, and a forklift. Not a pretty combination. Bashed in my leg and they sent me here. Not by forklift, thank goodness. Would have been a bumpy ride." He rubbed his eyes and looked puzzled.

"Now wait a minute, I'm not thinking straight. Must be this blasted painkiller they have me on. What are you doing here? Where are the others? And what'll I tell *Effie?*" He plopped his head back on the hospital pillow and groaned.

"We came with the cops," Will blurted out. "I saw Father Casey in the hall. The ghost got Ariel in the well, and Meg was down there, too. And you're wrong about ghosts. They're horrible." The excitement of finding Shep faltered. Will's mind raced, all the events of the afternoon jumbling up, plus all the pent-up questions.

"Whoa, slow down. Why are you kids at the hospital? Is someone hurt?"

"Ariel. It's her leg."

"Ariel?" said Shep. He struggled to prop himself back up on his elbows and stared hard at Will.

"We've been trying to find you all day. There's two ghosts. And we need to sleep at your place. We have to." He spilled the rest of the story out—his night attack, the fast exit through the roof, Ariel missing, and all the adventures at the well.

Shep was quiet for a moment. He looked pale, and there were no cheerful winks. He stared directly at Will. "The ghosts I saw as a kid never did this, Will, I swear it. That ghost girl is Katherine Croft, a girl who used to live in the Griffinage long ago back when it was Cook's Cottage. She hasn't been active in years, so I'm mighty surprised you'd see her. Fact is, she's a distant relative of mine, cousin of some sort. I played with her as a child—conkers, hide-and-seek, no harm done. But always only playful. Never anything else. Something unusual has stirred them up. We've got to quiet them down again."

"Do you think she's safe here in the hospital? Ariel, I mean?"

"Yesterday, I would have said she'd be safe sitting in a ghost's lap. But something's changed. I can't say what. But I do know this: The doctors can't help. They're focused on bodies in *this* world. Not the souls that slip out. Doctors don't know anything about ghosts."

Will's stomach clenched. The easy feeling he'd enjoyed being in the modern hospital evaporated.

"I won't leave you alone on this," Shep went on. "I'll just have to get myself out of this place somehow or other." He kicked at the hospital sheets, then winced as the movement jostled his injured leg.

Will winced too. Meg would be furious with him for being gone so long. What if something was happening right now to Ariel? He leapt to his feet.

"I've got to get back to them," said Will.

"Go!" said Shep. Will tore off down the hall.

Around the corner, there was a cluster of teal-jacketed nurses. Will sped up. It wasn't Ariel's room, or was it? He'd only left a few minutes ago, and everything had been fine. Will reached the knot of people and heard Meg's voice through the crowd. It sounded strained and strange. *She's frightened*, he thought. *Something's happening.*

"Blood pressure's dropping!" a nurse called out.

"What's her pulse?"

"Sixty, forty, thirty . . . I'm losing it."

Will pushed his way through the legs blocking the doorway and squeezed into the room. Ariel was lying on the hospital bed as before. Meg was at her side, squeezing her hand and calling out her name. A nurse with a dark bun stood by with a blood pressure monitor wrapped firmly around Ariel's arm. On the other side, a stocky male nurse with black-rimmed glasses kept glancing at the monitor in dismay. Two other staff encircled the patient.

Ariel groaned and tossed to one side. Just then, a nurse shifted to the right so Will could finally see.

Straddled across Ariel's chest sat the manor ghost.

Her legs bent and tucked back in a kneeling position, her hands cradling Ariel's cheeks, the ghost was sitting astride the little girl. Green velvet spilled over them both. The sight of green velvet made Will's stomach twist, bringing back all his terror from last night. Long black hair tumbled over Ariel's small frame. The curtain of hair mostly blocked the ghost's face, but it looked as if she were whispering.

Meg sat inches away from the ghost. Her shoulder almost touched the manor ghost's knee. Will sucked in a breath between hiccups, only to realize he'd been hiccupping in a low, steady stream and the air smelled of burned matches. How could no one see? Meg and the nurses were so *close*.

"She's here!" he called to Meg.

The nurses ignored them, immersed in their discussion of blood pressure and hypotension.

"What? Which one? How do you know?" Meg sat bolt upright. She swiveled her head from side to side as if looking for something and then stared desperately at Will.

"The manor ghost. Inches from your nose! She's sitting on Ariel!"

Meg drew back instinctively.

"What's she doing?" she asked.

The manor ghost was crooning over Ariel now, stroking her hair. With each stroke of her fingers, the color in Ariel's face faded a bit more. And, as Ariel's skin paled, the ghost's aura brightened. Will threw his arm across his face to hide the glare. His hiccups were gone now. Meg suddenly gasped and said "Oh my gosh, she's right here! I can see her now."

The nurse who was monitoring heartbeat, breathing, and other vitals suddenly moved fast. "Pulse is dropping . . . breathing shallow." She pushed a bright red button located next to Ariel's bed. A moment later, a new doctor and another nurse burst in.

"Dr. Fenster!" cried the nurse. "Five-year-old female, brought in for a fall, sprained ankle left side, but nothing else. Stable since she arrived at four twenty-seven. Now everything's dropping."

"Oxygen!" said the doctor. "And IV. Why isn't she

on an IV? Hook it up! It's not there for decoration."

Meanwhile, the manor ghost was inching closer to Ariel's face until she was sitting high on her chest. Her hands still stroked Ariel's cheeks, but her eyes also lingered on what Ariel held in the crook of her arm. She completely ignored Meg and Will.

"It's shock," said the doctor.

"It's the doll!" Meg cried.

"She wants the doll?" asked Will.

"No, she wants a child, but I'll bet the doll's the object that brought her here!"

"You're right," exclaimed Will. "The doll came in the chest, and she's totally focused on it. She won't even look at us with Ariel holding it. Can we get it off?"

Without waiting for an answer, Will grabbed for the doll, but his arm knocked sideways as one of the nurses shifted left and cut him off. Will squirmed to the side and tried to push at the ghost instead, but the manor ghost didn't move, and all Will felt was a blast of intense cold.

The doctor was monitoring the readout screen with her back to the kids. "Strange," she said. "You said she took a fall? All vitals down. Her heart rate seems like cardiogenic shock. I'll check again for head trauma. Give her a dose of dopamine." She turned and noticed the kids standing nearby.

"What are they doing in here?" she asked, flipping her thumb in their direction.

The next instant, rough hands landed on Meg and Will's shoulders, and they were propelled out the door by a big-bosomed nurse.

"The doctor will call you," she said. "The café's downstairs." And with that the door slammed, shutting in Ariel and the doll with one doctor, five nurses, and the manor ghost.

CHAPTER NINETEEN

Escape

Outside in the hospital's linoleum hallway, Meg and Will stared at the plain grey door marked ROOM 3.

"Shock!" said Meg. "They'll never save her. They don't know what's wrong, and they'll never believe us!"

"I know, but the doctors might delay the ghost a bit. Give us some time. All that oxygen and stuff," said Will.

Meg's face crumpled. She suddenly looked lost.

"I saw her that time, Will. I actually saw her. She's hideous. So much worse than the girl ghost. What are we going to do?"

"Listen." Will spoke sharply. "She's latched onto Ariel. The doll brought her here, but we know it's not really the doll she wants. Number one, we've got to shake the ghost off Ariel. Number two, we've got to connect the two ghosts. That's our solution. That's the only way they'll leave us alone: if they fix each other's longings."

"But both ghosts want Ariel!" wailed Meg.

"We've got to make a substitute," said Will with a determined look on his face. "We've got to change their minds. It's the only way."

Meg stared at Will stunned. She wiped her nose and smeared it on her pant leg, something she'd never do at home. Maybe her harrowing experience in the well was catching up with her. She slumped against the wall.

"So what can we *do*?"

Will wished he were anywhere but here. The fact was, he didn't know. How does a ghost change its mind? It was all a horrible nightmare. Worse than the manor ghost cornering him in the bedroom, worse than the girl ghost hovering by the well. Because now a ghost was cornering Ariel in the middle of the day in a perfectly respectable, modern British hospital and he couldn't do anything about it. They desperately needed a plan, but Meg usually helped him think up plans. Now here she was leaning against the wall, looking at him and expecting him to save them.

"Okay, plan A," said Will. He took a deep breath and watched as Meg lifted her head expectantly. He didn't know what he was going to say next, but the hope in Meg's eyes made him plunge on.

"Plan A is we go in and get the doll," Will said. "One of us sneaks into the room, grabs the doll, and the manor ghost comes with it. She's used to following the doll, so she leaves Ariel."

"Oh," said Meg. She wiped her eyes again but stopped crying. "Then we've got the ghost. What do we do with her?"

"Then we run. We run the doll back to the Griffinage, and, er . . ." His voice trailed off.

Meg looked at her brother. "We go back to the well."

"Yes!" said Will, just realizing it himself. He'd been hugely relieved to get away from the well, so it didn't occur to him at first. It had been so easy in the cop car, cruising away from all their troubles. Now they'd have to return, on purpose.

❦

Enacting plan A set them back five minutes. Meg slipped into the room with no problem. She was relieved to see Ariel looking somewhat better. Maybe the oxygen was working. At least there were fewer medical people in the room, which was helpful, and although the computer monitors were still blinking wildly, they weren't buzzing alarms. Ariel tossed on the bed, her cheeks rosy, and murmured, "Noodles likes marshmallow toast."

The big-bosomed nurse was busy on the far side by the window. She looked up and glared at Meg, but didn't say anything since two doctors were talking together in urgent tones. Meg smiled and tried to look her most innocent. She inched her way along the wall. Another nurse and the two doctors stood clumped together by the bed.

Meg darted forward and gave the doll's legs a tremendous tug.

To her surprise, nothing happened. Ariel held the doll with only one arm, but it barely moved when Meg pulled. It was as if an invisible lock had clamped down, binding the doll to Ariel.

It was horrible, too, because Meg could no longer see the ghost clearly. She thought she could see a fuzzy outline, but when she looked again there was nothing but empty space. Why couldn't she see her anymore? Was this what happened when you were eleven— almost twelve? Like radio on a bad reception. Intermittent. In and out. It just made everything harder, and scarier. *She's there all right*, Meg told herself, shuddering. *She's there just as much as ever.*

Meg tried again, bracing her legs this time against the hospital bed and yanking with all her might. Something did happen then. One of the doctors noticed her and spun around, knocking into the nurse with the dark bun, who crashed into the IV stand. Meg fell to the floor as the IV stand toppled on her. The second nurse leapt to right it. The doll stayed firmly clenched in Ariel's arms.

"What are you doing here?" demanded the doctor. "I told you to stay out!"

"I just need the doll," Meg pleaded from the floor.

"Out!" ordered the doctor.

"But . . ."

"OUT!"

The smaller nurse waved the others away and knelt down by Meg.

"That doll won't budge, sweetie," she said as she put her arm around Meg and helped her to her feet. "I tried when they brought your sister in. Best to let her keep it now." Then she marched Meg out the door.

Will didn't say anything when Meg appeared empty-handed in the hallway. It was obvious plan A had failed.

"The ghost has latched onto the doll somehow," said Meg, beginning to cry again. "It's stuck on Ariel. I can't get it loose."

"On to plan B," said Will.

"What's plan B?" asked Meg, wiping her nose.

"If we can't pry the doll off, we'll have to take Ariel, too."

Will had been thinking about that while Meg was in the room. When the crash came, he figured they would need more desperate measures.

"Are you crazy?" said Meg. "They'll never let us check her out! Her pulse was going nuts; there's still lots of doctors in there. They won't even let *us* go in, especially now. How are they going to agree to let her go home? They'll probably keep her for days doing stupid, useless tests. No one will ever believe us about the ghost, and she'll keep getting weaker. . . ." She paused. "That is, if she . . . Oh, Will!"

They both looked at each other, thinking the same thoughts. The fact was, Ariel didn't have days. She might have an hour or so at most, if the oxygen and dopamine and everything else kept her alive past the next few minutes.

"We won't ask, of course," said Will. "Just do an emergency checkout. But we'll need help and a big distraction."

"Uncle Ben!" said Meg. "He's big. In a place that won't let you cough or sneeze, he'll be a distraction all right."

Will fingered something in his pocket, and a plan began to form in his mind. Half a plan, but at least a way to get Ariel out of the hospital.

"Right," he said. "And we better get Shep's help too."

"Shep! But he's been missing all day. He's . . ."

"He's in the ward down the hall."

The door to Ariel's room opened, and a nurse stepped out. She walked casually, humming to herself.

"She wouldn't do that unless Ariel's stable again,"

whispered Meg. "That dopamine stuff must be working."

"Maybe," said Will.

"Look! It must be," said Meg, pointing, as the door opened again and a doctor walked out. "That's two gone. There's hardly anybody left in her room. Now's our chance."

Will nodded. The next instant, Meg and Will split up, one disappearing to the patient beds in Cadbury Ward, the other downstairs to the garden.

A terrific ruckus erupted on the patient wing of the hospital's second floor. Something brown, furry, and definitely oversized streaked down the hall, skidded on the linoleum, and slammed into a potted fig plant.

"A bear!" cried a nurse who was walking by. "A bear in the hospital! Help!"

"What?" called the matron, poking her head out of a patient's room.

"A bear! We're being attacked by bears!" screamed the nurse again. "Live ones! Big, hairy ones! Help!"

Feet came running from all directions. The nurse kept screaming, "Bear!" while the "bear" growled in all the confusion and barreled toward the nurse, who jumped behind a magazine rack.

No one could blame her for mistaking Uncle Ben for a bear. Newfoundlands aren't an everyday occurrence, especially high-speed ones. This particular nurse was fond of picking up the *Weekly Rag* at the grocery checkout. Just last week, they'd run a story about exotic pets. More and more British home owners were keeping wild animals as pets, animals like crocodiles, lions, and tigers. Imagine! Dangerous ones like that! A tiger named Teddy had even escaped from a house in Devon. If tigers could roam about Devon, bears might run wild in Somerset.

Uncle Ben swerved and bounded in the other direction. The excitable nurse yelped. She tipped over the rack, and magazines scattered and slid across the floor.

"What's all this?" cried a doctor, running up. The next moment he slipped on a glossy magazine called *Racing Ahead*, which slithered over *Wellness Today*, and he landed flat on his back.

"Oof!" he yelled. "What was that?"

"Bears!" yelled the nurse again, then added for good measure: "Tigers!" She scrambled to a new hiding spot behind a row of artificial potted plants.

The "bear," or perhaps, "Uncle Bear," was snuffing its great nose. All of a sudden, he leapt toward a gurney being wheeled down the hall by a porter, landing on top of the mattress. The porter yelled and let go, sending the hospital bed spinning and skidding down the hall straight toward the first nurse and her potted plants. She screamed and ducked.

The gurney hit the wall and bounced away again.

The bear was still balanced on the gurney, dropping globs of slobber on the neat, clean sheets.

"Hide your sandwiches!" the nurse cried. "Don't let it smell food. It might eat you!"

"Sandwiches?" came a doctor's voice. "Bears don't eat sandwiches. Whatever are you talking about, Fiona?"

"Hide your honey, then!" she cried and ducked again.

The speeding gurney spun in circles, knocking into chairs, fallen doctors, and spilled magazines, then hurtled to the opposite wall. It hit with a crash, narrowly missing the fish tank, then ricocheted toward the patient rooms.

At that moment, Dr. Fenster emerged from Room 3. She opened the door, took two steps, and—*slam!*—collided with the bear and gurney.

Uncle Ben had had enough. He jumped off the rolling bed, right onto Dr. Fenster, who tried to sit up, but collapsed again under 150 pounds of shaggy fur.

"The bear!" cried the porter, pointing at the mass of brown fur.

"The doctor!" cried a nurse.

"Wild animals!" called Fiona. "Exotic pets! Escaped from Devon!"

"Help! Police! Call the fire brigade!" yelled Dr. Fenster, her voice muffled underneath so much fur. Fiona, the first nurse, had sharp ears and ran to obey.

"Evacuate!" she cried, and pulled the fire alarm.

immediately. Quick! Emergency! Don't you hear all that noise?"

The door swung open again, ejecting the big-bosomed nurse. She stood out in the hall for a moment, then muttered, "Wait, we don't *have* a Dr. Gurney," and put her hand on the door knob to reenter Ariel's room. Just then, Uncle Ben came charging toward her, running away from the hospital bed himself as the wild gurney spun out of control. The nurse shrieked and leapt to the side. The empty gurney careened by and crashed into the wall beside Will. No one noticed Meg in all the confusion. She quietly slipped into Room 3. Will sent the gurney spinning back toward the pile of doctors. He would have loved to stay and watch the action, but instead Will dashed after Meg, spreading his last bits of Bowzer's Bones as he ran.

"We're in!" cried Will.

The heavy-footed nurse groaned and collapsed into the wheelchair as Will closed the door.

"About near killed my foot," Shep said. He threw off the nurse's uniform. "Quick, get her on."

Will and Meg heaved Ariel off the hospital bed, pulled away her oxygen mask, and placed her in the wheelchair on Shep's lap. The manor ghost remained tightly attached to Ariel. At least the ghost was following the plan so far.

"She's on," said Will, interpreting for the others, who

CHAPTER TWENTY

Across the Pastures

During this chaos, a new nurse approached Room 3 pushing an empty wheelchair. Will watched from behind a fake jade plant. This nurse was a big fellow, and he seemed to have steel-soled shoes, for every other step produced a huge *crash*.

Ariel's door opened. There was only one nurse in there now. Will heaved a sigh of relief. The rest were, well, distracted. He grinned and tossed a few more Bowzer's Bones to the far side of the hall. That would shift the action away from Ariel for a while.

"I'll take over," said the new nurse, marching into Room 3 with authority. He pushed the empty wheelchair into a corner and picked up the medical charts.

The big-bosomed nurse looked up. "But I just got here," she protested.

"Dr. Gurney's orders. You're needed outside

couldn't see the ghost. Shep nodded. Will half wished *he* couldn't see the ghost either. The sight of green velvet still turned his stomach.

They reached for the door, but the IV tube stretched like a leash. Meg ran back to the IV stand, which tipped, threatening to make another awful *crash*. She bent over Ariel's arm, fumbling with the tubes.

"Can't you hurry?" begged Will close to her ear. "They're going to see us! Someone'll be back in the room any second!"

"I know!" said Meg. The IV tube led to a small plastic port taped to Ariel's arm. The port could stay. Meg managed to disengage the tube from the port and left it dangling. Will swallowed. Now Ariel was free to move, but she was also without oxygen and whatever other life-sustaining treatments the doctors were trying to put into her. Time was even more precious.

Shep draped a hospital blanket over Ariel's small form on his lap. Now to get past the doctors. With any luck, they'd slip down the hospital hallway with Shep the Nurse now posing as a patient. As for the blanket blob on his stomach? Well, that was just a big blanket.

Meg and Will each took a wheelchair handle and shoved from behind.

"Ufh," said Shep, though gritted teeth. He raised his bad foot higher, clunking the purple cast against the wheelchair. "Turn right. Take the back way, to the lifts."

Meg and Will maneuvered the wheelchair out into the hall. They were totally exposed now, in full view of two doctors and five or so nurses. Two had their backs to them and were looking away. The others were looking at . . . Uncle Ben.

Ben the "bear" was sitting in a pile of Bowzer's Bones, crunching and smacking his lips. Will saw dog drool sticking to his muzzle and a small puddle of slobber pooling by his paws. Good old Uncle Ben. Ben looked up. He saw them. His ears pricked up in a friendly way, then he growled, dropped a half-chewed Bone, and lunged in their direction.

Will dropped his side of the wheelchair handles, leapt toward a hospital cart full of cleaning supplies, and gave it mighty push. "Sorry, old boy," Will muttered as the cart spun away. Much as he wanted the ghost off Ariel, Uncle Ben might *really* scare the manor ghost off. That could ruin their plan—their slim, but only hope—of getting the ghosts together.

The cart careened toward Uncle Ben. Two hospital staff sprang up to grab it. One tripped in his excitement. He fell on the cart, giving it a burst of speed as it screeched forward and collided with the spinning gurney.

Mops, cleaners, and trash bags tumbled out. Toilet paper rolls launched in the air. The rolls unraveled, flying like long white pennants, and covered four people who were now sprawled on the floor. Uncle Ben barked. He was fenced in by buckets, mops, and overturned furniture. From under the toilet paper, a nurse glared straight at Will and Meg and yelled.

The children gripped the wheelchair handles and ran. They bumped Shep's leg into the wall trying to make the turn, and Shep clapped his hand over his mouth to stifle a yell. Behind them came a tremendous crash and more barking. Through the noise, Will heard an elevator ding.

"Quick, inside!" said Meg.

Will lunged into the elevator with the wheelchair and Meg pushed the close doors button. Behind them came more barking and a nurse's raised voice. "That's no bear—it's a Newfoundland dog! My granddad had one."

As the elevator doors slid shut, Shep let out a suppressed groan.

"Who gave you a driver's license?" he grumbled. "Nearly took my other leg off."

"*Now* what do we do?" said Will. He glanced at Ariel's limp form and the shimmering green velvet encasing her, then looked away again. "They'll be downstairs in a minute. Do you have your Jeep, Shep?"

Shep shook his head. "Left it at the timber yard. Came here by ambulance, but I couldn't drive anyway. We'll just have to figure something out." At that moment, the fire alarm began to wail.

Will squinched his eyes shut as the elevator doors slid open. They'd reached the ground floor. He fully expected to see the doorway framed by a phalanx of angry doctors and nurses blocking their way. He opened his eyes. Nothing. Meg already had her head stuck out and was peering around the corner. She motioned them forward. With Meg pulling from the front and Will pushing from the back, Shep, Ariel, and the manor ghost rolled out of the hospital elevator.

They were down in the lobby with five or six people on their feet talking excitedly about the fire alarm. Some stared in their direction, but the person at the reception desk was leaning into a phone, fully occupied. Muffled barks echoed from the stairwell, audible even through the alarm's blare. No one seemed worried about a man in a wheelchair with a lumpy blanket on his tummy.

"Over here."

Meg pointed to a door marked STAFF EXIT. It was the same door they'd seen from the memorial garden, Will realized. They pushed through and found themselves on a stone pathway next to a parked motorcycle and the azaleas.

Will scanned the scene. What was the quickest way to the Griffinage? Ariel needed help fast. Going back to the well was going into the thick of it, but it was the only way he could think of to save Ariel. That girl ghost was connected to the well, and they needed the girl ghost to make this plan work. The squad car was still parked by the hospital entry doors, but Officer Targent was nowhere to be seen. If they could find him, would he give them a ride?

"Don't be ridiculous," said Meg. She must have seen his look. "He's the one who brought us here. No way would he drive us *away* from the hospital, especially not with two patients."

"One runaway patient and one kidnapped patient," added Shep. "I'm afraid she's right."

"Oh, hurry! Hurry and think of something," said Meg. Ariel was groaning and tossing under the blanket. Will was glad he couldn't see her face.

"Speed," muttered Shep. "Speed, that's what we need. Simple speed. That's it!" He scrambled up from the wheelchair. "Here, hold Ariel. Never mind the blanket. We've got speed right here." Shep hobbled a few steps and heaved himself up on the parked motorcycle.

"Yes!" said Will, pumping his arm in the air. He saw at once what Shep was up to. The motorcycle. It wouldn't be stealing in a ghost emergency; obviously even Shep didn't think so. With Shep's help, Will hauled Ariel over to the leather seat and lifted her up, then swung up behind her. Meg stood on the path wringing her hands.

"But your leg?" said Meg. "Can you drive?"

"Drive by hand with a bike. Right leg works the brakes. Just can't shift gears."

"But we don't have a key!"

"It's Father Casey's. Happen to know he always leaves the keys." Shep tapped a junior-sized bumper sticker that said: THIS BIKE PROTECTED BY GOD. "Hop on."

Shep revved the engine. Will knocked back the kickstand. Meg jumped on behind Will and secured herself by hugging Will and Ariel around the middle. They were scrunched together like a giant foursome sandwich: Shep in front at the handlebars, then Ariel, Will, and Meg. Fivesome, actually. The manor ghost clung to Ariel in the midst of them, her green velvet dangling down.

"This is going to be bumpy," Shep said over his shoulder. "Hang on!"

"Where are you going?" yelled Meg.

"The shortest way!" Shep called back.

"Cross-country!" Will said with a shout.

Of course. Shep was a local. Officer Targent's words came back to Will in a rush: *By road it's twenty minutes, but it's a straight shot through the pastures; you could walk in half the time.* He looked past the garden toward the back of the hospital. There was a collection of air-conditioning units, blowers venting heat with a noisy hum, a line of plastic garbage bins, and beyond that, sheep pastures.

A hand clamped down on Will's shoulder. He

cringed and turned, expecting to see Officer Targent's belt and the padded black vest of his uniform. Instead he saw blue jeans, a black shirt, and tennis shoes: Father Casey.

"Just a minute, now. You can't . . ."

"Sorry, Casey," Shep yelled without looking back. "Gotta go. It's a spiritual matter!"

Shep gunned the motor and the bike leapt forward. Will gripped Shep's chest, squeezing Ariel between them. They tore out of the hospital grounds. Behind them, the fire alarm blared and Father Casey waved madly, yelling "Wait! Wait! Stop!" after them. Riding in a cop car with the sirens on *and* stealing a minister's motorcycle? His friends would never believe this. Of course, soon the cop car sirens would be chasing after *them*, turning the escape even more wild.

They squealed past the air-conditioning units as Shep's hospital gown blew in Will's face, its green and pink polka dots flapping wildly in the wind. For an instant, Will breathed in hot air and the stench of garbage. Then the bins zipped by. There was gravel and a skid of tires. Then a bump, the grating of a gate, and open pasture.

CHAPTER TWENTY-ONE

Stampede

The motorcycle's roar invaded Meg's ears. She'd never been on a motorcycle before, but this was louder than she'd imagined. What was it Shep had said about gears? It sounded as if the motorcycle was straining. She was straining too, to hang on. It was a roomy seat, but with Shep and three kids there wasn't much space. What would her mother think of them tearing off across muddy fields with no helmets or seat belts?

Shep had unlatched the gate, and they were hurtling across McBurney's first pasture. The stone fence ahead joggled into view. Just one more pasture to cross before reaching the Griffinage.

"Blast it!" Shep yelled and twisted the handlebar grips.

The motorcycle leapt, bumped, then made a

thutt-thutt-thutt coughing noise. Their speed dropped. The engine roar sank to a hum. Then the entire motorcycle stuttered forward, Meg slammed against Will's back, and the engine died.

"Out of fuel," said Shep.

The motorcycle wheeled forward silently, wobbled, and stopped. Shep put his good foot down to steady it, and the children scrambled off, leaving Ariel draped over the leather seat. Shep glared at the motorcycle. Meg felt her body vibrating from the wild ride. It had been hard to gauge distance with so much bumping, but she could see they'd covered more than half the distance to the Griffinage. McBurney's second west pasture was next, and it was the smaller of the two. The empty-tanked motorcycle had skidded to a halt a few steps from the stile and gate between the fields.

"It's up to you now," Shep said, looking at Meg and Will. "Think you can do it?"

"You mean run for it?" asked Will.

Shep nodded and looked down at his foot.

"'Fraid I'm stuck here. I'll follow as I can."

Meg stifled a sob. It had been so comforting to have Shep back with them again. It was true he didn't know everything about ghosts, but he was real, solid, and grown-up. She hadn't realized how much she'd relaxed just having him with them. It was the feeling of taking off responsibility and just being a kid. A kid in a dangerous situation, but still just a kid following an adult's leadership. Now it was up to them again.

Will bent down with his back to the motorcycle. Shep placed Ariel on Will's back, but when Will tried to take a step, he collapsed on the ground.

"I can't stand up!" he cried with surprise. "There's something wrong with me. My legs won't work!" He wriggled on the ground and groaned.

Shep lifted Ariel off Will and rested her on the motorcycle seat again, his arm around her. Will struggled to his feet.

"Let me try," said Meg.

For some reason, she knew she could do it. Will was good at seeing the ghosts, but she could understand them. The way she'd been able to connect with the ghost girl in the well gave her courage. The manor ghost wasn't visible to her now, but Meg realized she could still feel her. The deep, wafting sense of loneliness she'd experienced in the well surrounded her again. There was loneliness in the manor ghost too, mixed with another deep aching, a lostness—not being lost exactly, but a loss of purpose.

Meg marched up to the motorcycle. Will stepped aside, opened his mouth as if about to protest, then closed it again. Shep said nothing, but grabbed Ariel under her armpits and hefted her onto Meg's back. Meg braced both arms against her thighs, her head down.

A crushing weight made her stagger.

She swayed but stayed upright.

"She's doing it," she heard Will whisper.

Meg felt the weight seep into her body. It was easier as it spread out more. She took a tentative step. Each time she lifted her foot, it felt as if she were fighting intense gravity. It certainly wasn't Ariel's weight. She'd carried Ariel piggyback plenty of times before. A far, far heavier mass was pressing her down. How could a girl and a ghost be so unearthly heavy?

Meg wobbled forward. Ariel's body hung limp, draped over Meg's neck. Wedged between Ariel's chest and Meg's back was the hard china head of the doll. Meg felt its unyielding head dig into her backbone with every step.

"That's a girl, Meg," said Shep.

Shep opened the gate so they wouldn't have to climb the stile. At first Meg used her hands to lift each leg forward. Her leg muscles alone weren't strong enough. Lift, step. Lift, step. They'd never get anywhere at this pace. Besides the intense weight, she felt an ache of sadness seep into her body. It seemed to be coming from the ghost. But as the ache poured into her, Meg discovered the weight on her back became more bearable. She stumbled forward faster, each step a little more sure and steady. She was running now. She could do it. The more she opened up to accept the sadness, the faster she could go. The key wasn't to think about carrying the body—it was to carry the feelings.

"That heavy?" said Will. He was running easily beside her.

"Like nothing I've ever carried," said Meg. "Feels like I'm carrying a car on my back."

After that, she saved her breath and concentrated on running. Meg ran with her head down, counting on Will to guide her. Every now and then he'd call out a direction—more right; left now—and Meg adjusted and ran on. As she ran, she heard a new sound. A kind of murmuring. It wasn't Ariel or Will. It sounded like a voice chanting from far away. She couldn't tell where the voice was coming from. It seemed to surround her.

"What's that?" Meg asked.

"She's talking," said Will. "She's got her mouth over Ariel's ear."

Meg shuddered. What a combination. She was the one who could carry the ghost's weight, and Will was the one who could see and hear the ghost clearly.

"What's she saying?"

Will didn't answer. "More left. Can you go faster?"

Partway across the pasture, Meg leaned against a shade tree to rest. They'd made it across the bulk of the muddy field and the last stile was in sight. Meg's breathing was hard and jagged. Will felt helpless running unburdened beside her. Why couldn't he carry the ghost? He looked at Meg, then flicked his eyes away. It was too awful. The ghost's eyes were bright silver now, her green velvet shining vividly. Those silver eyes landed on him sometimes, bringing back the terror of the night, but the manor ghost didn't dwell on Will. Her focus was Ariel. After the wild motorcycle ride, her hair was even more untidy and tangled. She looked like a gruesome gargoyle or vulture perched in a dreadful piggyback.

"Can you make it?"

Meg nodded grimly. "How's Ariel?"

"Fine," said Will. He didn't meet Meg's eyes. One glance at Ariel's face told him the ghost was getting her way. Were they right to take her away from the hospital medicine—dopamine, or whatever it was? How much could Ariel endure? Did they even have time to get to the well? There was no way to know. They had to keep running.

McBurney's sheep flock had seen many strange sights. There was the time a fox had snatched a newborn lamb in broad daylight. Once a hawk had dive bombed the flock when they'd grazed too close to her new nest in the oak, and the time Mr. McBurney had bought a new tractor. But nothing had ever spooked them as much as the sight of a creature running hunched over through the pasture with two things latched onto its back. It was a triple human, three bodies stacked on top of one another. The bottom one was groaning and bent over, the middle one was deathly quiet, and the top one was the most fearsome of all. It screeched and shimmered in green light that made the sheep's spines twitch and their ears flick. The flock shuffled nervously and stamped their front feet.

Then they did what all sensible sheep do when faced with an unknown menace: They panicked.

Will and Meg were two-thirds across the last pasture when they heard a low rumble.

"What's that?" asked Meg, unable to look from side to side because of the load she was carrying.

"Don't look. Keep running!" called Will.

Will, however, turned to look. Over the crest of the hill came the rumble. It was the sound of one thousand ovine hooves pounding the pasture.

"Sheep!" called Will.

"What?" asked Meg. The rumble was getting louder, and she couldn't hear properly.

Hundreds of sheep were running at them. Will gauged the distance to the pasture fence and the stile. An easy run if he were on his own. About fifty yards—the same distance as a quick sprint from the half line to the soccer goal. He'd done it many times. But Meg couldn't run that fast with Ariel and the ghost on her back. If she set Ariel down, Ariel would surely be trampled. No good saving her life from the ghost just to lose her here in the mud. Maybe they could make it. Will grabbed a stick from the ground.

Will clutched Meg's arm and dragged her toward the stile, trying to reach the edge of the field before the frenzied flock hit them. The sheep moved in one mass, like a swarm of insects, swaying as a group first left, then right, then barreling down at the children with increasing speed. Will waved his stick, trying to make them swerve.

"Sheep stampede! Run fast!" Will shouted in Meg's ear.

They ran. Meg stumbled after Will. The thundering noise gained on them. Will turned and saw the clear outline of the black muzzles on the front line of ewes. The sheep didn't seem to care about his stick. They just came charging forward. The children were still too far from the pasture's edge. There was nowhere to hide. They would be trampled. Trampled to pieces ... maybe to death ... by a crazed fluffy mob.

Meg squeezed her eyes shut. Will stared in dread as the wall of wool coats charged them. He felt a swoosh as if from a storm's gust, and his feet vibrated from the pounding hooves, but there was no impact. At the last second, the sheep swerved and dodged around the children, leaving a teardrop-shaped hole in the flock's middle.

"They missed us!" he cried, his face shining.

But as he said it, Meg's body suddenly lurched. A new sheep had appeared, not running in terror, but charging purposefully with its head down and thick horns curled back. It was Caesar.

Mind you look out for Caesar. Aunt Effie's words came back to him. Will watched now as Caesar rammed the two girls. Meg hit the ground. Ariel flew off. He saw a flash of green as the girls fell directly in the path of the running sheep.

The sheep kept pounding by. Will couldn't move. A mass of wool backs surrounded him, flowing by like a lanolin river. He craned his neck to spot Meg and Ariel, but was forced to stay stuck in his place until the last waves of ewes drummed past. When the sheep mob released him, he scrambled over to the girls.

Ariel lay tossed on the ground beside Meg. Her eyelids fluttered, but she didn't cry out. The flock huddled at the far end of the pasture, panting, their lambs between their legs. Caesar stood in front of the flock, his head lowered and ears trembling.

Meg sat up and rubbed her thigh. *Good,* thought Will. *Meg's all right.*

"Where is she?" were her first words. "Is the ghost still there? I don't feel her."

"She's off! She's on the ground between you and Ariel. But stunned, I think. Almost feels like she's dormant," said Will. "Whew. Can you believe it? The ram flung her off! And the sheep missed *us*."

"We're not there yet." At the end of the pasture, the sheep stamped their feet and shifted uneasily. They looked panicked enough to charge again. Caesar stamped his foot.

"Come on. Can you stand? I bet the manor ghost will follow us in a minute. I can take Ariel now that she's light."

Together they lifted Ariel over the stile. They'd only been a few feet away from its safety when the sheep stampeded. *Thank goodness we weren't out of the pasture,* thought Will. *Turns out we needed Caesar.* Meg scooped up Ariel and draped her over Will's back in a fireman's carry. The doll's head banged against his ear. Ariel stirred and clutched his shirt collar. Was she whispering his name? "It's me," Will told her and patted her leg.

Then Will charged forward. He ran with a burst of new energy buoyed by relief. The ghost was off. Not sucking Ariel's life any longer. They had some time again. And, incredibly, they'd accomplished the first part of their impossible task.

CHAPTER TWENTY-TWO

Back to the Well

Upstairs in the hospital, Officer Targent was pleased with himself. He'd bested his personal response time (a record-setting three minutes) by responding to the South Mendip alarm in a mere twenty-one seconds. There he found Dr. Fenster standing in a cluster of medical staff and toilet paper, brushing dog hair off her sleeve and sneezing. There was no fire. Not even a hint of smoke.

"Someone get this devil of a dog out!" ordered Dr. Fenster. She sneezed again and the fire alarm blared. "And turn that thing off!"

"No fire, then?" inquired the policeman. "You called emergency services because of a dog, Doctor?" The enormous Griffinage dog was padding in agitated circles, muddy paw prints covering the floor, matching the ones on the seat of Offier Targent's car.

The doctor glared at him. The dog stopped pacing and wagged his tail.

"Gotcha!" said Officer Targent, making a show of grabbing Uncle Ben's collar while the dog nuzzled him in a friendly way. Officer Targent watched as the hospital staff reset the fire alarm, then he headed downstairs with the Griffinage dog beside him. From the second-floor ward above, voices started yelling: "What do you mean she's gone? Wasn't anybody looking? What kind of hospital is this? Search the premises! Call the police! Call the fire brigade!"

Officer Targent sighed. So many emergency calls were simply false alarms from people overreacting. Whoever they were looking for, she'd probably just gone to the bathroom.

⟡

As the Griffinage garden and walnut tree came in sight, Will slowed down. It was all well and good to escape from South Mendip hospital and run across McBurney's fields. Up until this point, a strong idea had been driving him—the idea that they ought to get back to the well. Meg agreed, and Shep hadn't questioned it. The well seemed right. Now that they'd arrived, Will suddenly wasn't sure. He wasn't sure of anything. Well, he knew the manor ghost was following them, he could see her drifting form, but there was no sign of the girl ghost.

For the second time that afternoon, Will wished he had a more complete plan. A few paces away, the dark mouth of the well shaft yawned. He set Ariel down as gently as he could at the base of the walnut tree and scanned the area for ghosts. He wasn't hiccupping, but he could feel a tingle in his neck and that whooshing sound again. The ghosts must be near.

Ariel didn't stir. Her face was drained, and her cheeks had zipper marks from being pressed against Will's jacket. The doll was still clutched in her arms. Will tugged fruitlessly at the doll, but it wouldn't budge. Not even Caesar's ramming had shaken its uncanny grip. Suddenly, Will felt foolish. He was in over his head. What if Ariel never got better? What if she never woke up? Why had he and Meg been so sure they could help Ariel if they ran away from the hospital? All their lives, Will and Meg would have to live with the haunting thought that they had stolen Ariel's last chance for survival. The doctors and nurses might not know about ghosts, but they knew all about human bodies. Surely they could have saved her. Shep would be ages hobbling with his foot. It was all up to them. Two kids. And Will had no idea what to do next.

"What do we do next?"

Will realized Meg was looking at him expectantly. He gulped.

"Okay," he said. "Um, next, we . . ."

"You don't know," said Meg.

"I have no idea," admitted Will miserably.

Meg walked the last few feet to the old well. She didn't know what to do next either, but Will was right: The well seemed to be the center of things. Maybe the well would have answers.

The well entrance was clear now. It was easy to see there was a gaping hole in the grass. The loose dirt had been trampled into a soft mud by the emergency crew when they'd lifted Meg out, and there were paw prints circling too. The rope from the toolshed stretched out nearby like an unruly snake. No question it was frayed. Several strands had snapped. Had she really trusted her life to *that*?

Meg looked away from the rope and followed Will's gaze to the stone wall. Perhaps he was seeing something there. It was frustrating, being dependent on someone else to see for her. Then Meg saw a shape. Just a flash, really, but something was definitely moving along the stone wall.

She strained to look. It was the glimmer of the child ghost. Gradually, her form became clearer until Meg could see a stained white pinafore flapping slightly over her indigo-blue dress. Her face had a forlorn look. *Poor little thing*, thought Meg, again. *She wants a friend. All those years down in that well.*

The next moment, her sympathetic thoughts vanished. Will called out. Meg was just in time to see a greenish-white wind rushing toward her. It wasn't the girl ghost; it was much larger.

The manor ghost.

Meg screamed. The manor ghost glowed brightly, her body outline gleaming in a halo of greenish white so intense that Meg could clearly see. The manor ghost paused before Meg and hovered there, as if undecided. Then she spun suddenly as if she'd been lassoed and veered sideways to land on top of Ariel.

Ariel still lay propped by the walnut tree, where Will had left her, her legs and arms sprawled out in an unnatural sleep. As Meg stared, the manor ghost slid down beside the girl, lifted Ariel's head into her lap, and began to stroke her hair.

"My darling, my darling," she crooned. "Come to Mama. Mama's here now."

For an instant, they all stood very still.

Then Kay Kay glided over and reached for Ariel too. *No, no!* thought Meg. *This is all wrong.* The two ghosts were supposed to want each other. How could they be ignoring each other and stealing her sister? Will lunged at Kay Kay, and Meg watched in satisfaction as the ghost girl backed away. He hadn't pushed her, just spooked her. But it wasn't enough. Kay Kay retreated to a branch above their heads, but a moment later began drifting down again, drawn like a magnet toward Ariel's inert form.

Will lunged at the manor ghost too, but the grown-up ghost was not so easily spooked. She continued to stroke her prize.

Then Meg knew.

She'd done it once today, in the well, by mistake. She'd have to do it now on purpose. Meg walked toward the walnut tree where her sister lay. Her sister, who always delayed their trips, spilled things, followed her, and took her time away from Will. Her fabulous, creative, very own sister.

"What're you doing?" asked Will.

Meg walked forward purposefully, each step closer to the manor ghost. She was near now. She felt a well of fear rush up her throat and forced it down. The ghosts were attached to the wrong things. If she and Will wanted to change the ghosts' minds, they'd have to understand the ghosts' true desires better. She'd have to get to know them. Know their feelings. What was it Aunt Effie sometimes said? *Know thy enemy and know thyself and you shall win a hundred battles.* Well, she didn't need a hundred battles. Just one. She reached out a shaky arm.

"Meg! No, stop!" yelled Will.

It came from touch. The ability to merge herself with the ghost's soul. Before, when she'd been carrying the manor ghost, the ghost's body was latched onto Ariel, and she'd only absorbed some of the feelings. Now she would invite the full manor ghost into her body. Meg lifted the manor ghost's cold fingers from Ariel's head and gently placed them in her own hands.

Coldness. Surprise. Meg felt herself sucked in as the manor ghost clutched hungrily at her soul and enveloped her. She felt a tug on her heart, a chaotic, wild tug laced with pain and terror. Meg struggled against her instinct to pull back. She willed her hands to stay and clenched them around the ghost's fingers.

Then the cold crept up her arms and through her shoulders. She sank into a swirl of inner feelings. She'd done it. She was inside. *Trees. A lightning flash. Something silver. A bleeding horse and a blue hair ribbon pressed into the mud.* At first she saw a confused blur of images and noise. *There were bells, men shouting, an anguished squeal. It seemed to come from the horse. Spirit. The horse named Spirit. Then nothing but the rushing stream, and her voice shouting, "No! No!" above the bells. Gillian. Gillian.* Meg probed for more, and the scene repeated. *Horse, storm, muddy stream bank, blue hair ribbon. Aching grief and anguish.* There must be more. She didn't know how much time she'd have. How long did it take for a ghost to absorb your soul? The power tugging her heart intensified. She felt a surge of cold energy threading into her muscles. She couldn't feel her own body clearly, but had the vague notion she wasn't standing anymore, maybe floating. She wanted to run but couldn't feel her legs. The scene repeated. Wasn't there anything more? If the ghost was longing for her dead daughter, it was impossible. They couldn't bring her back. *Horse. Stream. Silver saddle buckle.* Of course, not a belt at all. The silver thing they'd found was a saddle buckle. Meg pushed deeper. She thought back to their sprint across the pasture. How much lighter her steps had been when she'd opened up to the ghost's longing. Meg took a long breath. Then she opened her heart as wide as she could, and gave herself up fully to the manor ghost's soul.

And there it was. The scene of the dying horse and wild creek waters lifted. She was deep inside the manor ghost now. She saw. She knew. She knew why the manor ghost had attacked Will and why it wanted Ariel. She knew exactly what the manor ghost was longing for.

She knew. But she could not tell Will. She could not move or speak.

Complete coldness crept through her, icy tendrils numbing her mind.

The manor ghost was taking her soul.

CHAPTER TWENTY-THREE

The Bells

Will watched as Meg's body trembled. First, her arms shook, then her head bowed, then she crumpled to the ground beside Ariel. Meg had touched the ghost willingly. She'd entered the ghost's spirit willingly. The question was whether she could get out.

Will clenched his fists and unclenched them. There was nothing he could do this time. No Uncle Ben. No sirens. Not even Shep, who could only limp and was probably blocked by Caesar. He was able to see both Meg's body and the ghost's body clearly, but not what was going on inside. Now the manor ghost was clutching Meg. She had her in an embrace, weeping, her tangled black hair pressed against Meg's neck. Her velvet dress flared violent green. Beside her, Meg looked deathly pale, paler than Ariel had ever been.

Will felt he would burst. He hopped from foot to foot, battling a surging wave of fear and frustration. Now *both* his sisters were lying there. Would he be next? Was Meg all right? Was she ever coming back? The manor ghost had no right to her. He must stop what was happening. In a rush of hot feelings, Will thrust his hands toward Meg and the ghost to pry them apart.

A jolt shot through Will's hands the moment he touched Meg. The force knocked him down. Meg and the manor ghost were joined together in some private, intense energy. He was blocked out.

Will sat rubbing his hands and heavy sobs escaped him, part pain, part fear. Just then, Meg's body shivered. She seemed to be talking. He crept forward and bent his head low to listen.

"I know," mumbled Meg. "She's here."

The ghost glinted. She was whispering in Meg's ear again.

"I will. I will," Meg muttered.

The words seemed to have an effect on the manor ghost. She turned a shade dimmer. Then, with a shuddering sigh, she released Meg.

Meg's eyes fluttered. She heaved a deep breath, as if she were finally coming up for air after being submerged underwater. Will dived in again and yanked at the two bodies—or semibodies. They separated easily this time. No jolt of energy. The manor ghost drifted back toward the daffodil garden, and Meg sat up and opened her eyes.

"Are you all right? What happened? How'd she let you go?" Will's head was a mass of questions.

Meg looked dazed and pale, but otherwise unhurt.

"I made her a promise," she said slowly.

"You what?"

"I listened and told her I'd help her." Meg rubbed her head and pushed her hair out of her eyes. She sat still for a moment. "She's sad about Gillian, she's still grieving her death, but that's actually not what she's longing for. She's longing to be a mother again. To be needed and to care for someone. Plus, she wants to do one last thing for Gillian. I said I'd help."

"Right. Okay. So you went inside her soul to find that out." Will was incredulous. He remembered the sheer terror he'd felt when the manor ghost had entered him. He'd never have the guts to do it on purpose.

"Now I just have to find out what the little girl wants." Meg scrambled to her feet.

"What!"

"You know, your plan," said Meg, walking forward. "Get the two ghosts together. Before we get them together, we have to see what they each want."

"But you can't! You nearly died. I was watching; you couldn't see . . . ." Will's voice trailed off. "Meg, *please*." Will was begging now. He wrapped both hands around her arm. "You can't. I won't let you. You just can't."

Meg pushed his hands away and stepped out of his grip. "Don't be silly. I have to." She headed purposefully toward the well, where Kay Kay hovered in the walnut branches. Will trailed after her. It was clear Meg could see both ghosts again. The manor ghost was also watching her intently. Meg turned and looked back at Will for a moment.

"Don't worry. I know how to do it now."

The ghost girl was sitting on a great branch that extended over the well, kicking her legs. She frowned at Meg. *A promise is a promise*, Meg thought fiercely. *Even if I wanted to break it, I couldn't. The manor ghost would come back for me for sure.* Meg walked faster. If she didn't do it right now, she'd lose her nerve to do it at all. Meg summoned up her best big-sister voice and tried to coax the ghost down from the tree.

"Kay Kay," she said. "Come on down, Kay Kay." For a moment, she felt like her father trying to lure their cat back into the house. Kay Kay wriggled on her branch. Then she dropped down on the trampled grass next to the well and scowled at Meg.

"You spoiled my party," said Kay Kay.

"I'm sorry."

"No, you're not. You did it on purpose."

The ghost girl sniffed. Meg thought she looked

about to cry. Kay Kay hadn't stepped toward her, but hadn't moved away, either. This might be the best chance she'd get. She reached out and grabbed each of the girl's hands with one of hers.

Kay Kay yelled when Meg grabbed her. Meg ignored the girl's angry looks, gritted her teeth, and braced herself for the coldness that would come.

Nothing.

Meg adjusted her grip and tried again. She felt a whisper of cool where Kay Kay's fingertips lay cupped in her hands, but nothing more.

"I can't get inside," she whispered to Will. "She's not letting me." Will had come up behind her. She could hear him breathing, gulpy, choked-up breathing, but it was comforting to have Will nearby. They were standing about five steps from the old well. Ariel was still only a few feet away, curled up at the base of the walnut tree. Meg wished she could hear *her* breathing. There was no time for that. Meg focused on the ghost in front of her.

Kay Kay was wiggling, and the ghost girl's arms were barely visible to Meg now, just a slight shine. She needed to concentrate. It was hard to hold on to something you couldn't see. Will could probably see her clearly, but for Meg the picture had started blinking in and out. Like trying to hold on to a dream when you were waking up: wavering and elusive. She focused on her glinting silver eyes. That was the brightest part of Kay Kay. Something was drooping over the ghost's left eye, partly obscuring it. The bow. Ariel's. The red-and-pink bow that was forever slipping and sloping into Ariel's eyes. Meg was always repinning it. For an instant, she saw an image of Ariel gazing up at her, holding out the bow and saying, "Here, Meg. It came off again." The memory gave Meg a renewed sense of courage. She took a deep breath and plunged in as far as she could go before Kay Kay slipped away.

The silver eyes flickered. Then they disappeared.

Meg couldn't see the ghost any longer.

Instead, she saw the familiar dank surface of the stone shaft of the well. She knew she was still standing next to Will outside in the muddy grass, but the well engulfed her. Meg trembled as the narrow walls of the well encircled her, conjuring back her recent terrors: the ledge, the frayed rope, Ariel being hoisted away, and Meg left forgotten. Then she gathered her strength. This was good. She was in! She couldn't feel the grass anymore. All she could feel was the ledge and the tree's roots rubbing her leg. A stone dropped off the ledge and hurtled into the pit below. She heard it splash. She was inside Kay Kay's spirit, and Kay Kay's spirit was in the well.

Bells and shouting. It was all the noise that had made her trip. Now she'd fallen down in here. Would anyone ever come? In all the commotion, it was plain she'd been forgotten. Everyone was so frantic about the other girl. The manor girl. The whole village had turned out looking for her. Her own family, too. Where was her mother? Cooking at the manor again, or out looking for the rich little girl. The one everyone loved so much. No one paid attention to her, a girl from Cook's Cottage. No one even knew she was missing. Bells, bells . . . She wanted to put her hands over her ears, but something was wrong and her head hurt. Bells. No company except the bells. She was alone. She needed someone beside her. Someone who would stay with her. Someone who would hold her hand and be with her when the bells rang. Be with her forever. She wanted . . .

"I don't want you!"

The ghost girl spat the words out.

Meg gasped and fell. The girl ghost had shoved her. Pushed her out of her soul and onto the muddy ground. She'd been on the verge of reaching something vital, something deep inside, when she'd felt a sting, like an angry wasp. Meg lay flat on her back. How close was she to the well? Tentatively, Meg rolled her head to the right. Her nose touched the well's stone rim. She'd fallen at the brink. One arm hung over the gap. If Kay Kay shoved again now, she'd tip over into the pit.

Meg knew she should move, but her muscles jammed. She lay where she was, too frightened to stir. A single pebble disengaged from the rim and plunged down the shaft. Meg listened, horrified, and waited to hear it strike the walls or splash.

Then rough hands were on her again. Tugging on her body.

Meg screamed.

She clenched her left hand in the grass and dug in, gouging soil under her fingernails and pressing her heels into the churned-up earth. She swung her right arm out of the pit and grabbed the well's rim itself, scraping her knuckles and scrabbling for a grip on the unrelenting stone. The rest of her body went rigid. She fought against the hands, trying to make her body a dead weight, and continued to scream.

"Oh, shut up!"

It was Will. And Will's hands. He was saying something too, but she couldn't understand. His voice was coming out in a high-pitched squeak. He rolled Meg away from the well edge. Meg relaxed in relief, but Will was shaking her shoulders again.

"Did you get it?" he repeated.

"Some. She won't let me."

"I won't let you myself in a minute. Geez! Look at you." Will's voice was still squeaking.

Meg struggled to her feet. Every cell in her body felt drained. Will was right. She couldn't do that again, especially not so close to the well. Kay Kay stood defiantly in her ragged pinafore, her legs spread wide, balancing impossibly on the empty air over the pit.

Meg rubbed her forehead. She felt foggy, and the

sharp sting still smarted inside her heart. Will was
talking and tugging her sleeve, hopping from foot to
foot. He did that when he was agitated and desperate
to know something.

"Well?"

"There were bells again, and we were in the well . . . ,"
she said.

She shook her head. There was no time to tell him
what she'd learned. The ones she had to talk to were
the ghosts. The ghost girl was now clear, as vivid as an
ordinary person. That was helpful. Was it just Meg's
age that made the view come and go?

"Kay Kay," Meg began, taking a step forward.

Kay Kay turned her back on her.

Meg hesitated. She tried again. This time Kay Kay
spun around and picked up rocks in each hand. Not
good. Meg ducked as the rocks came sailing toward
her. The ghost girl darted from the well to the walnut, where Ariel sat pressing the doll to her chest, still
groggy. The manor ghost had been watching Meg from
the daffodil garden, but when the ghost girl moved in
she swept back to Ariel, the hem of her green gown
swishing, covering Ariel's head.

"That's not your little girl!" Meg cried. "Leave her
alone! She *has* a mother."

The two ghosts circled Ariel. Their chins jutted
forward, their silver eyes fixed on her. Each step was

menacing and deliberate. They looked like two angry wolves defending a kill.

"They're not listening!" protested Meg.

Will was silent. Then he lifted his head and began to sing.

It was a wordless tune: la de de la da. His song wavered. He swallowed and sang again, but louder this time, with more confidence.

The bell song.

Meg realized where she'd heard the notes before: in both the ghosts' minds. And also from her sister. Ariel had been humming it all week. The bell tune was in both the ghosts' stories. Their lives and deaths were linked by this.

Under the spell of Will's song, the ghosts stopped circling and stood mesmerized. Will's high-pitched treble voice was nothing like the enormous church bells, but still, they were listening.

Meg stepped toward the ghosts and Ariel's hunched form. As she passed Will, he squeezed her shoulder, but never missed a beat with his singing. Meg walked closer until she was within inches of the ghosts.

"That's not your little girl," she said, pointing to Ariel. "That's the wrong one." Then Meg pointed to Kay Kay. "She's the one I told you about. She's the one who needs you."

"Ah!"

At first, Meg wasn't sure who'd spoken, but it came from the manor ghost. A thrill of hope surged through Meg's heart. Was it working? The manor ghost quivered. The music seemed to be holding the ghosts' attention, but Kay Kay's silver eyes were still locked on Ariel. Will sang louder, his voice cracking on the high notes.

Meg watched eagerly. The manor ghost glanced at Kay Kay. Meg hoped to see true love or rapture, but Kay Kay scowled and lines of suspicion darkened the manor ghost's face. The manor ghost draped her green sleeves over Ariel, and Kay Kay descended to Ariel's other side. They both placed their hands on the little girl's chest. Ariel moaned.

Meg felt frantic. As long as the music was there, the ghosts were ready to listen, but what was the right thing to tell them? Beside her, Will was singing desperately. His voice strained, replicating the dinging and donging in an endless rhyme. If only she'd truly found out what the ghost girl wanted. If only she'd had time . . .

She had half an answer. She knew what the manor ghost wanted. She'd have to guess at the rest. She'd been in the well herself. How would she feel alone and hurt in there . . . possibly dying? She let the feeling wash over her.

"You don't need a playmate," she said slowly, feeling

out the truth of the words. She spoke directly to the ghost girl who was on the right side of Ariel. Meg took another step, then knelt beside her. Behind her, Will continued to sing.

"You're lonely." She paused. This much she knew. "You think you need a playmate." Then it came to her. "But what you really need is . . . a mother."

The ghost girl froze. Only her eyes moved, two quick dots of silver. Meg gathered her courage. She knew she was right.

"You need someone to take care of you," said Meg, plunging on, more gently now. "You want to be loved, not forgotten."

For a moment, the ghost girl flicked her eyes back to Meg.

"The well's horrible," Meg continued, hurrying on. "You don't want to stay down there. You don't want to bring another child down with you. You just need someone to be brave with."

She was about to go on when something startled Meg. A movement close beside her.

Deep down, from somewhere far away, Ariel heard music. The sound stirred her. She shifted and moaned. The song. The sad one Kay Kay was always singing. But it wasn't Kay Kay singing; it was Will's voice. She was all mixed up. It was a dream, and she was asleep. But why was she sleeping outside? She felt something hard pressed under her elbow. The party—that was it. She'd been outside at Kay Kay's party. Ariel reached for the doll, and for a panicked moment didn't feel the familiar knobby head, then her fingers closed on the doll's hair and she pulled it close and nuzzled it. Again, the warm feeling spread through her chest. She gave a contented sigh and settled down once more. Here she was as snug and secure as being inside her mother's best hug.

The singing changed. More desperate. More Will. He was frightened. His fear poked into her warm blankety feeling. Why was Will scared? His fear kept prodding her. Her big brother. She struggled against the tug of the doll's cozy embrace. She had to be with him. She blinked, kicked her legs and forced herself to sit up. She blinked again. She couldn't see Will. For some reason, there was too much prickly green cloth in the way, plus there was Kay Kay blocking her view. Kay Kay was kneeling beside her, not singing, not humming. Simply staring. Staring fiercely and hopefully at Ariel, staring with those silver eyes.

She wants something, thought Ariel. She shook her head, trying to think, but her body felt slow, weighted down with rocks, or half asleep. *Something from me. Of course. She thinks I forgot. I never gave her a birthday present.* Her original gift, the silver buckle, was nowhere to be seen. It must have dropped when she fell. She'd have to give her something else. Ariel ignored the sharp twinge that shot through her heart and forced her arms forward.

"For you," she said, and handed Kay Kay the doll.

Kay Kay sat back on her ankles, clutching the doll. Warm blue light pulsed through her chest, her silver eyes sparkled and her shoulders relaxed. She flung her head back, her face tilted at the sky, and made a choking cry.

"Mama?"

Her voice startled everyone. It was small and child-like, just like any lost child.

With a bustle of green velvet, the manor ghost stood up and abruptly swung her gaze away from Ariel. Then she backed up several paces. Even from that distance, her eyes zeroed in on the doll buried in Kay Kay's arms.

"Mama!" Kay Kay called again.

At the first "mama," the manor ghost had dropped her menacing embrace of Ariel. But at the second one, she froze. Meg watched breathlessly as the manor ghost shifted her eyes up until they left the doll and settled fully on Kay Kay's face. At last she was looking at the ghost child.

Meg's hope surged. She waited. Two seconds. Five seconds. Will kept singing, croaking out the tune. The two ghosts were watching each other intently. Then the manor ghost stirred.

"Poor child," she said.

"Mama," said Kay Kay, stumbling toward her, tripping on the hem of her own blue dress. "I don't like it. It's cold and dark." Tears streamed down her dirty face. She tucked the doll under her armpit to free her hands and lunged forward. "Mama, hold my hand. I'm scared to die."

That was it. What Kay Kay really wanted. Someone to be with her as she died.

Off to the west, the bells began to ring. The ghost child reached out both hands. The manor ghost was now a vibrant green. Kay Kay was glowing and trembling, blazing with blue light. As the manor ghost continued to gaze at her, the silver light in the little girl's eyes rippled throughout her body, sliding over her smudged face, grubby pinafore and hungry hands, transforming them. Kay Kay was shining as only a child who's been seen and treasured can do. Meg blinked at the brilliance. Kay Kay stood before them, the bare beauty of her soul exposed.

"Oh, darling!" the manor ghost cried, and rushed forward.

"Mama!"

The two ghostly figures met. Child hands and mother hands grasped each other in a shriek of passion. Kay Kay crumpled against the green dress, more than a century of tension released at once, and the manor ghost cradled her shimmering head and rocked her.

The ancient sound of bell song surrounded them. Will's song mixed with the *clang* of the tower bells as the ghost tune rolled over them. A gust of chilled air brushed Meg's shoulders.

A flash of green burst forth.

"They're going, they're going!" cried Meg.

The two figures dissolved into one. They lifted above the ground in a dazzling blur of green-blue flame. The flame whirled above the well, then shot to the sky. A primal sound, raw and final, lingered around them: the sound of two people's innermost longings breaching into the open sky.

CHAPTER TWENTY-FOUR

The Weight of Longings

The Griffinage garden erupted in a cacophony of sirens, shouts, and squealing brakes. Officer Targent's squad car pulled up, followed by two yellow ambulances from South Mendip Community Hospital. Uncle Ben burst out of the squad car, barking joyously, and bounded at them with dried mud-clotted paws. Officer Targent and Father Casey climbed out of the squad car too. No one heard the golden Mini pull into the driveway.

"We did it!" cried Will, pumping his fist in the air. "We absolutely completely did it!"

"Did you ever hear such a wild yell?" asked Meg, laughing.

"Better than fireworks," he said. "Light show, music, primal screams."

Beside them, Ariel sat up, staring wide-eyed where the ghosts had been. Color flooded back to her face. Her nose bubbled, and she wiped it. Meg threw her arms around her little sister. Will hugged her too, even though Ariel's snot got all over him. He quickly backed away, and as he did so, a shiny glint of metal lying in the dirt caught his eye. The ghost's copper brooch. *I guess metal doesn't vanish the way ghosts do*, thought Will, and slipped it into his pocket.

A freckled hand nudged him aside. Officer Targent knelt down in front of Ariel. He felt for a pulse and, ignoring the hospital staff who came hurrying up with a stretcher, scooped Ariel up in his arms and hustled her into the house.

"He's probably trained in first aid," Will said to Meg. "Police officers usually are. Did you see how fast he tore over here? And listen to those sirens! Oh look, here's Shep. He's by the stile. Shep! It's okay! We're over here!"

Aunt Effie stood bewildered, the blue flash of emergency vehicle lights turning her hair a vivid shade of blue, her clothes spattered with fresh mud. She nodded vaguely when Officer Targent called out that the kids were all right. Then Shep hobbled into view in his hospital gown using a stick for a crutch, and Aunt Effie burst into tears.

⟨✦⟩

Aunt Effie spent the next few minutes collapsed in the burgundy armchair, pulling at her sweater buttons. The medics swarmed around the Griffinage until Officer Targent marched them out.

"But, Officer!" protested one of the medics. "Cardiogenic shock, nonresponsive, shallow breathing! That was the hospital report. And they just took her against doctor's orders! We can't leave her here with no medical care." The medic was a young fellow, raised in Birmingham. He hadn't grown up on Somerset ghost stories. Officer Targent shook his head.

"Find one thing wrong with that girl," he challenged. "Find one! Never mind, you won't. Nothing more than a sprained ankle."

Casey, Shep, and Officer Targent spent a long time huddled in the hall talking.

"That's what I was trying to tell you, Shep, when you peeled out so quickly," Father Casey said. "Low fuel! There's a petrol station across the street."

"So *that's* why . . . ," Meg began. She and Will were hanging by the door frame, listening in. Officer Targent turned when she spoke and cornered them. "Never move a person who's fallen by yourself," commanded Officer Targent sternly. "What if your sister had broken her back? Then you might have hurt her worse. She could be paralyzed."

"But you did yourself!" said Will. "You carried her in here."

"Never mind that," he said, blushing. "I mean before. They just told me what you did with the rope when she was down at the bottom of the well."

"The well!" cried Aunt Effie. "What *is* going on here? I'm responsible for these children. Will someone kindly tell me what's been going on at the Griffinage behind my back?"

"Ghosts, Effie," said Shep. "Your family's been part of a Somerset ghost story."

Half an hour later, Ariel was propped up in the big kitchen chair wrapped in a plaid blanket. She was chatting nonstop, glad to be the center of attention. Uncle Ben had his chocolate head in her lap, and next to her was a plateful of ginger nut cookies and another variety with jam inside called Jammie Dodgers.

"I told you about Kay Kay, you know," Ariel was saying, with a mouthful of sticky crumbs. "Kay Kay's been my friend ever since we came."

"Well, next time you make friends with a ghost, tell us," said Will.

"But I *did* tell you. An' I didn't know she was a ghost," said Ariel. Her face drooped. "Now who will play with me?"

"I will," said Meg, squeezing her hand.

"Me too," said Will.

Aunt Effie had been uttering words like "dash it all" and "confoundnation," which Meg was pretty sure wasn't in the dictionary. Finally, she announced she was completely "flummoxed," and rummaged in the pantry for supper food. "No time to cook after all this," she said. "We'll have to see what's in the cupboards."

What was in the cupboards was tinned ham and two Battenberg cakes, which Aunt Effie had been saving for the children's last night at the Griffinage.

"Cake for supper, anyone?" she asked, sounding more like her old self. So they all sat down, including Shep, to ham sandwiches and thick slices of checkered Battenberg cake for dessert.

"I can't believe it," said Will, licking marzipan off his fingers. "They really went for each other. After all this time living in the same village. After all those hundreds of years."

"Yes, if all this ghost business is true," said Aunt Effie, "why didn't the mother and child ghosts simply find each other on their own ages ago? According to you, they've had nothing else to do all these years except look for their heart's desire."

"I think they couldn't see each other," Meg said slowly. "The manor people and the cottage people lived such separate lives. Plus, they were so caught up in their own feelings, they weren't able to see anything else." *How close together people can live*, thought Meg, *and not really notice each other. Neighbors. Kids at school. Sometimes even brothers and sisters.* She looked at Ariel stuffing pink and yellow sponge cake in her mouth and smiled.

"I'm still finding it a hard story to swallow," said Aunt Effie, now on her third cup of tea. "Targent just accepted the whole thing and walked out of here meek as a lamb. Not an argument!"

"He's a local boy, Effie," said Shep. "Used to chase ghosts himself as a lad, same as me. But I'll admit he's a bit stumped. Doesn't know what to put in his police report. Come to think of it, I'm stumped too. Don't know why the ghosts behaved so differently with you kids." His eyes drifted to Will. "Maybe it's got something to do with your Samhain birthday."

No one had an answer to that. It was silent for a while. Then Uncle Ben left Ariel's lap and nuzzled his head into Aunt Effie's. She sighed and rubbed his ears.

"Yes, you're forgiven for running away, Uncle," she said. "Even after I stomped about the muddy fields of Somerset traipsing after you. And me without my wellies! Protecting your puppies, I know."

She glanced at his dog dish. Uncle Ben had devoured his dinner and licked the bowl clean. She beamed. He was also partially de-mudded. "Leg wash today, full bath tomorrow," she declared. "No need to add a bath to the day's excitements."

"But, Meg, how did you know Kay Kay wanted a mother?" asked Will. "I thought you never learned her real longing."

"I didn't. I just guessed," admitted Meg. "But I'd been in the well myself, so I thought it was right. Plus, everyone needs a mother." She reached for another slice of the checkerboard cake. "Ugh, my back feels sore. That manor ghost was impossibly heavy! I would have thought a ghost would be light—just air, I mean. But she was crushing."

"You felt the weight of the ghost's longing," said Shep. "A crushing weight, indeed. That's the burden she was carrying for more than a hundred years, then you carried it for her."

"That weight was just her feelings?"

"People carry heavy burdens in life," said Shep. "Frankly, I'm surprised you could bear the weight." He shook his head and looked at Meg with new respect. "Not sure I could have done what you did—run all that distance from the hospital, and everything else."

"She's young," said Aunt Effie. "That might explain it."

"Maybe," said Shep. "But it's still remarkable." He looked at Meg again, so intently she blushed.

"Many things have been remarkable today," said Aunt Effie.

"Not every day you banish a ghost," said Meg.

"Two ghosts!" said Ariel.

"Or go down a well, dodge the police, and escape from the hospital on a stolen motorcycle," said Will, grinning.

"Or decide to believe in ghosts," added Shep, giving his hostess a sidelong glance. "Guess you're a local now, eh, Effie?"

Just then, the phone jangled and everyone jumped.

"That'll be the police, I'll wager," said Aunt Effie, going to answer it. "No one else would call at this hour. Hello, the Griffinage. Oh, Marie!"

"It's your mother," she said, cupping her hand over the phone. "She wants to know what we did today. What on earth should I tell her?"

CHAPTER TWENTY-FIVE

The Last Day

Meg heard voices and laughter the moment she woke up. They seemed to be coming from the Griffinage kitchen. Will padded in from down the hall, and Ariel appeared from her alcove.

"What's going on?" Will asked. "Sounds like a party."

The Griffinage kitchen was blazing with lights and filled with the aromas of coffee, toast, and eggs. Plates and tea bags were scattered about, and in the midst of it, Shep and Aunt Effie were sitting close together.

"Morning!" Shep called out.

They were dressed in the same clothes as yesterday. Shep even had his hospital gown still on, though he had thrown a sweater over it. Aunt Effie's big outdoor sweater, Meg noticed. They were holding hands.

"Afraid we stayed up all night," Aunt Effie said. "There was simply so much to talk about. Never got around to bed, and look, now it's breakfast."

"Best night I've ever had," said Shep.

Aunt Effie blushed and laughed.

"Been doing that all night," said Shep. "Ever since I asked her to marry me."

"You . . . what?" asked Will.

"Who did the asking?" demanded Aunt Effie.

"Well, it came out just the same," said Shep. "We've decided to quit being neighbors and take up marrying. Isn't that right, my dear?"

"You . . . what?" said Will again.

"Oh, Aunt Effie!" said Meg.

"An uncle!" said Ariel. "A real uncle!" Uncle Ben barked. "Oh, sorry, Uncle Ben," Ariel said, and hugged his furry neck. "Two uncles!"

Aunt Effie didn't eat a thing at breakfast, but the children and Shep made up for that. Ariel insisted on sitting on Shep's lap and calling him "uncle" at every opportunity.

"He's not our uncle *yet*," said Will.

"Well, he's our almost-uncle," said Ariel.

"It won't be too far off," said Aunt Effie. "At our ages, there's no sense in waiting. I'll be forty in May, and that's old enough to marry. Just think! I'm going to be a June bride."

Will plowed into his eggs. He was pleased Shep was joining the family, but all the wedding talk was distracting him from his breakfast. Weddings were fine, but not like the adventure of ghosts, and if he heard Shep say, *Effie, love,* one more time, or Aunt Effie say, *Shep, my dear,* he might lose his appetite.

Meg tugged him out the door after breakfast. "For our good-bye tour," she said. "Plus, you know, one more thing to do."

Together they climbed the familiar path through the pasture. Ariel came too, carrying violets in one hand and a paper bag in the other. She tripped over her shoelace before they reached the first stile, but Will didn't mind. He stopped and tied it for her. They waved to the sheep ("Even Caesar," said Ariel. "Especially Caesar!" answered Will), and looked once more at the manor and its towers. Their last stop was St. Giles. They stood for a moment by Lady Mendip's tomb, then entered the Chapel of Innocents. A wash of rainbow colors from the stained-glass illuminated the chapel.

"Ooh," whispered Ariel, who was seeing the little chapel for the first time.

"Funny that Shep and Kay Kay are cousins," said Will. "I bet he's the one who usually puts flowers here."

Meg nodded, then turned as Ariel tugged her sleeve.

"Meg?" she asked. "Can you still be friends with someone when you can't see them?"

"Yes, I think you can," said Meg, giving Ariel's hand a squeeze. "I think it happens all the time."

The three children turned and solemnly looked at the small slate grave in the corner. Ariel placed a bunch of purple violets she'd picked from the Griffinage garden on the grave, next to a bouquet of bell-shaped lily of the valley that was already there. They all watched the word "missing" deepen to a royal blue as the sun pulsed through the tinted windows.

"Good-bye, Katherine," said Meg. "I'm glad we found you."

Next, they faced the manor girl's tomb. For a moment they watched the stained-glass window turn the angels shades of red and orange. Then Meg rustled in the bag. She took two steps forward and placed a wedge of cake on Gillian's grave. "For your birthday," said Meg. "From your mother." She laid more violets beside it. "And this is from us."

The cake looked warm lying on the grey stone. A crumb broke off and skittered down the side. As they watched, the cake began to shimmer. Then it rose in the air and sank gracefully into the grave.

Back at the Griffinage, Aunt Effie greeted them dancing at the door. She held a teakettle in one hand and an oversized envelope in the other. She waved them into the kitchen.

"Listen to this!" Aunt Effie cried, setting the kettle down on Uncle Ben's water dish, which was up on the counter to be refilled. She caught Will in a bear hug until he grunted.

"Is this what love does?" Will groaned to Meg as he escaped. "If it is, I think I'll go back to St. Giles and play the piano."

"From Mrs. Carmichael!" said Aunt Effie, doing a little spin. "She liked it! The Griffinage won. We won the grant!" She waved the envelope in front of them and produced a single sheet of paper. There it was: an official letter from the Somerset Historical Society, Mrs. P.M. Carmichael, chairperson. At the end of the letter was a personal note written in blue ink. *Congratulations—your historic value combined with authentic ghosts made you the clear winner.*

"Eighteen thousand pounds!" Aunt Effie cried. "For historic renovations! That's the new thatch and windows and more! Wait till Shep hears this."

The next morning was a bustle of bags and suitcases. Ariel kept running over to pat Uncle Ben one last time and to gaze at the new doll Aunt Effie had given her to replace the ghost one. Shep leaned on a set of crutches, grinning ear to ear, and shook David Griffin's hand. Their father grinned back, the same overwide Griffin grin that Will had inherited. Their mother, Marie, kept flitting from one child to another and ruffling their hair with kisses, then wringing her hands and saying, "Oh!" every time she looked at Shep or Aunt Effie.

"Kiss Uncle Ben, too, Mama," said Ariel. "And my new doll. You forgot the doll. I've named her Kay Kay."

"Kay Kay," said their mother. "That's an unusual name."

"I named her after my ghost friend, see," said Ariel and launched into a story about the ghosts. Will nudged Meg. They'd already decided the best policy would be to let Ariel tell the truth. Then it would be up to their parents whether or not to believe the story.

"My, that sounds exciting, Ariel," said Mama. "You can tell me more about your little friend later. Now, where's your suitcase?"

But when the bags were actually packed, and their father had slammed the trunk shut, it was suddenly hard to leave. The Griffin family stood awkwardly around the rental car from London, and no one made a move to get in. Will scuffed his feet and sank his fingers into Uncle Ben's thick brown coat. Ariel sat cross-legged on the ground and said she missed her alcove. Shep stood silent, and Meg began to cry.

"Well, here's a gloomy lot!" said their father. Aunt Effie came up to Meg and put her arm around her.

"You'll be back before you know it," she said, giving her a squeeze. "It's April, and June's just around the corner. I talked to your mum and dad, and you're all coming back for the wedding. As I said, no sense in waiting. Took us this long to hold hands; we can't be shy of the altar. Besides, if we wait, who knows what might happen? Shep here might fall down a badger hole before I've even squirmed into my wedding dress. What a pity that would be," she said, looking at Will. "No cake for you lot to eat!"

"Now," said their father, when they were all packed into the car, and Ariel was still waving to Uncle Ben long after she could see him, "I'm sure you kids are tired of the country. What do you say to a couple of days seeing the sights in London? Tower of London? Madame Tussauds? Plenty of history, and they even say some places are haunted. . . ."

Ariel stopped waving. Meg gasped and Will suddenly sat back. The whole back seat became silent.

"What?" their father asked. "Why are you all so quiet?"

"Perhaps they've had enough history for the moment," suggested their mother.

"Ah yes, I forgot," said their father. "Effie probably had a heyday stuffing their heads with tales of British battles and revolutions. Don't you want to go to the London Dungeon and learn tales about ghosts?"

"Uh . . . ," said Will.

"Sounds scary," said Ariel.

"It's just that . . . ," Meg said.

Their mother turned around and scanned the three faces in the back seat. "How about the beach instead? Weston-super-Mare is close by, and it has a Ferris wheel and pony rides."

"Yes!" shouted Will, punching his fist in the air. "Weston-super-Mare, Dad. Let's go there! We might even find some cool rocks in the sand."

"Thank you, Will, but I don't need rocks wherever I go," said their father, chuckling.

"Pony rides! I love ponies," said Ariel.

"They're donkeys, actually," said her father.

"I love donkeys!" cried Ariel.

"Frivolity over history," said their father. "Whose offspring are these?"

"They look as if they could use a rest," said their mother.

"Right then, to the Grand Pier!"

An hour later, they'd reached the coast and tumbled out of the car. "Two days at Weston-super-Mare! Can you believe it?" Will asked Meg. "The ghosts were good, but I can't wait to ride the Super Looper."

"There's the donkeys!" cried Ariel. She slipped her hand away from her mother and reached out for Meg's instead. Meg felt a warm glow rush through her insides as they headed toward the beach. Ever since they banished the ghosts, she'd been surprised by how much she liked holding Ariel's warm little hand and listening to her chatter. Being a big sister seemed like the most wonderful thing in the world.

"And then home," said Meg. "I'll be glad to be home. No ghosts there."

"Not exactly," said Will.

Meg stopped walking and looked at him. "What do you mean, 'not exactly'?" she demanded. Ariel was tugging her hand, and the smell of salt and seaweed beckoned.

Will grinned, his broad, goofy Griffin grin which stretched from cheekbone to cheekbone. "You know when we walk over the Water Street Bridge? I always get hiccups."

"Hiccups!" cried Meg. "I guess this won't be the end of the ghosts."

"Race you!" called out Will. Then the three Griffin children ran toward the ocean waves crashing on the ancient Somerset beach.

Author's Note

Castle Cary is a real town in Somerset, England. You can take the train there and step out on the same railroad platform where Meg, Will, and Ariel met Aunt Effie. But the resemblance ends there; I've created a fictional version of the town for this story. Castle Cary has been moved north and west, and I've generally rearranged things. If you visit, you will find a ruined castle and an old manor house in Castle Cary, but the manor is quite different from the one the Griffin children explore. As for the ghosts, you'll have to see if you start hiccupping.

Acknowledgments

Hugs to my first readers, the children who read early versions of the manuscript, added ideas, and told me exactly what they thought: Tess Barker, Alexander and Elizabeth Fey, Emerson and Charlie Hammersley, and Amabel and Ellen Schwaiger. Also to Alexander Shumaker, who was eight when he first met the ghosts and Uncle Ben, and had to wait until he was quite old to hold a published copy in his hands.

Special thanks to the lovable Mosey Brown. Her giant furry brown head and drooling tongue inspired the character of Uncle Ben. The idea for the rest of the story came to me while I was out cross-country skiing.

Deep thanks to Krista Vitola, editor at Simon & Schuster Books for Young Readers. You are an honorary member of the Griffin family. Thanks also to Catherine Laudone and the whole team from the book-lined walls of Simon & Schuster.

Thanks go to the parents, teachers, and children's librarians who read early chapters, sometimes reading ahead at the spooky parts: Kathy Fey, Kate Madigan, Mary K Montieth, Michele Rudd, Ana Ruesink, Zane Schwaiger, and Aaron Stander. Thanks to the Inkhearts, Powerfingers, and other writing critique partners: Karen Anderson, Patrick Fairbairn, Ann Finkelstein, Bronwyn Jones, Mardi Link, Jillian Manning, Stephanie Mills, Cari Noga, Anne-Marie Oomen, Teresa Scollon, and, of course, Angie Treinen, writer and pumpkin farmer extraordinaire. Thanks to Jen Costello of My Brown Newfies for all things Newfoundland, and to my intrepid trio of UK readers: Hannah Hiles, Nicola Keller, and Kay Weetch who made the whole book better by reading with British eyes. Hugs to the hardworking folks at the Society of Children's Book Writers and Illustrators, on both sides of the pond, and heartfelt thanks to my agents, Jacquie Flynn and Joëlle Delbourgo, who guided me from writing about children to writing for children.

As always, love to Rick, Xander, and Luke. Finally, to my parents, who read aloud to me all my life, shared the wonder of words, and introduced me to crumbly old castles.